THE BELIEVERS

TRAVIS GULBRANDSON

"The most common of follies is to believe passionately in the palpably not true. It is the chief occupation of mankind."

– H.L. Mencken

"What the eyes see and the ears hear, the mind believes."

– Harry Houdini

She threw open the door and shouted for her husband. The smoke was so thick in the wind she could not hold her eyes open without crying. Only the top third of the barn was visible, and the flames danced and licked their way along the frame of it as the horse screamed like a siren from within. The woman dashed down the three narrow plywood steps to the ground and the dried dead grass crackled beneath her heavy black shoes as she ran along the outer edges of the fire and called and called. The air tasted like soot and straw. Gagging, she waved her hands before her face and closed her eyes. She bent toward the ground and spat, her throat wheezing all the time like a broken whistle. She wiped her mouth and took a few tentative blinks, but she could see nothing but the billowing thick gray cloud in which she had become enveloped. She tried to call again but her lungs felt like they were encased in concrete. Her throat seemed coated with dirt. Dropping to her knees, she began to crawl, uncertain of which way to move. As she went forward the smoke grew denser and she heard the sound of the fire snapping and popping like bacon grease. She moved to escape the sound, but her legs were like a pair of heavy logs tethered to her waist as they dragged behind. Her fingers tingled with static shocks and her upper arms quivered with nonexistent cold. She could no longer breathe. Frothy cupfuls of saliva spilled from her mouth when she tried to call one last time. No noise escaped. Silent, slow, she rolled onto her side. Then she stopped moving. It almost looked as though she had fallen asleep.

ONE

Bryant was a sleepy town, remote enough to go unvisited by most travelers, and small enough to remain uncharted on most state maps. Indeed, the single reason its presence was notated on the map hanging in the red-bricked cube city hall building was because the mayor had marked it there himself in splotchy blue ink. Although the faded green sign that welcomed the community's few visitors proclaimed a population of just below four hundred, in reality it was somewhat smaller, as many of the people included in this tally resided amongst the elaborate checkerboard of farm places that stretched up to twenty miles beyond the city limits.

The main street did not consist of much. There was a general store, a diner and a bank, two bars and a post office. A gas station stood near the road that led into town. Three churches were scattered in the area, two of them Lutheran, one Catholic. There was a small school and a small fire station. There was no police station, although a state trooper made a quick pass-through each Tuesday and Thursday. If any other policemen were needed, it would have taken them more than an hour to arrive.

The young man's lips curved into a tight smile when he looked upon the scene for the first time. He set down his battered brown case of cracking imitation leather and clenched his cigarette in his teeth as he took his jacket, slung now over his shoulder, in both hands and shook it free of dust. Breathing smoke, he cinched up his tie and fixed the angle of his hat. He pulled on his jacket and took the lapels in his hands, waving them back and forth, cooling himself with the brisk

7

morning air before he fastened the buttons. He checked his fingernails and grasped the cigarette between his thumb and forefinger and inhaled a final time. Then, wetting his lips, he dropped it and ground it into the dirt with the heel of his shoe until the filter came apart.

Before he picked up his case, the young man considered looking at the note once more. He knew what was written on it, as he had carried the crumpled scrap of yellow blue-lined paper in his front left trouser pocket for weeks. 114 Oak Street. He had written the words in the exact center of the paper. He did not write the woman's name, but he still could remember it. His brain was a storehouse of names. They had only to be spoke or read a single time. Mathilda Bramble. Leland Edwards. It was easy.

Her name was Edith Parker.

An oil-stained attendant was sat behind the gas station counter. He wore a red ball cap with a broken bill and wrinkled army green coveralls, the material of which was worn so thin that it looked five decades old. Standing across from the attendant, the young man looked slightly incongruous in his gray suit, dusty and sweat-stained as it was. A small white portable radio sat blaring on the countertop, its speakers so distorted that it rendered all sound unintelligible. The attendant took no notice of the young man. His eyes were shut and he swiveled in his chair and nodded his head over the grating noise.

"Excuse me," the young man said. He repeated himself a moment later, his voice raised close to a shout.

The attendant opened his eyes and jumped, nearly tumbling out of his chair when he saw the young man standing before him. He soon regained his balance and stood, erect and alert, like a soldier.

"Hello!" he said with a bit too much enthusiasm. "I didn't see you pull up. You need some gas?"

"Would you please lower the volume of your radio?"

The attendant nodded and turned down the dial.

"Sorry about that. Thought I was alone."

The young man eyed the radio.

"Turn it off. Please."

The attendant fumbled with the control. It switched off with a snap and then the room was quiet. He smiled in an easy-going way.

"How can I help you? You need a fill-up?"

"No, thank you, I have no car. I was wondering if you might be able to offer me another form of assistance."

The attendant placed his hands on the counter and leaned forward, leaving thick black streaks of axle grease.

"What can I do for ya?"

The young man took the paper from his pocket and held it several inches from the attendant's face.

"Would you be so kind as to tell me how to reach this address?"

The attendant squinted as he read.

"That's Edith Parker's place, right?"

"That is correct."

The attendant stood back and put his hands on his hips.

"How you know her? You related?"

"No, I've never met her before."

"What you wanna see her for, then?"

"I have a message for her."

"What is it?"

"I'm afraid that's private."

The attendant smiled sheepishly.

"I'm sorry, mister. I guess I'm just too damn nosey for my own good."

The young man's face remained impassive.

"That's all right. Can you please instruct me as to how I may reach her home from here?"

"I sure can, but it won't do you no good."

"Why is that, please?"

"She ain't home."

9

The young man tilted his head.

"She's not home."

"Nope."

"How do you know?"

"Filled her car up before she left town."

"Is she traveling far?"

"Full tank."

The young man closed his eyes and began to think. The attendant stared at him with a look that expressed neither sympathy nor concern. He pulled a pack of Wrigley's Spearmint from his pocket and unwrapped a stick with his inky fingers.

"Have you any idea when she'll return?" The young man's eyes remained shut. "It is of the utmost importance that I see her today."

The attendant folded the gum once before he popped it into his mouth.

"Don't know. I didn't see no bags in her car, so I'd say she's prob'ly comin' back sometime today. Course, I didn't look in her trunk."

The young man opened his eyes. The attendant grinned and chewed open-mouthed with wet smacking sounds, the grease spreading across his front teeth.

"I guess I can't tell you one way or the other," the attendant said with a trace of embarrassment.

"Do you know of anyone who might?"

The attendant shrugged and stopped chewing. He stuck a finger in his ear and began to dig.

"You got me, mister. You could ask around, I guess. Maybe you'll find out that way. Talk to one of her neighbors or somethin'. Course, they might not be home, neither. Don't know what to tell you, I guess."

When he stopped speaking, he pulled his finger from his ear and wiped it against his chest without looking.

"Has she any family?"

"Here in town?"

"Yes."

"Nope. She's got a son. He got married a while back. He and his family, I'd say they prob'ly live about twenty miles away from here. Maybe a little more."

The young man took a step away from the counter and stared out the big picture window at the front of the gas station. His gaze fell upon a young woman in a blue dress who strolled up the narrow sidewalk with her two small children. A car passed them, trailing dust, and the driver stuck his arm out the window toward them and waved. They returned the gesture, smiling and shouting hellos. The young man turned back to the attendant.

"Would you still be able to tell me how to get to her house? Just in case she arrives home today?"

The attendant scratched the back of his neck.

"Could be there now for all I know."

It was a large house, the biggest in the neighborhood. It was tall and white with green trim, with ridged wedding cake banisters on the porch. Beside it sat a large garage, open and empty. The young man frowned and continued to scan the property. The lawn was a healthy green and clear of leaves and debris. The sidewalk and driveway were spotless, too, smooth as polished granite and without spiderweb cracks or oil stains.

The interior of the house looked even nicer, from what the young man could see of the living room through the prismed glass panel on the front door. The furniture was well-stuffed, clean and soft and new. The walls were lined with shelves, all of which were crammed with tiny glass animals and porcelain people. There were ornate hand-carved boxes on the end tables and flowery pictures on the walls. In front of the smooth red sofa sat a long oak table with three crystal bowls set in a line, each filled with irregular bits of potpourri.

The young man left the porch and followed the sidewalk to the edge of the yard, where he deposited his suitcase. The house next door was not as large or as well-kept as Mrs. Parker's, but there was a Studebaker Starlight coupé sitting in the driveway. The young man straightened his jacket and tie and checked beneath his nails before he rang the doorbell.

"Just a second!" called a woman with a voice like stale cigarettes and razorwire.

The young man heard the sound of approaching footsteps – loud, clumsy, stomping – and he removed his hat and held it against his chest.

The door opened. A large woman stood behind it. Not even five-foot-five, she weighed more than two hundred-fifty pounds. Her face was flushed, like she had eaten a hot pepper, and her hair was red and cropped close to her scalp. Her housedress was red, too, magenta. It made her appear overheated, an impression that was reinforced by her labored breathing. It was impossible to guess her age.

"I apologize for disturbing you, ma'am, but I was wondering if I might ask for your assistance. Have you any idea when your neighbor, Mrs. Edith Parker, will return home?"

He pointed toward her house with a flattened palm.

The woman said lifted her hands and held them mid-air close to her chin. She had fingers like swollen dough. A long smoldering cigarette protruded from them, its firecherry tip glowing hot.

"Oh, that's no trouble," she said, holding the door half-open. "I'm Mrs. Colman. I'm her neighbor. I'm her best friend. She comes over for tea every afternoon. Not today, though. She's with her family. Her son and his wife, they've got three little ones. So I'm all alone today. Tomorrow, too. Oh, well. Nothing I can do about that. We carry on as best we can."

She took a hard drag off the cigarette and blew the smoke out fast over the young man's head.

"Have you any idea when she will return?"

"I'm sorry, honey, I don't. Sometime today, that's all I know. We won't be having tea tomorrow, but I know she'll be around. What'll she be doing? I couldn't tell you."

"She'll be back by the end of the day, though? That's definite?"

"Oh, sure. She never goes anyplace overnight, thank goodness."

Mrs. Colman moved her hand and a clump of ashes fell from her cigarette and powdered into nothing on their way to the ground.

"I see," the young man said, and nodded. He backed away from the door and took a step off the porch.

"Is there anything I can help you with?"

The young man shook his head.

"You've already helped me," he replied, and moved backward down the walk. "Thank you for your assistance."

"Any time," Mrs. Colman said with a sad smile. She put the cigarette in her mouth and waved before she began to close the door.

Just then, a large cat scampered out of the house. It was the biggest cat the young man had ever seen, twenty pounds at least, with thick rolls of fat that jiggled when the cat moved. It was a creamy brown-gray tom with crystal blue eyes, and it stumbled down the steps of the porch on stocky legs, and onto the lawn, where it stopped, staring and meowing.

Mrs. Colman screamed like she had been stabbed.

"No! Charlie! Charlie, get back here!"

"It's all right, Mrs. Colman. I'll get him."

He trotted toward the cat, which stood inert in the grass, watching nothing, like a miniature cow. The young man bent over and picked up the cat with an involuntary grunt and lugged it back to the house under his arm like a sack of flour. It felt like a sold ball of fat, and it did not move. It just hung there, bored.

"Oh, thank you."

By this time the front door was closed and Mrs. Colman stepped out of the house and onto the porch. She held out her arms as though she were drowning.

"Thank you, thank you, thank you, thank you," she repeated in jagged gurgles.

The young man handed the cat over.

"It's nothing. I don't think he was going anywhere."

Mrs. Colman flipped the cat onto its back and held it like a baby as she wagged her index finger in its face.

"Bad cat, bad cat. Bad cat, Charlie. Naughty, naughty boy."

The young man watched her for a few awkward seconds, until he heard the sound of other cats beginning to meow from inside the house. He turned to leave.

"Again, thank you."

Mrs. Colman flashed a manic smile.

"You, too. If you hadn't been here to catch Charlie for me, I don't know what I'dve done."

The young man nodded.

"Have a pleasant day."

The young man walked, case banging against his thigh with each step. Once he was a few blocks from the house, he slid a hand into his left front trouser pocket. He felt the corner of Edwards' business card and gave it a flick. He glanced left and right and pulled out the card and read it one last time. He crumpled it into a tight ball and smiled. Then he dropped it into the gutter, never once slowing his pace.

The diner had a baked-in greasy smell of ten-thousand hamburgers, all fried on the same uncleaned flattop grill, mixed with the sweat of decades' worth of stifling summer days. The place was virtually

14

empty, as the lunch hour had passed some forty minutes previous. A single old man sat at one of the tables, and turned his head when the young man entered. He continued to stare after the young man seated himself. He placed the case near his chair at a perpendicular angle and ordered a cup of coffee.

"You lookin' for someone?" the old man asked.

The young man shook his head as the waitress returned with his coffee. "Be back in a sec," she said, and ambled away. The young man lifted his cup and took a sip. The coffee was good, and strong.

The waitress returned with a clean pad of paper. She pulled a dull pencil from the pocket of her apron and tapped the eraser against the paper three times. She sighed. Despite her youth, her face was tired. There were lines beneath her eyes and at the corners of her mouth, which was fixed in a permanent sagging frown. She straightened the front of her golden brown uniform and addressed the young man.

"You ready? You want anything else?" she asked in a flat voice.

"Have you any sandwiches?"

"We got hamburgers. You want a hamburger?"

"What else do you have?"

"Cheeseburgers."

"That's the same basic sandwich. What else is there?"

"Grilled cheese," the waitress said with a cold stare. "We have patty melts, hot ham and cheese, cold ham and cheese, turkey club. We might have some chicken, but I think we're out. We have hot beef."

"What is that, please?"

"What it sounds like. Chunks of beef on a couple pieces of bread with gravy on top. I guess it's not a real sandwich. You can't pick it up or anything. They just call it that for some dumb reason."

"I suppose I'll order a hamburger."

"Didn't need to hear those other ones after all, did you?"

The waitress walked away, scribbling on her notepad. She moved in a slow, tired shuffle toward the window to the kitchen. She tore off the sheet on which she had written and tossed it with disinterested nonchalance onto the dull metallic base of the windowframe.

"Order up!"

The young man watched as a stubby hand appeared in the window and grabbed the ticket. It looked like it belonged to a giant, aged baby. A crown of frizzed black hair poked into view, swaying back and forth as though its owner were sitting atop a pendulum.

"This all?" a voice boomed through the opening. "Just a burger? Nothin' on the side? No fries or anything like that?"

The waitress leaned against the counter, eyes cast toward the front door.

"I don't think so."

"Did you ask?"

The waitress sighed and rolled her eyes toward the young man.

"You want anything else?"

"No, thank you."

"He said no," she called through the window and ran a hand through her mousebrown hair.

"Just makin' sure."

"I know."

The waitress tossed her notepad onto the counter and walked toward the rear of the diner, where there was an empty doorway which led to a darkened corridor. "I'll be outside a minute," she said as she disappeared through the opening.

The young man stared at his reflection his coffee. He blew, cooling it, and sipped.

"He ain't a midget, you know."

The young man set down his cup. He eyed the old man, still seated nearby.

"I beg your pardon?"

"I saw you lookin' through the window. He ain't no midget, but he's goddamned close."

"To whom are you referring?"

"In the kitchen," the old man said, pointing. "Guy that's makin' your burger. He's goddamn short but he ain't no midget. Has to have a crate to stand on, so he can see the goddamn griddle. I seen it myself. Otherwise, he wouldn't know what he's cookin'."

The old man laughed and took a cigarette from the inside breast pocket of his coat and stuffed it into his mouth. The coat was thin, navy blue with tiny black buttons. A brown cap, its inside stained yellow with old sweat, sat on the table in front of him. He struck a match and lit the cigarette.

"You want one?"

He gave the match a hard shake and threw it over his shoulder.

The young man shook his head and sipped some more coffee.

"Joe Nickles. Who're you?"

He did not remove the cigarette, and it flopped in his mouth when he spoke, flicking white ash down the front of his coat.

The young man paused before he made his reply.

"Jacob Peterson."

"You related to Carl and Alma?"

"No."

"You sure?"

"Yes."

Nickles nodded at the young man's case.

"You headed somewhere?"

"No."

"You got that case, you must be headed somewhere."

The young man looked toward the kitchen.

"You can't see him from where you're sittin'. Too short."

"I'm sorry?"

"He's too short."

"Who?"

"Guy who's cookin' your damn burger."

The young man nodded.

"Go on, get up and take a look at him."

The young man shook his head.

"You ever seen a midget? Like I said, he ain't no midget but he's as close as you're gonna see today. Why don't you go on up to the window and sneak a peek?"

The waitress reappeared from the back entrance and approached the ticket window.

"This isn't a zoo," she said. "Say Vern, how's that burger comin'?"

"Just a sec."

"I know it ain't a zoo. Besides, you don't see no midgets at a zoo, you see 'em at the carnival. You ever seen a midget at a zoo before?"

As Nickles continued to speak, the waitress brought the young man his hamburger. It was cooked well. Still juicy, but not too raw. A thick slice of strong purple onion sat on top of the meat, absorbing grease. The young man slathered some Heinz 57 on the bun, which he then planted on the burger. He bit into it, chewing slowly.

"Taste all right?" the waitress asked.

He nodded.

"I'll get you some more coffee."

"Get me some, too," Nickles shouted. "Dyin' of thirst over here."

His cigarette, now burned out, remained lodged in the corner of his mouth. When he was sure the waitress could see, he spat it onto the floor.

The waitress growled as she passed his table.

"I'm not telling you again. Use the ashtray."

She hissed like a snake through her teeth as she emphasized each word. Without stopping, she picked up the butt and walked away.

Nickles smirked, and cleared his throat and spat into a white paper napkin, which he crumpled into a tight ball and set on the edge of the table.

"Got a fresh one for you!" he laughed.

The waitress returned with the coffee pot. Her face was dark and there was visible tension in her jaw. She filled the young man's cup in silence, and then she turned and walked to Nickles' table. She stopped and stared at him. The young man could not see her face. The waitress filled Nickles' cup and reached for the balled napkin, but before she could take it he flicked it to the black and white tile floor with a playful smile. He laughed. The waitress said nothing, and bent over to retrieve the napkin. Nickles waved to the young man and pointed to her rump with his thumb. His fingers were long and thin, and his nails were a yellowy orange, like old packing tape. All the time he continued grinning and winking, his head bobbing like an obscene jack-in-the-box.

The young man looked at his plate.

"Whaddyou think of that?"

Nickles' voice was just above a whisper. The young man glanced up to see the waitress had gone.

"She's got it in all the right places, don't she?"

Keeping his voice down, Nickles began to laugh in a hoarse cackle, exposing his teeth. The top four were crooked, with the appearance of having been jammed into his mouth without the proper space to accommodate them. The particular angle at which the two front teeth touched each other made them a catching point for saliva, which was either deposited in a frothy white pool on his lower lip or spat across the table in long, clear strands.

"Got a terrible attitude, though. Nothin' you can do about that. Try jokin' with her – well, you seen how she gets. Don't know what her problem is."

The young man chewed in silence.

"Just get into town, didja?"

The young man nodded.

"Say, you hear anything about that thing that happened? That guy with the church?"

"No."

"Happened maybe two hundred miles from here. Maybe two hundred miles to the south?"

"I came in from the north."

"Too bad."

Nickles lit another cigarette and tossed the match behind him.

"When you get in? You come in this mornin'?"

The young man nodded and brought his cup to his lips. He emptied it, but continued to hold it in place, studying the heavy sedimentary stain at the bottom. He put down the cup.

"But you're not headed nowhere? You said you're not goin' nowhere. You got family here? You stayin' with them? You gonna stay at that table?"

The young man put the last bite of burger in his mouth and chewed. After swallowing, he lifted the cup and pretended to drink.

"You don't say much," Nickles said after the young man set the cup down again.

The young man looked for the waitress.

"She goes off all the time, never know where. Good luck gettin' a second cup. You're still hungry you'll probably starve before she gets back. I owned this place I'da fired her by now."

He scrunched up his face.

"Smell somethin'?"

The young man turned his head back toward Nickles' table. Plumes of smoke like morning fog rose from the table behind him. The young man stood and Nickles turned quickly and stumbled out of his chair, grabbed his coffee cup and poured its contents onto the table. The smoke spread across Nickles' side of the diner, bitter and dense. He grinned.

"Napkin. Goddamn match."

"What happened in here?"

The waitress appeared in the door to the hallway, her lips curled in exasperation.

"What did you do?"

"Don't worry, it's out."

The waitress walked about the diner, opening windows. She went to the door and, grunting, opened it and propped it with a broken brick.

"Everything's all right."

He elongated his words in a way designed to soothe.

The waitress found a towel and began to mop up the mess. She did not speak. Her mouth was shut, and the young man could hear her breathe hard and sharp through her nose. A sootblack mark had spread across the table where the napkin burned, and she rubbed at it with a white rag until it was dark as coaldust.

"Yeah, you're gettin' it all right," Nickles said as he observed her progress. "But I better get goin'. Money's on the table, for the food. But I bet you want a tip, huh? You want a tip?"

The waitress kept working.

"You gotta get outta this racket!"

Nickles laughed and shook his head. He took his cap and put it on, and tipped it when he passed the young man, still standing awkwardly by his table.

"See you, friend."

After he'd gone, the young man sat and watched as the waitress finished her work. When the tables were clean, she put the change Nickles had left in the ancient cash register at the counter. When she reset both tables she headed once more for the darkened hallway at the rear of the diner.

The young man cleared his throat, and the waitress spun back to address him.

"Yeah?"

"May I have another cup of coffee, please?"

She retrieved the pot.

"You want your ticket, too?"

"That would be fine."

"How long you stayin'?"

"I don't know. For a few days, I suppose."

"I mean at your table."

"I have no idea. Perhaps thirty minutes. Why do you ask? Are you on the verge of closing up?"

"I'm on the verge, all right."

She took the coffee pot back to its place on the counter.

"I'm sorry about what happened. I didn't know what was going on until the event had already transpired."

The waitress stood in the door of the hallway, framed in darkness. Her skin was pale, with a shiny film of bacon fat on her elbows. She crossed her arms and stared, one dark eyebrow arched imperiously on her forehead.

"I'm sorry. I can leave if you want."

"That's all right."

"I didn't mean to offend you in any way."

"You didn't. No more than anybody else."

The young man made it back to Mrs. Parker's house just in time to see a sparkling black Mercury pull into the driveway. It was her. She was sixty-five, he knew. There were lines around her eyes and her once-dark hair was swirled with gray. She stepped out of the car with no difficulty and stood, smoothing the wrinkles from her sea green dress.

"Mrs. Parker?"

The woman brought a white-gloved hand to her head, in line with her white pillbox hat, to shield her eyes from the glare of the late afternoon sun.

"Yes?"

"I have a message for you."

"What is it?"

The young man set down his case and stood before Mrs. Parker. He put one palm on her shoulder before he spoke.

"Your husband says that he's fine, and that he loves you and he misses you."

The second these words left the young man's lips, Mrs. Parker lost consciousness.

John Parker was late coming home from work. Mrs. Parker eyed the pork chops and sliced potatoes frying on the stove and watched the clock. It was twenty-three minutes after five. He was eight minutes late. Turning from the stove, Mrs. Parker looked at the heavy black telephone that hung on the wall by the kitchen door, cord hanging loose below and free of tangles. It did not ring. She returned to the stove, frowning, and lowered the heat on the pork chops. The potatoes sizzled in the pan as she jostled it over the burner and added some salt from the tiny bluebird-shaped shaker. She lifted one of the potatoes with an old wooden spoon. "I cut them too thick," she said and flipped the potato slice, exposing the dark butterbrown side. "Oh, well. Too late now." She flipped the other slices too, and soon the air was filled with hissing steam and the kitchen smelled warm and good. A glance out the window and Mrs. Parker moved the pan of chops from the burner.

She hoped John would not take much longer. She loved the creak of the back door when he opened it, and the thick hollow clattering of his keychain when he placed it in the green ceramic bowl on the kitchen counter. "I'm home!" he would shout even if she was there waiting for him. It was Mrs. Parker's favorite part of the day. It made up for everything.

The telephone rang.

"Parker residents, this is Mrs. Parker speaking."

She wiped her hands on her cream-colored apron, the receiver cradled beneath her left ear.

"Edith!" It was Gloria, John's receptionist. Her words tumbled in a mass of gurgled syllables. "You have to come here now, this second!"

"What's happened?"

"Please, just come down here. I can't talk. Just stop whatever you're doing and get here quick as you can."

She hung up.

By the time Mrs. Parker arrived at the office her husband was already dead. Gloria sat in a chair by the desk next to the examination room, and she stood when Mrs. Parker entered. Gloria's face was wet and there were strawberry patches around her eyes. A thin layer of slime coated her lip just under her nose. She wiped it with a crusty tissue she kept balled up in her palm.

"I'm so sorry, Edith."

"Where is he?"

"I'm just so sorry."

"Where is he?"

Gloria pointed to the door, frosted glass in impossible to see through apart from the vaguest of shapes.

"The coroner told me to stay out here. It was lucky he was in town, otherwise you'd have to wait a lot longer."

She gasped and brought the tissue to her mouth.

"Edith! I didn't mean that it was lucky! That's not what I meant, you have to believe me! It just slipped out that way. I would never say anything like that on purpose!"

"I understood what you meant."

"I just don't know what I'm saying."

Mrs. Parker nodded.

"Maybe you should step outside and get a breath of air."

Gloria waved the wadded tissue in wild swoops. Her arms were long and thin with elbows that stuck out like the handlebars of a bicycle.

"Maybe I should. It's so close in here I feel like I could smother to – Edith!"

When she was alone, Mrs. Parker knocked three times on the door to the examination room. Although it was latched and heavy the door was loose in its frame and it rattled for several loud seconds. Then it opened and the coroner stood there, light shining off his bald head, glaring the thick lenses of his glasses and hiding his eyes. Beads of sweat covered his jowls. He did not speak, and he held the door firm.

"May I–?" Mrs. Parker stuttered.

The coroner breathed through his mouth. His thick fingers drummed on the glass in the door.

"I know you got a right to. But I want you to wait out here a minute. And I need you to think about this. He doesn't look like himself, and you should think about whether you want this to be your last picture of him."

"What happened?"

"Heart attack. Gloria out here? She could tell you."

"She stepped outside for a minute."

"It happened fast. There wasn't even time to call anybody. I know you can't take much comfort in that, but at least it's something."

Mrs. Parker said nothing.

"I won't be ten minutes," the coroner said.

The sound of the closing door echoed like a gunshot in the empty office. Clutching her handbag, Mrs. Parker went to the second of the three chairs that lined the far wall and sat. Everything was quiet, save the heavy thud of the coroner's footsteps from the next room. A sudden choked sob broke the silence and Mrs. Parker tore into her handbag and grabbed a white handkerchief with a tiny green-stemmed tulip embroidered in the bottom right corner. She held it to her face, covering her mouth and eyes, heaving soundless and alone for the next minute. Then she regained her posture and placed the handkerchief back in her handbag.

Three minutes later there was a wet sniff at the office door.

"I'm sorry about before. Sometimes I just get that way. I get so upset I don't know what I'm saying, and then I end up saying the exact wrong thing."

"Don't worry, Gloria, I understand. Come in now and have a seat."

Gloria sat and blew her nose into what remained of the tissue.

"When my brother's wife was going to have a baby I told her she didn't look too fat. Not that she didn't look fat. That she didn't look too fat. But you don't want to hear about that. I'm sorry, Edith."

"I know it's difficult, but could you tell me what happened?"

Gloria nodded.

"I was there at the desk, and Mrs. Fisher had just left. She was the last appointment." She held her hands in her lap and tugged at her fingers. "He always stays in back a little while you know, just getting everything put the way he likes and getting his papers and everything straightened up. Then the coroner came in, I don't know why. He never called or anything, just showed up, and he wanted to know was Dr. Parker in. He wanted to see him. I don't know why, I said before. So I said, 'He's in back, I'll see if he's busy,' but he must've heard the coroner because he hollered to send him right in. So he went in and he closed the door, and I guess they were talkin'. Don't know what about. They were talkin' a while, and then I heard him – the coroner – go, 'John?' I guess he had trouble breathing. I don't know. I guess so. He was pourin' out sweat, I know that. His coat was like he'd walked neck-deep through a lake. I still have it right here. We took it off him."

She stood and lifted a white bundle from the desk. A puddle had collected underneath, and wet drops trickled off and spattered on the floor as she handed it to Mrs. Parker. The coat was sticky to the touch.

It smelled like him. Mrs. Parker unfolded it lengthwise and placed it in the chair to her left, and stared. It hurt to breathe. It hurt to sit. She did not move.

The door opened and the coroner appeared.

"What's your decision?"

"I want to see him." She stood, her gray eyes alert.

"You've really thought about it now."

"Yes."

The coroner stepped away from the door.

"It's your decision. Take your time. We'll be out here."

John's face was purple, and his neck. From the chest up he was purple, like a finger with a piece of string twisted tight around the knuckle. His eyes were shut. That was a good thing.

Gloria was gone when Mrs. Parker emerged from the examination room. The coroner stood close by the door.

"I truly am sorry. There wasn't anything I could do. If there was, I would've done it."

"I know."

"You want me to call your church, get them started on planning the funeral? I can have them get ahold of you when they're ready, when his body is. I'll take care of that for you, too."

"Yes. That would be fine."

She went to the chair and picked up her handbag.

"What about your son?"

"I'll call him when I get home."

A fire truck was parked in front of the house, blocking the driveway, when Mrs. Parker arrived. A thin blanket of dark smoke covered the lawn while neighbors clustered around and muttered to each other in low tones. Others watched with open stares as Mrs. Parker pulled up to the curb and got out of the car. The front door was open and she made her way to it on brisk footsteps, her shoes clicking sharp and quick against the sidewalk. A fireman appeared, hand outstretched.

"I'm sorry, Edith, but you'll hafta wait a few minutes."

"What's going on?"

He stroked his bushy red mustache.

"You leave somethin' fryin' on your stove?"

The potatoes.

"Oh, no..."

"Now, don't worry about it. Wasn't any real fire, just a whole lotta smoke. You'll have to give that stovetop a good wash and let your windows open a while, but other than that you're A-1. You'll have to throw that old pan out, though."

The air was acrid and it made Mrs. Parker's eyes water.

"Must feel pretty relieved, huh? You know, you're real lucky."

The entire downstairs reeked of scorched metal and potatoes burned black. The open windows did nothing but provide transport for the smell to drift room to room. When Mrs. Parker's son arrived near seven-thirty, the odor still had not dissipated. Six and a half months pregnant, his wife spent the evening on the porch.

That night, Mrs. Parker awoke from dreamless sleep. She thought a moment, and frowned. Soon she rose and crept in her warm blue nightgown through the hall and down the steps, moving silent and slow to the kitchen. The room was cool, bisected by a strong shaft of moon that poured in through one of the still-open windows. Mrs. Parker went to the counter and picked up the green ceramic bowl and held it and thought. Then she placed the bowl in the cupboard, and returned to her bedroom.

"You must be feeling a lot better, Mom," Nathan said.

29

Mrs. Parker smiled. The white plates were coated with a thick brown layer of gravy and grease and she rinsed each of them before she placed them in the sink in neat stacks. She rinsed each piece of silverware and the glasses, too.

"I do. I feel terrific."

"That's great. It's been so nice having you here, helping us out with the baby and all."

"He's beautiful."

"Shirley and I both appreciate it." He sniffed. "It's funny. We were worried."

Mrs. Parker turned on the faucet and added soap to the water. She dipped in one of her hands and swirled it until a white froth of suds reached the brim of the sink.

Nathan tried to speak over the sound of the dishes clanking against each other beneath the foam.

"Mom? We didn't know how you'd handle being by yourself all the time. Mom?"

She turned off the water.

"I said Shirley and I didn't know how you'd handle being by yourself all the time."

"I heard you, dear."

She dunked a glass beneath the surface and pulled it out. Great bubbles of air gurgled and snorted as she repeated the motion.

"I wasn't sure. But anyhow, you seem like you're doing really well."

"I am."

Mrs. Parker continued to smile.

"That's good. That's really good."

She rinsed the glass and held it up to the light.

"Yeah, we're both really glad," Nathan said and cleared his throat. "Listen, Mom. I need to talk to you."

"What about?"

She did not move from the sink.

"Come here, sit down by me. The dishes can wait."

"But the water's just right. It's just hot enough."

"That's all right, Mom. We can always fill it up again."

Mrs. Parker took a breath. She dried her hands and took a seat across the table from her son.

"Now, Shirley and I have been talking, and we have something we want to ask you."

"What is it?"

Nathan smiled.

"Well, we wondered if maybe you might want to come and stay with us from now on."

"Why would you wonder that?"

"What?"

"You said you wondered if I might want to stay with you. Why would you wonder that?"

"Well, we just – you know – you'll be all alone in that big house. I – we just want to be sure you'll be okay. You've never been by yourself like that before."

"I've been by myself these last few months."

"I know."

Nathan shifted in his seat. He cleared his throat once more and laughed a single discomforted "ha." His smile began to fall.

"You just said it seemed like I was doing well."

"I did. You do. You are."

"Then why would you want me to move in here – if you think I'm doing so well? It doesn't make any sense."

Her shoulders were rigid. Her voice was calm, but dry. It sounded as though she needed a drink of water.

"We just thought you might want to live with us. That's all. You've seemed so happy here with us that we thought you might just want to stay on. That's all. We didn't mean anything by it."

Mrs. Parker nodded.

"Would you at least think about it? Please. Just think about it."

"Please don't talk down to me."

"Mom, I'm not."

"You are. You just don't think I can see it. Or maybe you don't even know you're doing it. But you are."

"Mom–"

"People have been talking down to me for the last three months. If I go to the store, everyone tells me how well I look. Then they whisper to each other about how difficult it must be for me now. What's difficult? I've been to that store ten thousand times. I know what I'm doing. I can take care of a house. I can take care of myself. I didn't become an old lady overnight just because your father died."

She slid her hand across the table and touched Nathan's sleeve.

"Darling, Bryant is my home."

"I'm sorry, Mom. I didn't mean to upset you. But if you change your mind, just tell me. We'll always have a place for you here. All right?"

Mrs. Parker stood and wiped her forearm. She lifted a finger to her nose and sniffed it before snaking out her tongue for a brief taste.

"Mom?"

"I have to wipe down the table. Somebody spilled the gravy."

Mrs. Parker pulled the car into the driveway. Her heavy brown suitcase thudded on the floor behind her against the back and front seats when she slowed, and then parked. She sat a minute thinking and listening to the low rumble of the engine. Nathan and Shirley had spent breakfast asking her to reconsider leaving so soon. It did no good. With a frown, she turned the key in the ignition and the engine went quiet. She sat. She stared at the big empty house. She took the keys and dropped them into her handbag, and clasped it closed. The door handle gave way with a metallic buckling sound and she stepped out of the car. It was close to noon, she figured. The August sun hung high and hot overhead. It wasn't until she retrieved the suitcase from the back of the car and slammed the door that she heard Mrs. Colman's voice.

"Edith! Yoo-hoo, Edith!"

Mrs. Parker turned to see her neighbor approaching with a sharp pair of pruning shears in her hand. They were new and they gleamed like a mirror in the bright light of day. Although Mrs. Colman wore a wide-brimmed straw hat her face was red as the shell of a boiled lobster.

"Edith, you're back already. I thought sure you'd be gone the rest of the week."

"No. We had a change in plans."

"Well, that's a real shame, Edith. Here I thought you'd be with that cute little grandson of yours through Sunday. I'm so jealous, Edith, you have no idea. So jealous. You don't know how lucky you are to have him."

"Oh, I know."

She took a backward step to the house. Mrs. Colman moved two steps closer.

"I've had such a day. I've been out here puttering around with my flowers since eight this morning. Since eight. And I've not been back in the house, not even for a cold drink of water. And believe me, I sure do feel I could use one about now."

She took out a cigarette and lit it and pulled on it with deep drags.

"Maybe you should get one."

"Not 'til I'm finished, Edith, not 'til it's all done. If I go in now I'll get so cozy and relaxed I won't ever wanna move again, ever. You know what time it is?"

"I'm not sure. It's around noon, I suppose."

"Noon! That's four hours I've been out her so far today, Edith. Four hours! Can you believe it?"

"I don't know that it's exactly noon. It was only a guess."

"And a good one, I'll bet! It sure does feel like four hours. You should come see. I started in the front since that's what everybody notices. That's what they tell me, anyhow. But the back is just as important – it is to me. Even though not as many people can see it. I can see it. It makes a difference to me."

Mrs. Parker switched her suitcase from one hand to the other.

"I had no idea there was so much work back there, though. It's just unending. But it's so worth it. Come and look."

"I can see the ones in front, and they look very nice."

"Oh, you have to see them up close to really see them! You have to see them up close! I mean to really see them! It's just not the same all the way over here. You can see how bright they are – the sun is just right for it now – but you can't tell how <u>big</u> – how big and how full. It's their bigness, their size that sets them apart. It really is."

"I'll tell you what. I'll go home and unpack and have some lunch. You should eat something, too. You should take a rest. Then in the afternoon perhaps I'll give you a call, or maybe I'll just come knock on your door and you can show me then."

"That sounds wonderful. I'll see you then."

"All right."

Mrs. Parker hefted the suitcase toward the house and began to trudge up the drive.

"Oh, Edith!"

She stopped, turned back.

"Yes?"

"How was he?"

She smiled.

"He was perfect."

"I'm so jealous, Edith. So jealous."

Once Mrs. Parker was inside the house, she dropped the suitcase and shook her arms until they stopped hurting. Then she went to the living room and sat in her chair until it was time to fix dinner.

The house was black and quiet. It was like being locked in a cramped closet. Outside the air was thick, still. Nothing could be seen in the cloud-covered sky. Mrs. Parker turned in bed, taking care to stay on her side of the mattress. She opened her eyes wide but she could not see the clock. It felt very late. She wondered if she would ever sleep well again. Folding down the blankets, she sat and thought and then got out of bed. She knelt on the floor and folded her hands, interlocking her fingers and holding them tight. She prayed for her husband to hear her. She knew she would pray again the next night, and the night after. She was very still and quiet. She prayed for a very long time.

Mrs. Parker awakened to the feeling of dozens of pointed green fingers tickling at the back of her neck. The smell of chlorophyll was strong. She blinked several times before her eyes regained focus. The young man knelt at her side, face lined with tension, and held one of her hands, patting it gently.

"What happened?"

Her voice was groggy.

"You collapsed. You've been out for the past two minutes."

Mrs. Parker said nothing.

"You don't appear to have hurt yourself. How do you feel? Are you in any pain?"

"I don't think so. Who are you?"

"My name is Jacob Peterson. You said you feel no pain. Tell me, are you light-headed? Do you feel dizzy?"

His voice was clear and strong and his eyes were intense, blue like ice.

"No. I'm sure I'm fine"

"Are you able to stand?"

"I think so. But you'll have to help me up."

"Of course."

He helped Mrs. Parker to her feet. She brushed bits of grass from her dress and straightened her hat.

"Here's your bag."

"Thank you."

She opened it and glanced inside before closing it again fast.

"Would you help me to the door?"

The young man walked alongside, arms spread as if to snatch her as she scaled the porch steps. There was an unbalanced feel to the way she moved, as though one of her legs were an inch longer than the other.

"Do you need something cool to drink?" the young man asked after he had led her into the living room and helped her to recline on the sofa.

"No, thank you. I think I just need to lie here a minute."

The young man stepped back toward the front door and bumped into a narrow wooden stand about three feet tall, on top of which sat a framed photograph. The stand was top-heavy and began to wobble as soon as the young man touched it.

"Oh, be careful!" Mrs. Parker's voice was frantic.

The young man turned and caught the stand before it could topple over and pushed the picture frame flat against its podium with a crisp metallic snap.

"Be careful!"

"I have it, don't worry."

"Did you break it? Is it broken?"

The young man checked the glass.

"No. It's all right."

"Thank goodness. I don't know what I would have done if it was broken."

The young man set the photograph upright on the stand. In it sat a man with a black mustache and thick dark hair that was pushed to one side and close-cropped around his ears, which made them appear to stick out. He wore a white coat. The young man turned from the photograph to Mrs. Parker and stepped forward. One hand she held to her chest and the other to the side of her face.

"I'm sorry I've upset you. I didn't mean to. I was unsure of how you would react outside, and what happened with the stand a few moments ago was clearly an accident. I meant no harm, and I do apologize."

"What did you say your name was?"

"Jacob Peterson."

"Mr. Peterson, just what is it that you want?"

The young man had a shy smile.

"I'm sorry. I just came to give you the message. I should have made you better prepared for it, I suppose, but I never fully understand the significance of these things."

"What do you mean?"

The young man's eyes sharpened and Mrs. Parker felt the urge to look away from him when he spoke.

"I don't know how to explain it other than to say I can see things others cannot. Mind you, it isn't any traditional sense of vision – it's more of a feeling. I'll be minding my own business when I'll be struck by it. All at once, I will hear a voice. It is not the voice of a man, or of a woman. I cannot explain exactly how it sounds. It may not even be a voice in the traditional sense. But this voice – when I hear it, it tells me things. It will tell me a message, and although the message might not make complete sense to me, I know it is something to which I must listen."

The young man folded his hands as if in prayer. His voice was soft and warm and Mrs. Parker sat up partway on the sofa to better hear him.

"For example, I was once told to find a Mr. Reed in Montana. His son had gone missing for some time, and the voice told me where to find this Mr. Reed and what to tell him. I'm sorry to say the news was not good, Mrs. Parker, but the man was glad to receive it, and finally feel a sense of closure in his life.

"Another time, the voice told me to travel as far west as California and tell a family by the name of Johnson where they might find a car of theirs that had been stolen. I am happy to report that they found the car, and apart from the mileage that had been accumulated, it was in the same condition as when it was taken."

He smiled in bewilderment.

"I don't fully understand what all of this means, Mrs. Parker, nor why the lord might have chosen to bestow this gift on me, but I do know that when I hear the voice and hear its instructions, I must follow them. I don't know if I could live with myself if I didn't."

By this time, Mrs. Parker was sitting up. She did not move or speak.

"It's strange, but sometimes this thing – this spirit, if you will – will speak through me so that others may hear. I can never tell when it's going to happen. I never know it has happened until it's over, and I can never remember what has been said. I am simply overtaken. My back becomes rigid and my eyes open wide and I begin to speak. The voice is mine, but the words are not my own. I'm told that the words I speak are of those who have passed on – words of friends, family, spouses."

Mrs. Parker's voice quivered.

"What are you trying to tell me?"

"That's just the thing." The young man knelt before her. "I don't know why I've been sent here, but I feel it was for a purpose only you or your husband may understand." He smiled. He looked embarrassed. "I know you think all of this sounds crazy. I can hardly blame you."

Mrs. Parker swallowed. "When you heard this voice, what did it say? What were you supposed to tell me?"

The young man closed his eyes. He took a breath and folded his arms at his chest.

"It told me I was to come to 114 Oak Street in Bryant, where I was to find Mrs. Edith Parker and tell her that her husband can hear her. The voice said Mrs. Parker's husband is fine, and that he loves her and misses her very much."

Mrs. Parker's eyes began to fill.

39

"Wh-what else did the voice say?"

The young man's eyes remained closed, his arms folded.

"The voice said that I must come find you on this day. That was the most important thing – that I find you and relay the message today, on this specific day." The young man opened his eyes. "Tell me. Is this day in any way significant to your or your husband?"

She nodded. Tears streamed down her cheeks and collected at the point of her chin and hung there without falling. "Yes. This was the day he died. Ten years ago."

"His death was sudden, wasn't it?"

"Yes." She sounded as though she were breathing underwater.

"You had no time to prepare, is that correct?"

She had trouble speaking.

"Yes. Yes it is."

The young man nodded slowly and watched as she continued to cry. He reached for her hands, which she held out to be accepted. She had skin like ice. It was wet with tears and her delicate bones trembled beneath the young man's touch.

"I think perhaps your husband has another message for you."

Mrs. Parker whimpered. A thick dripping ooze began to seep from her nose and the young man pulled a handkerchief from his back pocket and used it to wipe her face.

"I'm sorry."

"You have no reason to apologize. You've been through so much." He placed the damp cloth in her hands.

"I've just– It's–" Her voice broke. "I've waited so long. I've just waited for so long."

"I understand."

"And-and you think you'll hear more? Will there be more?"

"It would be unfair of me to give you an answer, positive or negative. For all I know, that first message may have been the end of it."

A single trickle dribbled from her right nostril. "When will you know for sure?" She sniffed.

"Not until I hear the voice again. And remember, there is no guarantee that I will."

Mrs. Parker looked at the floor when she spoke.

"Mr. Peterson, would it be too much for me to ask that you stay here for the next few days, just to be sure? I would hate – Could you?" She stared at him. Her expression was filled with such naked yearning it was almost painful to watch. Her eyes were like glass and she seemed afraid to breathe.

The young man nodded once.

"If you think I must," he said in a soft voice.

"I do."

"All right. I shall."

"Thank you. Thank you so much."

She reached out as if to hug him, but pulled her arms back before she could make contact.

The young man raised his hands.

"I think that to begin with, we must say a prayer together."

"Yes. Yes, I do, too."

"Please. Kneel down with me."

Mrs. Parker fell to her knees with a thud that rattled the trinket-filled shelves. Her bones creaked and popped but she felt no pain. She closed her eyes and cried and held her interlocked fingers to her chest.

"Come," the young man said. "Let us pray."

Mrs. Parker apologized for not making a fancy dinner. There was very little food in the house and the grocery store had closed before it was time to fix anything, so they ate some chicken she found in the refrigerator. The chicken was baked and the juices that collected at the bottom of the dish congealed into a heavy waxlike paste that made wet schlurping sounds whenever a piece was taken. There was bread, too, cut into fat slices with firm pats of butter that tore the bread when Mrs. Parker attempted to smooth them with a knife. Before eating, the young man closed his eyes and bowed his head in silent prayer. Mrs. Parker followed his example. Then they ate.

The food was salty but good. Mrs. Parker added more salt to the food on her plate until it looked like it was coated with thick morning frost. She ate with unselfconscious enthusiasm. She dipped her bread into the dripping on her plate and tore into the chicken. The young man was careful. He took a bite of bread, then swallowed. Then some chicken. Then he drank some milk. Then he repeated the process. Neither of them said much.

Throughout the meal the young man noticed Mrs. Parker looking past his seat to a wooden stand in the corner of the room. It was identical to the one at the front of the house, except it was empty.

When the meal was finished Mrs. Parker washed the dishes. She refused to let the young man help so he sat at the kitchen table and watched in silence.

Later in the evening they went to the living room, Mrs. Parker in her chair, the young man on the sofa. The room smelled strong of roses and he felt a headache developing. He rubbed his eyes and grimaced.

"Do you feel all right?"

He put down his hands and smiled a weary smile.

"Yes. Thank you. I'm fine."

"You look exhausted."

"I traveled quite a long way to get here."

"How far did you come?"

"More than seven hundred miles."

"My goodness! And did you walk that whole way?"

"No." The young man spoke in a shy voice. "I managed to hitch a few rides."

"Oh, my. Isn't that awfully dangerous?"

"No. I can handle myself. And most people are pretty friendly. To godliness brotherly kindness; and to brotherly kindness charity."

"It's good that you can still rely on people."

The young man nodded.

"I'm sure you'll sleep well tonight."

"I'm afraid not. I've not slept through the night in more years than I can remember."

"But after coming all that way–"

"It makes no difference."

"It's funny. I never used to have trouble sleeping."

"And now?"

"I can't do it, just like you."

The young man's eyes moved to the stand near the door and the photo resting on it. When he returned his gaze to Mrs. Parker twelve seconds later he found her staring at him, bent forward in her chair with lips pursed tight and body still as death.

"I won't all of a sudden begin to speak in his voice. That isn't how it works. I sound like myself for the most part. That's what I've been told."

43

"How did you–?"

"I told you," the young man said with an embarrassed smile. "I'm not entirely sure myself."

"I guess I'm just anxious."

"That's understandable. I would imagine you have quite a lot of questions you want to ask him, things you want to say."

She let out a chuckle of surprise and then shook her head.

"I never really thought about it before."

"I've found that's often the case. People will go through their entire lives wanting something, but when you ask them why they can't say."

Mrs. Parker sat in silent thought.

"I'm sorry," the young man said. "I didn't mean to imply anything. If I insulted you I apologize."

She looked up.

"You didn't say anything wrong."

Watching him against the fine clean fabric of the sofa accentuated the age and poor condition of his clothing. The cuffs of his jacket were the faint brown of road dust stained foul with layers of dirt and sweat that could not be washed out. His shoes seemed newer, but they did not match the suit. They needed to be polished and Mrs. Parker was certain the soles were beginning to wear through.

"I just realized. I never asked about your bags."

"Of course."

The young man sprang from the sofa and walked at a brisk pace to the front door.

"I forgot it outside earlier."

"It?"

Mrs. Parker stood as the young man stepped onto the front porch. She followed him and stopped in the doorway to watch as he picked up his pathetic-looking case. Taking a few steps back, she bumped into the stand again and nudged the photo off-balance. She grabbed it before it could fall and she held it close with both hands. She felt afraid to move, afraid to breathe. She heard footsteps and the closing of the door and she turned and saw the young man standing behind her, case in hand.

"Here it is," he said.

When they returned to their seats Mrs. Parker brought along the photo and placed it between them on the coffee table so she could watch both her guest and her husband simultaneously. She smiled at the thought. The young man balanced the case on his knees, palms held flat against its side. The case was in worse shape than his suit. Only one of the clasps remained, and some fabric dirty white like a used handkerchief protruded from a hole in the bottom corner. The young man ran his hand along the edge until he found the hole and felt the cloth, which he pushed back in with a quick thrust of his index finger.

"You don't have much, do you?"

"No, I surely don't."

"Hmm."

"I don't mind doing without." He smiled. "Take head, and beware of covetousness: for a man's life consisteth not in the abundance of things which he possesseth."

"You certainly know your Bible."

With a look of pride the young man opened his case and pulled out an old tattered book. Its cover was black and frayed strings dangled along the spine like the dry roots of a dead plant. The words "Holy Bible" were stamped on the front in faded gold lettering and its pages were thin, almost transparent, and looked as though they would crumble into powder if they were touched.

"That's because of this," he said. "This book has been in my family for many years. It's always been very precious to me. It's all I have left of them. Since I was a young boy I've made it a point to read it and learn a new verse each day, to absorb what I could so that I might be able to lead a decent Christian life."

"That's good to hear. So many people don't seem to feel that way."

"I know. I've been all across the country and I can tell you with certainty that more and more people are abandoning the Christian values. They would sooner look out for themselves than help their fellow man – even in a small community such as this one. And in the cities – in the cities I've seen sights to make you wonder how the lord could let such things continue. It is not for us to question his ways, but at the same time it pains me to see such acts go unpunished, and often rewarded. People behave like depraved animal. They do and they take what they want when they want without one thought to consequence."

Mrs. Parker clicked her tongue.

"It is a changing world," the young man said, "and we are the poorer for it. A man could lie bleeding in the gutter, agonizing on the verge of death, and be completely ignored by his neighbor. I can assure you it happens each day. And those souls who pass through this life with their eyes shut and their hearts closed off, believe me when I say that they sleep better than you or I ever have. When I think of it I often remember the words of President Roosevelt, rest his soul. Do you know what he said? 'The virtues are lost in self-interest as rivers are lost in the sea.' He was so right, Mrs. Parker, he was more right than he knew."

He took the case by its loose handle and set it on the floor by his feet. He held the Bible in his lap.

Mrs. Parker hesitated. "May I ask you a question?"

"Of course."

"I don't want to make you feel out-of-sorts."

"I am twenty-four years old."

"No. I was wondering about that, but it wasn't what I wanted to ask you."

"Ask me anything you like," he said with a smile.

"How long have you heard voices?"

"I hear only one voice."

He turned the Bible in his hands and balanced it on its spine.

"It sounds like nothing I know. I am not sure I can properly explain – it's more of a feeling. I get the feeling – or rather, it is given to me. I receive it. If it is necessary for others to hear, I speak it. And the words arrive as I speak them."

"How does it feel? Does it feel like anything?"

The young man closed his eyes. His face was peaceful, beatific. "It's warm. It's like basking in the brightest, purest sunlight you can imagine. It feels safe. The only thing of which I'm truly aware when I receive these messages is the feeling of calm that envelopes me. It's the best thing I can think of. It is total, absolute. I can't describe it any other way. I don't have the words."

He opened his eyes.

"How long has it been happening?"

"Since I was a boy."

"What was it like? That first time, I mean. Did you know what was going on? Were you afraid?"

"I was not afraid. The first occurrence was just as comforting as the many that followed. Fear is not a reaction I associate with this–" he searched for the right word "-gift."

"How old were you?"

"I was ten."

He looked away.

"What happened?"

The young man did not respond.

"You don't have to say." Mrs. Parker felt ashamed. Her face burned. "I shouldn't pry."

"I was ten." The young man continued to look away. "My family and I were eating dinner. My father sat at the head of the table, with my mother on the opposite side. Across from me sat my two older sisters, Mary and Ruby. I sat by myself. I was lifting a glass of milk to my lips when all of a sudden, I felt something. I wasn't sure what was happening. I dropped the glass and it shattered on the floor. My father was not an easy man, and he shouted in my ear and slapped me hard across the face. I remained still. Then I looked at him and I said, 'Your mother won't wake up tomorrow morning. This is her last day on Earth. Go to her now while you still have the chance.' My father didn't understand. He thought I was being insolent for his slapping me. He grabbed me by the arm and pulled me to him, hitting me in the face again and again. I didn't feel a thing. My sisters told me later that he continued to shout at me, demanding I apologize for what I had said. I remained expressionless. So he picked me up by the neck and hauled me to my bedroom, where he threw me to the ground and locked the door.

"Morning came. That entire day my ears rang so I could scarcely hear. Not long after I was let out of my room we received word that my grandmother had indeed passed away overnight. My father didn't believe me when I told him of the voice. No one did. Not my sisters, my mother – nobody I told. They all would ask, 'How could you say such a thing? What possessed you?' The fact that my grandmother really had passed away seemed beyond their comprehension. But still, I didn't know what to tell them. I was just as perplexed as they.

"The same kind of situation occurred so many times. So often I would feel that same presence within myself and I would relate my family what had been told me. Not once did they listen. Not once did they believe. I began to hear things that pertained to others from the town in which we lived, and I would go to them and tell them what I had heard. They were always so thankful. Even in the face of such overwhelming evidence my own family looked on me as though I was some kind of... I was a cipher to them. They seemed utterly bewildered by me.

"The messages became father-reaching, but I always managed to find a way to contact the people I needed to. At first I would write letters, but one day my father intercepted me when I was about to purchase a stamp for one of them. He took my money and he dragged me home, nearly dislocated my arm, all the time saying the most awful things you can imagine under his breath. When we arrived home he tore up the letter and threw it in my face. He beat me until he was winded but it did not diminish my resolve. That night once everyone was asleep, I snuck out of the house and began the journey to find the letter's intended recipient. You understand, I found this task to be too important to stop. I did not want to disobey the wishes of my father, but when the lord entrusts you with a mission, you must not turn your back. And so, I've devoted my life to following that mission. I've not had a real home since."

"Isn't that terribly difficult?"

"Now unto him that is able to do exceeding abundantly above all that we ask or think, according to the power that worketh in us, unto him be glory in the church by Christ Jesus throughout all ages, world without end."

"Did you ever see your family again?"

"Once. I felt something awful could happen, so I went to their home. Three years had passed. They had moved to a new town since I left. Still I found them. I never wanted anything more than to see them again. I traveled day and night to reach their new home, and I prayed that when they saw me they would forgive me of whatever wrongs they felt I had committed. Unfortunately, it was not to be. When I arrived at their home they turned me away. They wouldn't even let me step inside. My mother cursed me. My own mother. She cradled a baby in her arms as she spat out venomous words no child was meant to hear. My father said nothing at all. He stared at me, and spat at my feet. I stood there, listening, allowing my mother to continue. When she finally stopped I said what I had come to say. Then I left. I never saw them again. Their house burned to the ground the next day."

Mrs. Parker felt a chill and pulled the covering from the back of her chair and wrapped it snug about her shoulders.

"I've been moving ever since then," the young man said.

"Do you still think of them?"

"Of course. I think of everyone I've met. They're always with me. I'm sure you understand."

She frowned. "I do."

The young man picked up his case by the corners and opened it so Mrs. Parker could not see what was inside. He placed the Bible in the case and closed it and stared past her with guilty eyes.

"I was wondering if I could ask a favor of you."

"What is it?"

The young man's posture fell as though he were afraid she might lash out and strike him.

"By any chance, might I be able to wash out some of my things in your sink?"

"Of course you may."

He smiled and thanked her, straightening himself once more.

"But tell me," she said. "How much do you really have?"

"To be honest, I'm down to my last few shirts."

"That settles it. The first thing tomorrow, we're going to go out and buy you some new clothes."

"I couldn't let you do that."

"I insist. This is the least I could do."

"No. Thank you just the same, but no."

"Please. It would mean so much to me."

The young man considered.

"I just can't. When I began living my life in this way I made an oath to myself never to let anyone spend money on my behalf, regardless of who they were."

"Don't you worry a thing about it." There was a distinct finality to Mrs. Parker's voice.

"Thank you." Standing, he said, "If you'll forgive me, Mrs. Parker, I think I'm going to try and get some rest."

She looked out the window. The sky was black and floating clouds of bugs swarmed around the orange-glowing orbs of porchlight that lined the street.

"Goodness, I didn't realize it was so late."

"Time has a tendency to sneak up on you." The young man lifted his case. "I'll say good night, then," he said as he walked toward the door.

Mrs. Parker stood and the chair cover fell in a pile on the floor.

"Where are you going?"

"I intend to sleep on your porch."

"Nonsense." She scurried around the coffee table and blocked his path. "I won't hear of it. As long as you're here you'll stay in the guest room."

"I don't want to impose."

Mrs. Parker placed a hand on his arm.

"You're not imposing. It's my son's old bedroom. Nobody's slept there in ages, but I change the bedding every two weeks."

"I must admit, it does sound tempting."

"Then it's settled."

The young man rose some time after midnight. Cricketsqueaks of bedsprings echoed in the dark when he stood and stopped and waited, listening. No sound of stirring came from the room across the hall and he turned the knob and opened the door and paused to allow his eyes to adjust. When he could see again he stepped into the hallway, door still open, and crept on bare feet along the smooth softness of the rug and began to descend the stairs. The wood was sturdy and he could walk without making noise. When he reached the bottom of the stairs he stopped. He was right. The stand was empty.

It was morning when the young man awoke. He yawned and stirred beneath the sheets, sending a particulate cloud of dust above the bed, illuminated in the sunlight like fuzzy specks of gold. The mattress was firm and it felt good to lie on. The room was small but was not cramped and it did not have the stale smell of non-habitation. It was the room of a child, with a tiny writing desk against the wall and sports pennants of colorful felt hanging nearby. The walls were the shade of eggshells and a circular blue rug lay in the middle of the floor. The young man slept naked and his skin felt clean thanks to a steaming shower before bed. Sitting, he edged his way to the front of the bed before he stood near the open window and let the crisp air of daybreak cascade over his body. He rubbed his face and stretched and tried to wake up, sighing and turning and letting the morning breeze blow against his back.

The kitchen was warm and filled with sizzling and popping and pleasant smells. Mrs. Parker set a plate heaped with fried eggs on the counter near the stove and put a lid over it before she lifted a halfcooked strip of bacon with a fork and flipped it in a massive black iron skillet. Her husband's photo sat on a windowsill framed by a halo of sunlight. She turned when she heard the young man enter the room and she smiled.

"Did you have a good sleep last night?"

"It wasn't bad. Thank you."

"Sit down here at the table. I'll have breakfast ready in a minute."

The young man pulled a chair scuffscrape across the tile and sat. He placed his hands on the table and folded them.

"I always like to eat breakfast in the kitchen. The light here in the morning is so beautiful. It's too bright in the afternoon. Was the bed all right for you?"

"Yes, thank you, it was fine."

"I wasn't sure it would be. You're taller than my son, but I didn't think of it until the middle of the night. I didn't know if you were too tall for it or not."

"No. Sleeping in any bed is something of a novelty for me."

Mrs. Parker stacked the bacon on a dish, which she set in the center of the table. She placed the eggs there, too, and lifted the lid and went to the cupboard and found two plates.

The young man stood. "May I help you?"

"No, it just takes a second. It's only the two of us."

"There must be something I can do."

"You can sit down and enjoy your breakfast. That's why I made it. It looks to me like you don't get enough to eat, anyway."

He sat, waiting with patience as Mrs. Parker loaded his plate with food.

"Do you like coffee?" she asked when she gave him his silverware. "I made a pot, but I wasn't sure if you liked it."

"I do, yes. That would be nice."

"Would you like some sugar?"

"No, thank you."

The young man waited for Mrs. Parker to sit before he began.

"Do you have everything you need? Do you want anything else?" She speared some egg with her fork and put it in her mouth.

The young man bowed his head and closed his eyes.

"Let us pray."

Mouth full of egg, Mrs. Parker dropped her fork and it clattered on her plate. She did not chew until he was done.

54

The young man did not open his eyes.

Dishes washed and returned to the cupboard, Mrs. Parker dried her hands with a thin white towel.

"We'd better get going."

"I'm sorry?"

She hung the towel on the handle of the drawer by the sink.

"We're going to the store. They close at noon, so if we want to go buy you some new things to wear we should get down there."

"You've already done so much for me. Suppose I receive no further information. You'll have purchased these clothes for nothing. You've let me stay here, you've given me food – I can't possibly repay you for any of this."

"I don't want you to. It's a gift."

"But I told you, I've made a vow to myself–"

Mrs. Parker's voice was patient but firm.

"Mr. Peterson, I don't see how you can possibly ever have anything better if you keep going by this system you've set up for yourself. Those clothes will fall apart soon if you don't stop wearing them. How would you get the money to buy anything new? You don't take money, and I know you would never steal. You probably don't approve of taking charity, either, and that's fine. This isn't charity. I'm just doing you a favor. If I get you something nice today that'll last you, well, then you won't have to worry about clothes for a while."

The young man opened his mouth to speak but she cut him off.

"And don't worry about this costing me a lot of money, either. It won't be that much, and anyway, my husband was a doctor. He left me enough to be comfortable – more than comfortable. I have that nice car outside, I have this nice house. I'm not struggling at all. You don't need to worry a thing about it. If you want to do some work out in the yard to try and square it, you may. But remember, you don't have to. Now get your jacket. We're going."

The young man rose from the table and headed upstairs.

"I give money to the church, too," Mrs. Parker said as an afterthought.

The young man's new trousers were stiff like canvas as he ambled down the sidewalk. Clean clothes felt odd, new shoes like hooves clomping upon the pavement. His hat was pushed back and his hands hung low in the pockets of his tan jacket, halfway undone. The day was perfect. He took his hands out and pulled an unopened packet of cigarettes from the front of his shirt. He took care in peeling the cellophane from it, his movements clinical, specific, sliding off the thin clear plastic to retain its rectangular shape. Once it was off he folded it into thirds and opened the pack and put it carefully inside. He lifted the pack to his face and inhaled, savoring the sweetness of it, before he selected a butt and lit it. His first of the day. Closing his eyes, he smiled and replaced the pack in his shirt before he exhaled.

The diner closed at noon. Everything did, except for the churches. The young man rubbed his forehead and thought and began to walk again. There was not much to look at beyond main street apart from the houses, many of them no more than one storey. One block from the diner stood two brick apartment buildings with short iron patios not wide enough to stand on lining the windows of the second floor. From an open window in one of the buildings protruded the back of a woman in a red-checked shirt reclining against the grate in the sun, legs stretched into her apartment. Her hair was pulled back in a tight ponytail and her arms were crossed. In her right hand she held a smoked-to-the-filter cigarette, from which she took the occasional puff. It was her.

The young man drug from a fresh cigarette.

"Good afternoon."

The waitress did not turn.

"Good afternoon. Miss, good afternoon!"

The waitress gave a slight roll of her eyes to glance beyond the grating.

"When you failed to respond I thought perhaps I'd made a mistake. I'm glad to see it's you after all."

The waitress took the cigarette from her lips and flicked it at the young man's feet. A pack of Camels lay at her side. Continuing to watch the young man she picked it up and slapped it on the end a few times. Then she took another cigarette and lit it.

"Perhaps you don't remember me. We met yesterday at the diner. I'd say it was about–"

The waitress shook the match before tossing it away.

"Yeah, I remember you. Whaddayou want."

"Nothing. I simply recognized you and felt it might be nice if I said hello."

"Oh, gee, you did? That's real nice."

She looked back to her apartment.

"Excuse me, miss, but I don't know that I've said or done anything for which I should be insulted."

"You mean besides bein' here?"

"I beg your pardon? Your voice is so soft, I can't..."

"I said, 'You mean besides being here.' Yow get it now?"

"I don't see how I could have failed to miss it the first time."

"Head's up your ass."

"I'm sorry?"

"I'm not repeating that."

"I see."

"Why are you here?"

"I told you, I thought I recognized you and that–"

"-it might be nice. Yeah. I got that before. Other than that, do you have a reason to still be talkin' to me? 'Cause if you don't I'd just as soon you keep on walking. I don't get a whole lot of time to myself other than Saturday afternoon and all day Sunday."

"Don't you attend church services?"

"No. I do not."

The young man finished his cigarette.

"And why is that? If you don't mind my asking?"

The waitress glared, her eyes hard and cold.

"I do mind. But I'll tell you. I don't feel like spending my only full day off sittin' in a roomful of chumps who all think that some giant invisible man in the sky cares whether or not they do bad things."

"Chances are, he does not care. Is that what you mean?"

"Nope. Chances are, he ain't up there."

The waitress turned away from him.

"It's interesting. I don't attend services myself."

"Why are you still here? You're ruining my nice day."

"I haven't been to a church service since I was twelve years of age. Isn't that something? I've not returned since I was confirmed."

"That supposed to make us friends or something?"

"No. It just seems an interesting coincidence. That's all. A coincidence. Nothing more."

A faint trickle of smoke escaped the waitress' parted lips.

The heavy front door of the building creaked as it swung shut. Beyond the entryway was a solid hand-carved banister, worn with age and pockmarked with what looked like clumsy hammer blows. The stairs were old, too, and had absorbed so many footsteps the finish was worn off, leaving exposed the soft light brown underneath. The ceiling was high at the foot of the stairs, lined with dusty white tin tile with hexagonal patterns. Each step the young man took elicited a moaning squeak that rattled off the waterstained walls.

When he reached the door, he knocked. Soon the waitress appeared and flung the door open before she wandered into the kitchen area.

"Want some coffee?"

"Are you brewing some?"

"It's a yes or no question. You want some coffee or not?"

"Yes, if you're having some, I will. That would be nice. Thank you."

The waitress looked up from the counter. "You waitin' for a goddamned invitation? Come in."

The young man stepped inside and closed the door. The apartment consisted of one main living area containing an unmade bed, cooking supplies, a table and two wooden chairs. Above the stove was a small cupboard and a countertop space with drawers and a sink. Across from the bed were two doors. The walls were a sickly yellow, like pus, and two mismatched rugs lay on the floor, one blue the other orange. The pillows on the bed were filled with holes, and feathers stuck out of them like mouse nests. There were no pictures, no ornaments to be found.

"Shut up, you think I like livin' here?"

"I said nothing."

"Didn't have to say anything – I can hear you thinkin'. Now siddown, the coffee'll be ready in a minute or two."

The young man pulled out a chair and sat. His knees bounced in a steady, regular tempo, heels thumping.

"You have to do that?"

The young man stopped. Coffee bubbled into the percolator in gurgling spurts.

"You take sugar or anything?"

"No, that's fine, thank you. I prefer to go without."

The waitress eyed the pot.

"I always felt that people who add milk or sugar just don't like the taste of coffee. They mask it – otherwise they would never consume it. It is the same with faith–"

"Don't start."

The young man grinned and folded his arms and watched as the waitress went to the cupboard and brought out two white coffee cups. The rims were lined with a one-inch stripe of glossy blue paint. The waitress filled the cups and brought them to the table.

"These look familiar," the young man said before he blew and sipped.

"They oughta, I swiped them from work."

The young man nodded and took another sip.

"Got a problem with that? 'Cause if you do you can just clear out right now."

"It was merely an observation."

The young man set down his cup and examined the table. It was small and square. He touched a corner and it began to wobble.

"Don't do that. That leg's not hooked on. You push it too hard it'll just fall off and then my whole table'll fall over."

"You'll have to steal some new cups."

"Just don't do it. Please."

"What's wrong with it, exactly?"

"Leg's not hooked on, I told you."

"Is the bolt loose?"

"It's more than loose, it's broke."

"I can try and fix it for you."

"Don't bother."

"It would be no trouble."

"I said don't bother. I don't care about the damn table."

The young man took a bigger sip without blowing into his cup. The coffee was scalding hot and he felt a sharp pinch in the soft skin beneath his tongue as it began to bubble.

"Burn yourself?"

He nodded.

"It's hot," she said.

"It's all right." He set the cup on the table. "What's your name?"

"I don't like my name."

"What is it?"

"Sarah."

"Why don't you like it?"

She shrugged.

"Could it be that you don't like anything about yourself? I know some people who feel that way."

"I know what I don't like and I don't like my name, that's what I know. What's your name?"

"Jacob Peterson."

"Figures."

"What do you mean by that?"

"I don't know. Just seems like the kinda name you'd have, I guess. That's all. So whaddayou want, anyway?"

"Why should I want anything?"

"People are greedy."

The young man smiled.

"I just want to talk."

"Well, talk away. As long as it's not about Jesus."

"Do you think that's why I came here?"

"I'm not sure."

"Has that happened to you before?"

"Some people like to butt into things that aren't any of their business."

She picked up her cup and took her first sip. Sputtering, she coughed and stood.

"You sure you don't want any sugar?"

"No, thank you. As I said before–"

"Yeah, yeah," she said with a wave of her hand. "Mask, sugar, faith, bullshit, bullshit, bullshit. I heard you the first time. I don't care. I need sugar."

She went to the cupboard and found a tall glass dispenser with a shiny metal top half-filled with white.

"Yeah, I stole this, too," she said as she poured. She set down the dispenser and sat stirring a while before she drank some more.

"That's better."

"How long have you resided in this place?"

"You mean here in this building or here in this town?"

"Either one."

"Building, a couple years, town, all my life. Know how you can tell?"

"How is that?"

"Because nobody'd ever come to live here if they had a choice."

"I did."

Sarah grimaced.

"Why?"

"I'm afraid it would take too long to explain."

"Where d'you live?"

"Are you acquainted with a Mrs. Edith Parker?"

Sarah's grimace remained.

"Yes."

"At present I am living with her."

"You two related or something?"

"No."

"Then why you livin' with her?"

"It's rather a complicated situation. Why don't you like her?"

Sarah shrugged.

"I don't like her less than I like anybody else, I guess."

"But you don't like anybody else."

"No. I mean yes. I don't."

The young man removed his hat and set it on the table.

"That's right, stay awhile," Sarah said.

The young man grinned.

"Why don't you like anybody?"

"Whaddayou care?"

"I don't, I'm merely asking."

"Then what're you askin' for?"

The young man put his hand across the brim of his coffee cup. He held it there and stared and waited.

"I don't like people who think they know me."

"Do you find that quality in a lot of people?"

"Everybody I meet."

The young man said nothing.

"You gonna be in town long?"

"I have no idea. It's possible."

He removed his hand from the cup and draped his arm over the back of the chair.

"Let me tell you. It don't matter to these hicks what you do or who you are. Only thing matters to them is what they think you are. And they don't ever get tired of reminding you what they think. I'm sick of it. That's why I'm leaving."

"When?"

"Once I get enough money saved up."

"How much is enough money?"

"That's not any of your business. I'm savin' enough to get outta here. That's more than you need to know."

"It wouldn't take much just to get out."

"Not as far as I wanna go."

The young man pushed his chair onto its back legs and began to rock.

"And how far is that?"

"Far as I can get."

"You could travel in increments – move from town to town until you reach your intended destination."

"And get stuck somewhere else even worse than this place? No thanks."

"When you arrive at this mysterious destination, what will you do then?"

"I won't be a waitress, that's for sure."

"Why not?"

"If all you're good for is to bring people food and clean up after them you might as well be somebody's wife."

The young man let his chair fall to its proper position.

"I was wondering, may I use your, umm..."

"Toilet? You know, I've heard the word toilet before. You don't have to pretend to be a gentleman."

"What makes you think I'm pretending?"

"Seems like you're forcing it."

The young man chuckled.

"May I use your toilet? Your bathroom? Your restroom facility? Your shithouse?"

"No."

"Why not?"

"'Cause I don't want you to."

"You certainly aren't a very good hostess."

"I don't give a shit. I tell you I don't want you to use it, that should be enough for you."

The young man stood and walked toward the doors against the wall.

"Which is the bathroom and which is the closet..."

Sarah lunged between the young man and the doors and gave him a shove.

"No! I said no."

"Why is there such concern over this? Are you hiding something?"

"Just get the hell away from the door or get the hell out of my apartment."

"All right, I'm sorry. I apologize."

Sarah's shoulders drooped and she shook her head.

"The hell with it. Bathroom's on the right."

"I won't go in. It's all right."

Sarah opened the door and it creaked on rusty hinges. She took a step away to let the young man past. He stuck his head inside. On the mirror was a round adhesive label shaped like an orange with the word "Florida" printed on it in extravagant script, small black dots shading the bottom like bumps on a rind. Near one part of the edge was a tiny crease, as though someone had failed at peeling the label from the glass. The young man looked back at Sarah.

"What is–"

"Shut up. It's stupid."

The young man stared.

"Shut up."

She stomped back to the table and sat with crossed arms and a black scowl. The young man closed the bathroom door and resumed his seat.

"If you're gonna piss, piss. Just don't say anything about it. It makes me feel stupid. I feel stupid. I feel like a little girl. Shut up."

"It's all right."

"Go to hell."

The young man's smile returned.

"Have you any family?"

"Goddammit! Why are you asking me all these questions? What's it to you? Why do you wanna know? Do you have any family?"

"No."

"Where you from? Why you here?"

"You asked me before and I told you it was complicated."

"And I shut up about it, didn't I?"

The young man emptied his cup, and set it back on the table. He wiped his hands together with studied nonchalance.

Sarah stood, knocking her chair to the floor.

"Why are you here?"

"I just wanted to speak with you."

"Why?"

"I just had a feeling about you."

His smile remained. She eyed him.

"Whaddayou mean?"

The young man put on his hat and headed for the door.

"Thank you for speaking with me. I hope to chat with you again soon."

Then he was gone.

Mrs. Parker sat in the cushioned pew and waited for church to begin. It was her spot – on the aisle three rows from the front. The seat to her right was empty. She stared in silence at the light shining through the modest stained glass crucifixion scene at the head of the sanctuary. Brilliant blues and reds and whites, sharp yellows and muted fleshtones, beauty and pain intermingled, inseparable.

Three minutes after eight o'clock. He was late again.

The organist began to play, soon after which time the door behind the altar opened and two acolytes emerged. One was sixteen inches shorter than the other and every alternate step he tripped on the hem of his long white robe. The pair paused at the foot of the tall wooden cross. The smaller one tugged at his drooping sleeves in an attempt to free his hands and fumbled with his long goldshining candle lighter. When he stopped moving, the boys split apart to light the twelve white candles at the sides of the cross. The smaller one lifted his lighter to his first candle only to find it had gone out. He motioned to his companion, who gave an audible sigh. They pressed their wicks together and began again, this time with the smaller one attempting to light first the candle on the far side of the cross. "Psst!" the taller one whispered, too late. Moments later, the candles lit, the pair retired to the aisle seats of the front pews.

As the organ music ended, the door behind the altar opened once more and the pastor appeared. Ken Gruber. Mrs. Parker did not like him. She thought he had a face like a toadstool. Little more than thirty, he already had jowls. His nose was bulbous, with an enormous mole on the end of it, with several twisted strands of coarse black hair. He was blond, with a scalp like plastic, forever slicked down with a generous slathering of Brilliantine. He spoke as if his mouth was crammed with food, his fat, stupid tongue protruding from his fleshy lips at the conclusion of each sentence. He stood before the cross and bowed his head, pausing before he turned and faced the congregation.

He opened his mouth.

The young man. Words carefully chosen, true and right and good. Strong. Moral. Clean. Skin unblemished, smooth, perfect. His eyes, sharp like lightning. His mouth and his hands.

As the congregation sang the closing hymn seventy-five minutes later, Pastor Gruber made his way to the door at the rear of the sanctuary, all the time singing widemouthed like a moaning dog. When the song was over Mrs. Parker stood, handbag under her arm, and began the slow walk toward the door. She made it five steps before she had to stop and wait as the other congregants gathered at the door to shake Pastor Gruber's hand and talk. She turned and watched as the acolytes extinguished the candles, the smaller one beginning with the candle right next to the cross and moving outward. She shook her head with disgust and looked back to the line, since moved four inches and now deadstopped.

"And how are we this morning–" Pastor Gruber began when Mrs. Parker finally reached him.

"I'm well, but–"

"That's good–"

"-but you need to have some kind of discussion with your acolytes. You need to refresh their memories about how exactly they are supposed to perform their duties."

"Oh?"

"I don't know his name. The smaller one. Has he ever done this before? It didn't look like he knew what he was doing. Not at all."

"I'm sure he was just nervous. We all make mistakes, Mrs. Parker."

"That was all the boy made. He didn't do one thing right that I could see."

Pastor Gruber smiled. "I'll have a talk with him."

Mrs. Parker lingered between the sanctuary and the fellowship hall as Pastor Gruber met with the remaining members of the congregation. When they had dispersed the acolytes appeared. Pastor Gruber took the smaller one aside and began to speak. His hand came to rest on the boy's shoulder and although Mrs. Parker could not hear his words, his tone was awash in compassion. In less than half a minute, he let the boy go.

The base of Mrs. Parker's basket sagged under the weight of her groceries, boxes and cans and packages, and still more to buy. Her arm ached.

"Edith!"

It was Mrs. Colman. She wore a pink blouse and a magenta skirt, with a matching jacket and hat and she giggled as she scampered up the aisle.

"Hello. How are you today?" Mrs. Parker said as she set the basked on the floor.

"Good. Edith, tell me, tell me, tell me, how was your son Friday? And those sweet little grandbabies of yours?"

"Everyone's fine. They're keeping him busy."

"I'm so jealous, Edith. So jealous. I never asked, but how did you make out with your visitor? Did you see him when you got home? Was he still there?"

Mrs. Parker blinked.

"I'm sorry, who?"

"Your visitor, Edith. He came to my door Friday asking after you. I told him you were gone but that you'd probably be back soon. Poor thing, I'm sure he thought he'd missed you. He wanted to wait at my house, but I had things to do, you know. Broke my heart to send him away, but that's how things are sometimes. So, did you see him? Did he catch you?"

"Oh. Yes, he did."

"I thought he had. I could've sworn I've seen him over at your place since Friday."

"You have."

"I thought so. Well, who is he? After he left the other day I realized I never asked. I had a lot on my mind, sure, bein' so busy, but I could've kicked myself when I realized I never asked him."

Mrs. Parker looked down at her basket.

"He's–" she looked back to Mrs. Colman "-he's a nephew. He was a nephew of John's. He's going to be staying with me for a while." Her face burned.

"Oh, that's nice. It'll be a good change for you. I don't know how you do it, Edith, staying in that big lonely house all the time. Well, I guess I do know a bit of what it's like, but I have all my babies to keep my company. You don't have anybody. How long is he staying?"

"It depends."

"Depends on what?"

"On how long he feels like staying, I suppose. He's not in any rush to leave, so I'm just going to enjoy the time I have him here. I haven't seen him in such a long time."

"That sounds good. He's a good boy, too, that's for sure. When he was over the other day my Charlie got out of the house and your nephew chased him all over the neighborhood to get him back. I almost told him to forget about it, Charlie gave him such a time. He wouldn't listen, though, he just kept after him and finally he caught him. Charlie squirmed and squirmed so much I thought your nephew might not be able to hold him. But he did, and everything worked out. You have to thank him for me, and tell him I'm sorry."

With an involuntary grunt, Mrs. Parker picked up the basket and the women began to half-step their way to the front of the store.

"I see you're stocking up for him," Mrs. Colman laughed.

"I am. It'll be odd to have a full refrigerator for a change."

"Cooking for two people's a lot different than only making things for yourself. The money alone."

"I don't mind. It's nice."

"So, does this mean we won't be having tea today, then? I hope not. I've gone without it two days in a row now and I miss it so much already. It seems like it's about all I've got to look forward to anymore."

"I'm not sure what my nephew will be doing for the rest of the day, but I don't think he would mind if I spent a few hours with you this afternoon."

"I'll plan on it, then." She put her hands on the basket and Mrs. Parker stumbled and struggled to maintain her balance. "Edith! You should bring him along!"

"I don't know what he has planned." Mrs. Parker transferred the basket to her other arm.

"Ask him! Just ask him, Edith. Please. It would make me so happy. I wouldn't think he's up to anything too exciting. Do ask him. Please."

Bible in hand, the young man rose from the sofa and marked his page when Mrs. Parker entered the house.

"May I help you with that?"

"No, thank you," she said as she closed the door.

The young man approached and took the basket.

"Please, I insist."

"All right," she said, relinquishing it.

He went to the kitchen, with Mrs. Parker following close behind, watching him. The young man stopped at the swinging kitchen door and held it for her. He smiled.

"After you."

"Oh, no. I couldn't. It's so heavy, you go ahead."

The young man did not move. Mrs. Parker bowed her head.

"How was church?" he asked as she went by.

"I don't remember."

The young man remained at the door. He did not speak.

"It isn't that I don't remember – I just – I was thinking, and – Please, come in. I don't want you to strain yourself with that."

The young man stepped forward, door swinging, and set the basket on the counter. He began to empty it, placing the items with care in a row, none of them touching, none of them askew.

"I'm afraid I don't know where any of these go."

"Mr. Peterson–"

He turned. He wore a sad smile.

"Those who preach the Gospel are not always worthy of doing so."

"Yes. Yes, that's exactly right."

"We must remember never to blame the lord for the faults of man."

Mrs. Parker's eyes felt smoky, and they were suddenly blood red and poured out water. The young man moved slow toward her.

"What is it, Mrs. Parker?"

She drowned in speech. "I told a lie this morning. About you. I'm so sorry, Mr. Peterson."

"Tell me."

"It was my neighbor, Mrs. Colman. I saw her at the store this morning and she asked about you. I didn't know what to tell her. I didn't want to lie, but I didn't – I don't know."

"You didn't think she would understand."

"No."

He nodded.

"I told her you were my nephew. My husband's nephew."

The young man held her shoulders, which quivered with cold. Her eyes and her mouth twitched, her cheeks were flush and wet, her lips like pond scum.

"You did the right thing, Mrs. Parker. It isn't right to lie, but too often when people hear of such an arrangement as ours they try to twist it into something ugly and shameful. I don't mean to imply Mrs. Colman would do such a thing, but it's better not to chance it. I've seen friendships break up over far less. I wouldn't want to cause any of those troubles for you, especially after all you've done for me. I don't think I would be able to live with myself."

Mrs. Parker stained her white gloves as she wiped her face.

"I should have told you my first night here. I'm so sorry to have caused you such pain."

Hands folding and head bowed he knelt before her.

"I'm so ashamed, Mrs. Parker. I feel as though I've failed you. Please forgive me."

"You don't have to apologize to me."

His body folded into itself.

"I do. I do, Mrs. Parker. I've no right to speak to you. I've no right to look at you. Forgive me, please. I am vile; what shall I answer thee? I will lay my hand upon my mouth. Once have I spoken; but I will not answer: yea, twice; but I will proceed no further."

He covered his face with mangled hands and began to rock. Mrs. Parker took off her pasteslicked gloves. With tentative movements she

73

extended her hand to the young man. When he did not budge she placed her hand on his head and held it there a while before she began to stroke his soft dark hair. She closed her eyes.

"I forgive you."

The young man tried to sleep but even with the curtains drawn the room was too bright. He needed rest. His head ached and there was a tremulous tingling in his arms and legs. His stomach was sour as though he had swallowed a rotten egg. He felt always on the verge of sickness.

Light bled through his eyelids and he could hear the sounds of chirping birds and screeching children. Rubbing his face, he growled and sat. Soon he was at the window, curtains parted an inch, peering into Mrs. Colman's house. On the first floor she and Mrs. Parker sat talking and sipping tea from tiny China cups. Neither of them stopped to listen. They spoke over each other in a constant stream of words. A sweet breeze filled the young man's head, and he let the curtains fall.

At the end of the upstairs hallway was a white door, behind which was a wooden staircase that ran along the side of the house. The young man fingered the cold brass bolt shining and smooth above the knob. He turned it and it unlocked with a loud scraping click. Placing his hand on the knob he twisted it and opened the door. The hinges made no noise. He closed the door and waited. Then he opened the door again, slower this time. Still there was no sound.

The young man stepped onto the staircase. He shifted his weight on various points at the top to see if it would shake. He grabbed the rail and pulled. The structure did not move and it did not creak. He walked down the stairs, and back up. None of them made noise, either. Everything was solid.

He reentered the house and closed the door. He did not turn the lock. He smiled.

Sarah awoke at six-thirty to the sound of the alarm clock, jackhammer loud, ringing a foot from her head. She opened one swollen eyelid and stared. The sun was beginning to shine. She groaned and silenced the alarm. Springs screeched inside the lumpy mattress when she sat and coughed, arms stretched high above her head. Lowering them she shook the pieces of white down from her hair. With a groan she stood and stumbled to the bathroom, where she turned on the light and looked in the mirror. The sticker stared back at her.

By the time she arrived at the diner a crowd of five old men was waiting. They watched as she came up the street, shouting and fidgeting like little boys.

"Come on! Hurry it up already!"

Sarah did not change the pace at which she walked.

"I'm comin'. The coffee'll still be there, don't worry."

"Ain't made yet, though, is it?" Nickles called. "Lotta damn good it does me now if it ain't even made yet. Oughta hire somebody'll be on time Mondays. What a change that'd be, huh?"

Sarah inserted the key in the lock.

"I'm not late. You're early."

"Same goddamn difference."

Sarah turned back the key and pulled it from the slot. One of the old men grabbed the door and shoved her to the side as he went in, the others filing behind him. Nickles stopped in the doorway and looked at Sarah.

"I better have my coffee in five minutes."

"Or what?"

"Five minutes, that's all. I better have my coffee."

"Then get outta my damn way so I can start makin' it."

The old men walked with a sense of entitlement to their regular spot, taking ashtrays and stray pieces of silverware from other tables as they went. Sarah said nothing, went to the coffeemakers and began to brew two pots.

"You can come get our orders when you're done over there," Nickles said. "That is, if you got the time. I'm sure you got lots to do, like stand around with your hands in your pockets. Keep it up, girl, see if they promote ya."

Turning her back, Sarah stared at the coffee pots as they slowly began to fill.

Nickles took the handle of a butter knife and began to beat it slow and steady against the edge of the tabletop, growing louder as he went on. The other men joined in at a gradual pace until they were all going at it and it sounded like an indoor hailstorm.

Sarah picked up one of the near-full pots and held it while she slid coffee cups on each finger of her right hand. They jingled toneless notes against each other as she walked to the table, drowned out by the continued din of the knives and the men. She circled the table setting down cups and each man stopped his banging when his cup was filled. Nickles continued on as he took his first sip, stopping at last when he set down his cup.

"Oh, I'm sorry, was I making too much of a racket?"

He held up his watch.

"Six minutes. How much're they payin' you, anyway? I think it's too much, whatever it is."

Sarah's notepad stayed in the front pocket of her apron. She pointed a pinky at each man from her downturned fist as she spoke.

"Two eggs over easy, bacon, toast. Three eggs, medium, sausages, patties, not links, English muffin, butter, no toast. Two eggs,

77

scrambled, sausages, links, no patties, no toast, no English muffin. No eggs, bacon, five strips, toast. Three eggs, sunnyside, bacon, sausages, patties, no links, hashbrowns, crispy, toast."

"Come in here late every Monday. I don't know how long it was we were waitin' out there. It's always the same thing, too, ain't it? I always thought it was the waitress was supposed to get in first, not the customers. You know. So she could have the coffee ready and they wouldn't have to wait for it. That's how it's supposed to work, right? Ain't it? That's how it's supposed to work? That's how it's worked in other places I been to."

"Go to one of 'em, then."

Sarah walked to the order window and pulled out her notepad and began to mark it. Vern stood in the kitchen and held his stubby hands on his smooth scalp, waiting. He had the voice of a Rottweiler.

"Who is it?"

"You can't tell?"

"Never know. Anything different?"

She shook her head.

He whispered.

"Which one?"

"Scrambled."

"Any others?"

"Nah."

He sluiced a gob of saliva around in his pudgy cheeks.

"All right, can do."

Sarah tore off the order and put it in the window, sliding it all the way to the edge of the smooth metallic surface, static popping against her skin. The orange light was on and it warmed her bare arm.

"Can you reach it?"

"Yeah."

Sarah went behind the counter near the trays of silverware and began to fold paper napkins. A two-inch stack had accumulated by the time Nickles called again.

"Hey there, Sarah?"

She looked up.

"Could you come over here a second?"

She sighed and put down the napkins.

"What's a guy gotta do to get some sugar in this place?"

"You should have some there," she said as she continued toward the table.

"We're out."

At the foot of the table sat an empty glass container and its gleaming aluminum lid, in front of which lay a mountain of clean white crystals.

"I spilled it, see?"

Sarah said nothing.

"Don't worry, I can help clean it up."

Nickles extended his arm onto the table and with a smooth motion pushed the entire pile sprinkling like snowflakes onto the floor. He kicked at it with his scuffed black boots as the other men began to laugh with redfaced glee.

"There you go!"

Sarah turned without speaking and walked back to the order window.

"Vern!"

"Yeah?"

"Do all of 'em."

Leroy entered the diner through the back door, pausing to light a fresh cigarette from a dying one, and moved through kitchen, where he clapped one of his massive hands on Vern's shoulder before he went to the coffee pots, poured himself a cup and sat at his table near the door by the hallway. He had the frame of a bison and the legs of his chair bowed when he sat. Cigarette still dangling from his fleshy lips, he gulped his coffee with audible swallows.

Sarah nodded as she passed.

"Morning."

"What's with the mop?"

"Jackass thought it'd be funny to dump sugar on the floor."

"Hey, Nickles!"

"Yeah?"

"Do that again and you'll pay for it."

"Aww, it was a joke."

"Ha, ha. Don't do it again."

Leroy pulled a folded slip of yellow paper from the breast pocket of his white black-lined short-sleeved shirt, top two buttons undone. He had a silver pen, too, and he tapped it with Gatling gun clicks on the table. Sarah emerged from the back.

"Any interviews?"

"None that I heard about."

Leroy ran a hand across his thin black hair brittle with pomade and pushed his thick glasses up the bridge of his nose.

"Looks like you're by yourself a while longer."

"I can handle it."

Standing, Leroy emptied his coffee cup.

"See you in a few, then."

He stopped at the kitchen door and eyed the counter.

"Better fold some more of them napkins."

Vern and Sarah stood in the back doorway and passed a cigarette. It was ten-thirty and the diner was empty. The air was cool and it neutralized the garbage smell of the alley.

"Whaddayou think?"

Sarah took a puff and handed the cigarette back to him.

"If I think about it I'll kill myself," she said.

"Join the club."

The bells on the front door tinkled and she stuck her head inside.

"Be there in a second!"

She turned back to Vern and held out her hand with grasping fingers.

"Can I have one more?"

He gave her the cigarette and she closed her eyes as she drew.

"Thanks."

"I won't be long."

Mrs. Parker and the young man sat across from one another at a table by the window. Sarah frowned when she saw them and brought two menus to their table.

"How are you two this morning?"

Mrs. Parker picked up a menu and opened it.

"You're the most sour-faced girl I've ever seen. Hasn't anyone ever told you the day goes better when you wear a smile? Try it and you'll see the difference it makes."

Sarah's lips curled upward.

"How are you this lovely morning?"

"I want some hot tea," Mrs. Parker said, eyes buried in the menu. "And Mr. Peterson will have...?"

"I would like some coffee, if I may. Please."

"Okay. I'll be right back with that."

"No, wait a second. Don't go rushing off."

Mrs. Parker closed the menu and held it against the corner of the table.

"I know what I want. Do you know what you want?"

The young man's eyes scanned the column of text.

"Yes, I think so."

"All right. Get out your pad, we're ready to order."

The young man watched Mrs. Parker.

"All right. I want two eggs. I want them over medium. I don't want them over hard. I don't want them over easy. I want them over medium."

"Two eggs, over medium."

"I want hashbrowns. I want them crispy. I don't want them soggy. I don't want them burned. I want them crispy."

"Hashbrowns, crispy."

"That's all. Now read it back to me."

"Two eggs, over medium and crispy hashbrowns."

"There. Now, doesn't smiling make a difference?"

Sarah's face hurt.

"Yes, it does."

"What would you like, Mr. Peterson?"

The young man paused before making his reply.

"I would like two slices of toast, please, and some hashbrowns, too. Thank you."

"All right. Anything else?"

"No, thank you. That will be all."

"Is that really all you want, Mr. Peterson?"

"Yes, thank you."

"You should have more than that. You can have anything. Order anything you want. As much as you want."

"This is all I want. Thank you."

Sarah turned to leave.

"Wait a minute. Read it back to him."

"That's quite all right. I'm sure it's practically impossible to mix up an order of toast and hashbrowns."

"They're comin' right up."

Sarah drew slow breaths as she left the table.

"And don't forget our drinks!"

After she set the ticket in the order window, Sarah found a tray and loaded it with two cups, one empty, one filled with coffee, two teabags, a gray pot brimming with boiling water and some extra spoons. She lifted the tray and walked to the table, where the young man spoke in a quiet voice and Mrs. Parker listened, nodding. Sarah set down the tray and began to place the items between the two.

"All right, here's your tea, and here's your coffee. Be careful, the water's hot. You need more napkins?"

"Thank you. We're fine."

"Your food'll be ready in just a few minutes."

"Thank you."

The young man raised his eyebrows at Mrs. Parker.

"Yes," she said. "Thank you very much."

Her voice was soft and shivering.

"You're welcome."

The door opened bells clanging chinkclink and Nickles entered, sauntered to a table and sat, one foot propped on an empty chair, and lit a cigarette.

"Service?"

Sarah approached and gave him some coffee and bent to retrieve the curled black matchstick from where he'd thrown it. She faced him as she picked it up and he scowled.

"Hamburger?" she asked and stood. She placed the match in an empty ashtray and wiped her fingers on her apron.

"With a hunk of tomato on top, if you can find the time."

He ashed on the floor.

"Can you not do that?"

"You gotta mop anyway."

"I did it already."

"And you will again."

Sarah put the ticket in the window and went back to the counter. A tower of napkins. Pull, fold, stack. Pull, fold, stack. Her hands were chapped, dry skin like a lizard's back. Pull, fold, stack. Three customers. The buzz of the electric lights. Pull, fold, stack. Sizzling from the kitchen, clanging pans and heavy trudging footsteps upon the grease-coated floor. Tacky, like flypaper. Pull, fold, stack. The sun in the window warm and golden like honey. A breeze drifting in from the side door. Low mutterings. Coffeeslurping. Snort, cough, spit. Green spatter on the floor. Pull, fold, stack. Pull, fold, stack. Pull, fold, stack.

"Order up!"

Sarah brought the plate to Joe's table.

"Don't strain yourself gettin' me a bottle of ketchup."

"You already have a tomato."

"And now I want ketchup."

"Ass."

"What?"

"Ask."

"What?"

"Ask for it nicely."

"Get me the ketchup."

Sarah said nothing.

"Go on, get me the damn ketchup!"

She sighed. She got a bottle and brought it to the table.

"Thank you ever so much for waitin' 'til my food's gone cold to get me the things that I ask for."

"Don't mention it."

"I could have you fired!"

"Please, do it."

Mrs. Parker set her handbag on the table and gripped it by the strap with both hands.

"Waitress!"

Their plates and cups were empty, pushed to one side. The table was clear of crumbs, as though someone already had wiped it down.

"How was everything for you?"

"I'm fine, but I'm sure Mr. Peterson wanted another cup of coffee."

"No. That's all right."

"No it isn't. Didn't anyone ever tell you that you should always pass the customers' table several times throughout the meal to make sure they have everything?"

"I thought that since it's so slow right now you'd just tell me if you needed something else."

"No. No, no, no. That isn't how it works."

The young man made three soft taps with his knuckles on the tabletop. Mrs. Parker stopped talking.

"I'm very sorry," Sarah said. "I can get you something else if you want."

"No. That's all right. I'm sorry I snapped at you."

Mrs. Parker looked to the young man. He nodded once.

Sarah ground her cigarette into the redbrick wall and tossed the butt. A graystriped cat jumped onto one of the nearby garbage cans and mewed. It had green eyes and fur matted with grease, and the bones of its hips stuck out. It mewed again. Sarah lifted the lid of one of the cans and the cat jumped in. Turning back to the door, she checked her watch. She reached into her pocket and fingered the half-filled pack of cigarettes. Against the pack she felt the sharp corners of a card. She took it out and looked at it with a puzzled gaze. One side was blank and on the other was written a message in red ink.

Let's talk. J.P.

Napkins littered the floor like fallen October leaves. A smug smile played upon Nickles' lips as more customers began to enter the building.

"I didn't do nothin'!"

"Then who did?"

He shrugged and lit a cigarette.

"Maybe it was the wind."

Mrs. Parker stared at her husband and stared at the young man. The photograph rested on a table she had placed beside the sofa. It was narrow and three feet tall with legs that spread at the bottom. It made the photo easier to see. The coffee table was too short. The young man sat with perfect posture, the Bible held inches from his face. He was quiet and breathed through his nose and did not move his lips when he read. Mrs. Parker did nothing but sit her chair and watch. She cleared her throat.

The young man did not hear. He turned the page with care. His fingers were long and slim and the nails were clean, buffed. His skin was smooth, with the pink cheeks of a little boy. He did not need to shave. He wore his hair short on the sides, longer on top, with a part to his right. He closed his eyes and held up his head. Apart from the steady rising and falling of his chest he did not move. Eyes still closed he marked his page and set the Bible on his knees. Then he folded his hands and brought them to his face. His neck curled down and his hands became wedged between his chin and his chest and he remained very still.

Mrs. Parker nearly tore the fabric of the chair when she dug into its arms. She felt a ball form at the base of her throat but she did not swallow and she could not speak.

The young man straightened himself. He put down his hands and opened his eyes. As he set his Bible on the coffee table he looked out the front window, and the breathing white lace curtains that surrounded it.

"It certainly is a beautiful evening. Is it not?"

Mrs. Parker swallowed. Her limbs relaxed and she sank back into the chair.

"Yes."

"He hath made every thing beautiful in his time."

The young man smiled, his face golden and pure in the evening glow.

"I've enjoyed having you here. I never knew how lonely this house could get until John had gone. He was gone a lot for work, he was always making house calls. He had his office, too. Most doctors I've ever known had their office in their house, but John didn't."

She stopped herself, frowning.

"It's just nice to have someone around. It almost feels like it used to."

"What about your son?"

"What?"

"If I'm incorrect I apologize, but I was certain Mrs. Colman said you were visiting your son and his family last Friday."

"Yes. I was."

"I'm sure they've been a comfort to you in difficult times."

Mrs. Parker brushed some lint from the front of her dress.

"Would you like some tea?"

She stood and circled around the coffee table to the dining room.

"Thank you. I will if you're having some."

The young man put his hands on the sofa and began to boost himself up.

"No, wait here. I'll go put the water on and be back in a minute."

She hurried out, door swinging.

In the kitchen Mrs. Parker flicked the lightswitch without looking and went to the cupboard and took down the gleaming copper kettle. She held it under the sink and turned on the tap and the kettle echoed with a high hollow bubbling. Then she went to the stove and turned on the gas, lit the burner and set the kettle on top. She set the tea tray on the counter and placed two delicate rosepainted saucers and cups on it, along with a covered white bowl filled with sugarcubes. After she set the teapot on the tray she began to pack the strainer with coarse black leaves.

"Mrs. Parker?"

The young man's head poked out from behind the white kitchen door.

"What are you doing?"

"I thought perhaps you needed me."

"No. It'll be just a few minutes more, I think."

"May I sit with you while you wait?"

"Of course."

The young man took a chair at the table.

Mrs. Parker returned the red tin canister of tea to the cupboard. She stood with her back to the sink and watched the kettle. Thickening clouds of steam spilled from the spout and a low whine began to build. The young man stood.

"Stay where you are. I like to let it whistle for a minute."

He nodded.

"Would you mind if we drank our tea in here? I don't want to carry the tray back out to the living room."

"I can do it, if that's where you want to drink it."

"I don't."

The whistle grew too piercing to speak over. Mrs. Parker and the young man watched each other, motionless.

A minute passed and Mrs. Parker turned off the burner. With careful movements she lifted the kettle and began to pour. When the teapot was full she put the kettle back on the stove, clasped shut the strainer and lowered it dangling into the water. The young man stood once more.

"Please, sit down," Mrs. Parker said as she carried the tray to the table. "It still has to brew yet."

He resumed his seat. Mrs. Parker sat beside him.

"I wanted to thank you for being so patient. And you've been so kind to me. I'm sorry I haven't been able to tell you anything more regarding your husband. I'm sure it must be unbearable for you to wait so long."

"It hasn't been long."

"I've been here more than a week now."

"It hasn't seemed that long."

"All the same, I feel I should thank you."

"We used to drink tea. I used to. John would make it for me with sugar and a spoonful of honey. He drank coffee. I drink coffee myself, but not like he used to. He made it so strong I couldn't drink it. It was like dirt. He was good at making tea, though. I got sick when we were going to have Nathan and I had to stay in bed that entire last month. He made tea for me every day. I remember he was so worried about the baby. I would wake up at night and I'd hear him pacing up and down in the hallway. That's what he would do. If he was worried about something he would never talk about it, he would just pace. It's a wonder he didn't wear a hole in the rug. The baby was fine. I think the tea is ready."

The young man stood.

"Let me. Please."

"All right."

He placed one cup and saucer in front of Mrs. Parker and poured.

"I forgot the spoons."

"I'll get one."

Teapot in hand, the young man trotted to the drawer and returned with two long spoons.

"Thank you."

The young man held the other cup below the spout with his thumb and forefinger curled around the lip, his ring finger hooked through the handle. Soon the cup had overflowed and the outer edge of his hand was a grotesque white C-shaped blister. Tea spilled from the cup and poured out on the table before dribbling onto the floor. Mrs. Parker gasped and stood but the young man did not move. His eyes were fixed ahead and opened wide, and he showed no sign of pain or emotion. Before long the teapot was empty, its contents collected in a puddle at the young man's feet. He continued to hold it as though he were still pouring. The overfilled cup rattled on the saucer before it finally tipped over, soaking tea into his clothes and shoes.

"Mr. Peterson, what's wrong? What is it?"

She reached out, afraid to touch him.

He turned his head toward her, slow, lifeless eyes still wide.

"Edith?"

The voice with which he spoke was distant and not entirely his own.

"Mr. Peterson?"

"Edith, I'm sorry."

Mrs. Parker clutched a hand to her chest.

"Is it–?"

"I'm sorry, Edith."

She covered her mouth.

"John?" she sputtered through her fingers.

"I love you, Edith."

Her voice was dry. Her eyes were dry, and she tried to see.

"How–?"

"Goodbye, Edith. I have to go now."

"John, don't."

"I'll be back, Edith. I'll be back."

The young man's arms fell, sending the teapot and cups smashing to the floor, where they shattered into dozens of jagged pieces. Mrs. Parker stumbled back against the wall. The young man shook his head.

"Mrs. Parker, what's happened?"

The young man tore out of sleep. The dream was over. His heart beat strong and fast against his ribs and his mouth burned a sour bile taste. The bandage on his stinging hand was yellow with pus. He felt exhausted and exhilarated and he tried to calm himself, blinked his tired eyes and scanned the shapeless dark. He jumped once more when he reached the ghostglowing light at the window.

"Mrs. Parker?"

She sat watching him from the desk against the wall. She held the photograph of her husband face-up in her lap, the eerie light from outside reflected in the glass of the frame.

"I'm sorry, Mrs. Peterson."

The young man pulled the sheets to his chin.

"What are you doing in here?"

"I heard you – you were talking, or it sounded like you were. I thought it might be John again."

The young man wiped his eyes.

"What time is it?"

"It's late. After three."

"How long have you been sitting there?"

"Not long."

The young man raised up his knees and rested his arms on them.

"Mrs. Parker–"

"I'm sorry. I just didn't want to miss anything. But when I came in and listened I couldn't make out what you were saying – just a word here and there. It wasn't anything important."

"Mrs. Parker, I sincerely doubt the lord would try to tell us something at a time either of us could be guaranteed to hear it."

"And then I was afraid I would disturb you when I left. You were so restless I thought I might wake you up if I moved."

"Is that what happened?"

"No. You just bolted up – bolted right up like you'd heard something. And then I thought – Oh, Mr. Peterson, I'm so sorry."

She held the photograph tight to her chest.

"It's all right, Mrs. Parker. I would expect this has been very difficult for you."

Mrs. Parker sighed. Her breath fluttered out in a ragged burst and she continued to hug the photograph. Her shoulders shook and she began to whimper.

"It's all right, Mrs. Parker. Please believe me."

Her voice was like ashes.

"I just feel so foolish."

The young man looked to his side.

"I'm sorry. I can't get out of bed."

Leland Edwards jolted upright, shaking the last pew of the darkened church when he lurched into a sitting position. He was not sure of how long he had been out. It seemed like hours. The sun was down, and the sanctuary was too dark for him to read his watch. His back felt as though he had lain on a pile of jagged rocks and he kneaded the half-filled cushion of the pew as he looked to his sides and attempted to get his bearings. Stretching, he gave a loud long involuntary groan. His craggy voice reverberated in the empty space.

"Hello?"

No one answered. He smiled. He liked to be alone. It was Thursday. He reasoned the he could stay in the church the next night, too, without worrying about seeing anyone. It was good to be out on the road. He did not miss his wife or his children. He did not miss anybody.

The building was nice. It was dry and it was clean and unlike a lot of churches it did not smell like a loaf of rotten bread. And he didn't have to pay to stay the night. There was no sense in wasting money on some hick town hotel where the hot water never worked and the desk man asked a lot of questions. They were all the same, those guys. No bed in the world was worth talking to one of them. The pew wasn't great, but it beat the back seat of his car.

Edwards had not planned on staying. He entered the building around six in search of a restroom. After he used it he began to wander. He checked out the kitchen and the Sunday school classrooms. Then he came to the main hall, where he followed the

94

center aisle to the last pew, set his sample case beside it and lay down. The fading light of the evening was warm and comforting. The air was close, warm. He felt safe and tired and he closed his eyes and began to fall.

Yawning now, he rubbed his face, shook his head. Hands fumbling in the black he found his case and set it on his lap. He opened it and grasped with blind fingers for the bottle. He found it and lifted it and gave it a shake. A faint tickling on the sides of the glass. Almost empty.

"Goddammit, anyway."

He frowned, unscrewing the cap, and cursed himself for not getting another when he had the chance. He poured some of the whiskey into his mouth and held it there. It made his whole face tingle, hot and wonderful. Perfect. He swallowed a drop at a time as he lifted the bottle again. Two or three mouthfuls left. He replaced the cap.

He thought of his wife. He did not know why. She would be in bed by now, alone. He told her not to let the kids in the bed. She said it made her feel better. Less lonely or something. He wasn't sure. She never told him much. He thought of how she looked when he left. It was the way she always looked, even when he was home. It was funny how much she missed him when he was gone. He never missed her at all.

Edwards reached into his jacket and fished out a pack of cigarettes and a silver Zippo. He pulled one out of the pack and lit it. He inhaled deep and slow and held it in a moment before he sighed a feathery cloud of blue and smiled with glazed satisfaction.

He chuckled. If she could only see him. He never enjoyed church. Not until tonight. She always tried to make him feel bad for staying home. Weeks and months and years of begging. It wasn't so bad in the beginning, not until their first son was born. Then she decided they had to start going each week, not just Christmas and Easter.

"Don't you want him to know about God and Heaven and everything? Don't you think it's important?"

"I guess, but he's just a baby. He wouldn't get anything out of it now. He doesn't know what they're saying, much less what they're talkin' about."

"I don't always know what they're talking about, either–"

"Should tell you something."

"-but that doesn't mean we shouldn't go. We should go. We really should."

"Why? We know what's right and wrong. We're good people."

"Don't you think he should be baptized?"

"If you really want him to be, I guess, sure, but I don't see why that means we'd have to go crazy over the thing."

"It's not going crazy. That's not what I'd call it."

"What would you? Go a few years with no church, you have one baby and all of a sudden you're, 'We have to go to church every week, we have to go every Sunday.' Sounds crazy to me."

It got worse after the other two kids were born. Each week she would ask him, and soon she had the kids doing it, too. It made him want to vomit.

Edwards frowned. When he thought of his family it was never over something good. He drank some more. Then he took another drag on his cigarette, the bottle still in his hand. Perhaps half a swallow remained.

"Fuck it."

He drank the rest. It gave him no pleasure.

He dropped the cigarette into the empty bottle and screwed on the cap. He set the bottle on the floor and grabbed the back of the pew he was facing and hoisted himself to his feet. He was still thirsty.

He began to walk hollow footsteps on the carpeted floor to the front of the sanctuary. He pulled the Zippo from his pocket and flicked it, casting wavy shadows on the walls. Near the pulpit he saw a door. It was cut into the wall, with no frame and no handle. Edwards approached and placed his hands on it. The door opened with little pressure. Stepping inside, he removed his hands and the door swung shut.

Upon entering the room, Edwards flicked his lighter once more. The room was cramped, walls lined with dozens of rows of cupboards and shelves, and one empty white table in the middle of the floor. There were no windows and no visible lightswitch. Edwards opened eleven drawers before he found some Christmas Eve candles white with burntblack tops in glass holders. He took one and lit it and placed it in the center of the table. The Zippo he slipped back into his pocket.

He found a giant jug of dark purple wine and a silver tray of tiny Communion glasses in one of the cupboards. The jug was unopened. Edwards smiled and grunting heaved it onto the table, which shuddered beneath the weight. The jug was too big to drink from, and the Communion glasses were half-shot at most.

"Fucking Lutherans."

Edwards took an empty candle holder and scraped it free of its brittle melted crusting. The jug belched when he opened it, and he held it like a baby as he poured.

The wine was not good. It was like black vinegar. He searched the other cupboards but found no more wine.

Edwards grabbed the jug and the candle and the empty holder and lugged them through the sanctuary to the pew in the last row. He filled the candle holder and drank and lit another cigarette. He wondered if he had made the right decision. He only packed six days' worth of clothes.

"How long will you be gone?"

The car idled in the driveway. Dorothy and the kids stood watching him.

"A week, I told you before."

"Are you sure?"

"Yes."

She said nothing.

"You don't believe me, that's it?"

"Of course I do."

"Then why would you ask me?"

"I don't know. It's nothing. I'm just being stupid."

"Goddammit, you're not stupid. How many times do we have to go over this? You're not stupid, all right? For Christ's sake, why do you hafta do this whenever I'm goin' somewhere? You trying to make me feel bad? Are you trying to make me feel guilty?"

"No."

"Course not. You'd never do that, not you."

She pushed the hair from the eyes of their oldest boy.

"Honey, look. I'm sorry. I'm really sorry. I know you don't like me being away. I know it makes you sad. It makes me sad, too, why do–" He gripped the steering wheel. "The kids gotta eat. It's as simple as that. I don't know how to do anything else. I'm not good at anything, you know?"

She nodded.

"All right, I love you. I'll see you next week."

He shifted gear and started back down the driveway.

"Say goodbye to your father."

The kids shouted and jumped and waved their little hands in the air.

Edwards watched them all in the rearview mirror. He watched as they receded into the distance, until he could no longer see them.

One sandwich remained in Edwards' sample case. He took it out and sniffed it before the first bite. Its taste was off. The ham had the feel of slime in his mouth. He washed it down with some more wine, which did nothing for the flavor of either. The rest of the sandwich he tossed under the pew. He put the wax paper in which the sandwich was wrapped back in the case, now empty save for the undershirts. The other clothes were spread in the back seat of the car. He drank some more and refilled his makeshift glass. The wine was weak. It would take days to achieve the slightest buzz.

Edwards stared at the pew in front of him. On the back was a small shelf that held six books, three black and three green.

"What the hell."

Shaking his head, he took one of the green volumes and opened it. A hymnal. He closed it and put it back on the shelf before he took one of the other kind. He set it on his lap and opened it and read.

"O how great is thy goodness, which hast laid for them that fear thee; which thou hast wrought for them that trust I thee before the sons of man!"

He closed the book with a growl. Kiss-assy bullshit written by a crowd of idiots thousands of years ago who thought the sun wouldn't rise if they didn't pray hard enough. Talking animals, burning bushes, phony baloney all the way through. Love thy neighbor and thou shalt not kill were all right but rest of it could be thrown in the trash.

He opened the book again and flipped the pages.

"Thy lips are like a thread of scarlet, and thy speech is comely; thy temples are like a piece of pomegranate within thy locks."

He read the verse twice before continuing.

"Thy two breasts are like two young roes that are twins, which feed among the lilies."

Edwards closed the book and read the cover.

"I'll be goddammed."

He read to the end of the passage, skipping ahead here and there, and used one of the undershirts to wipe himself clean when he had finished.

Reopening the book, he held it close to his face and further scanned the text.

"I opened to my beloved; but my beloved had withdrawn himself, and was gone: my soul failed when he spake: I sought him, but I could not find him; I called him, but he gave me no answer."

Edwards closed the book. He frowned again.

TWO

Mrs. Larson snored through her nose, the still-burning cigarette stuck in her lips. Cool trickles of smoke curled out of her nostrils so that they look like fleshy chimneys, and she tilted her head and featherweight chunks of gray dust flaked down the front of her blue housedress. Her overstuffed green chair was pockmarked with ashy islands of burnt orange from other occasions when she had opened her mouth. Pastor Gruber sat nearby, ready to catch the cigarette should she do so again.

He arrived at nine o'clock with a bag of groceries. Bread, cornflakes, eggs, a red can of Hills Brothers Coffee. The bag sat untouched next to her chair, and the money was clutched in her hand. She had not moved from her seat to open the door for him, nor had she stood when he entered the room. Instead she eyed the bag, lit a cigarette and fell asleep.

Pastor Gruber stared at her. She had skin like a catcher's mitt, sallow with deep lines that ran deep across her forehead and out from the corners of her eyes down her cheeks, and cracked lips the color of wet clay.

She sniffed and opened her mouth in a wide yawn. The cigarette clung to her bottom lip until her top denture, stained brown at the roof, dislodged in her mouth and fell, loosening the filter tip. Pastor Gruber stood and caught it in his palm in time for Mrs. Larson to see him. She threw out her arms and began to cough and Pastor Gruber stood back and tossed the butt into the fireplace. A welt like a small raspberry rose on his palm.

"Do you need some water?" he asked after she caught her breath.

"What were you doing?"

"I had to take your cigarette. I was afraid–"

"Look what you did! You got ashes all over me!"

"Would you like a washcloth?"

Scowling, she brushed herself. "Siddown, you're making me nervous."

"Your cigarette fell. I was catching it."

"Sit down, for heaven's sake."

She took a new cigarette from a half-empty pack on the table beside her chair. The table seemed covered with black-speckled bird droppings and the ashtray on top looked like it was scorched in a fire. She tore a match from a white book and lit the cigarette.

"Sit down," she said as she exhaled. "And sit back. You're not at somebody's sickbed."

Pastor Gruber sat and crossed his legs.

"I am sorry," he said.

Mrs. Larson stared for a moment at the point where his knees intersected. She said nothing.

"How have you–"

"You talk that way too much."

"I beg your pardon?"

She aimed a stream of smoke toward his eyes.

"The way you talk. You don't sound like a pastor to me."

"How do you mean?"

"Your sermons. You go on too much about that kind of thing."

"What is that?"

The word was like a bad taste in her mouth.

"Forgiveness. And love. You talk about love too much."

Pastor Gruber began to laugh. She did not join him, and he stopped and waited.

"There's more to the Bible than damnation," he said at last.

Mrs. Larson shrugged and pulled the cigarette from her mouth, flicking it near the rim of the ashtray and sent a scattering of white powder to the floor.

"Maybe, but you should tell people when they're doing somethin' wrong. You can't let them be animals. They have to know they're going to pay for it sooner or later."

"Who's behaving like an animal?"

She shrugged. "Look around."

He stood and took a step toward her chair.

"Is there anything else I can do for you this morning?"

"You want your money, don't you?"

"I never said—"

"Before you leave, why don't you go out into the yard and trim my hedges? They're getting shaggy and I don't have anyone to do them for me."

Pastor Gruber looked out the front window.

"I just have two, right there by the door. One on each side. You can see them from here. What is it? What's wrong? You have to go? You want to come back?"

"I suppose I could, if it won't take too long."

Mrs. Larson stamped out her cigarette so the table shook.

"What are you looking at? I said you can't see them from here."

Pastor Gruber approached the window and pulled aside one of the tar-stained drapes.

"Who is that?"

On the lawn across the street the young man pushed a mower. The sleeves of his white and blue checked cotton shirt were rolled to his elbows so that is bare arms could be seen. They were tanned from the tips of his fingers to midway up his smooth forearm, at which point they were as pink as the cheeks of a small child. He moved with quick steps in precise rows as uniform as the lines on a legal pad. He had not begun to sweat.

"Who is who? Where? What are you talking about?"

"Across the road. At Mrs. Parker's house, mowing the yard."

"How should I know?"

"I thought he might be from the neighborhood. Come take a look at him."

"No," she said emphatically as she lit a new cigarette. She dropped the matchbook on the table.

Pastor Gruber turned away from the window. The cigarette was in the exact center of Mrs. Larson's mouth, poking out like a stiff white smoldering tongue. She frowned at him through the smoke.

"Are you going to trim the hedges or aren't you?"

"I'm afraid I don't have time this morning. I'm due at Mrs. Rops' house shortly."

"It won't take long. How short?"

"A quarter 'til."

She looked at the clock.

"Damn."

"I can always come back."

"Don't bother. It's just as well."

"Really, I can. If you want me to I will."

Mrs. Larson took the cigarette from her mouth and exhaled the thick gray cloud.

"Don't come back."

Pastor Gruber opened his mouth to speak, but she silenced him with the wave of her brokenveined hand.

"Shut up. I was going to say when you were done with the hedges, but since you won't do them I'll just tell you now. I'm not coming back to church."

She inhaled one-third of the cigarette and waited, letting the smoke spill slowly from her mouth.

"No, that's wrong. I'm not coming back to *your* church."

He began to sputter. "But why?"

"I don't like you. You should be able to see that. I think I've made my feelings very plain. You don't understand."

"But I do understand–"

"I don't care to hear what you have to say." She took the cigarette from her mouth and pointed it at him. "Let me be very clear about this. I am not rejecting God. I'm rejecting you."

"Because I preach forgiveness and love?"

"Among other things."

"You can't be serious."

"I am. Very."

Pastor Gruber folded his arms and took a breath. The air was foul and he felt like he needed to sit.

"I can't reason with you, then? You won't talk to me about this?"

"There will be no discussion. None whatsoever." She stubbed out her cigarette. "You can go now."

Pastor Gruber felt as though his shoes were nailed to the floor.

"Oh, right. Your money. Here."

With a sideways glance Mrs. Larson cast the coins to the floor, where they bounced and rolled, clattering against each other. Some went under chairs while others spun in circles or tumbled into the next room. It would be difficult to collect them all, and impossible to retrieve any of them without kneeling.

Pastor Gruber stepped out of the room, found his hat and left the house. On the front stoop he looked toward Mrs. Parker's home. The yard was empty. The pastor frowned.

Before he walked on, he noticed a bright yellow rose in full bloom growing near one of the hedges by Mrs. Larson's door. Its petals were full and thick, and it smelled sweet and rich like honey. He broke off the blossom and slipped it into his lapel. By the other hedge grew a second flower. He broke it off, too, and threw it into the street as he left the house. He smiled.

The young man pushed the mower across the grass. Its reel was well-oiled and it whirred smooth and clean, without squeaking. The grass was in need of cutting, but was not so long that the mower would simply flatten it. It was soft and healthy, and it smelled sweet. Although the air was not yet hot, the young man's shirt stuck to his back, and he stopped at the end of each turn to peel it from his skin. He pulled it from his shoulders, too, but it bonded itself to them as soon as he took up the mower again.

Through one of the kitchen windows he could see Mrs. Parker for half-second flashes as she darted from the stove to the cupboard to the refrigerator.

The young man licked his lips and craved a cigarette as he looked across the yard, one-third finished, with dark green trails consisting of clumps of cut grass. He wiped his sticky hands on his trousers and brushed back his hair. Then he lifted the handle of the mower and began to push it once more. Midway down the line he heard an irregular thumping noise. Frowning, he knelt and examined the cylinder to see if there was anything stuck in the green-stained blades. Before he could get a close-up view he heard the noise again – the sharp rapping of fingernails against glass. He turned and saw Mrs. Colman standing in one of her first-floor windows, lit cigarette in her fist. He smiled and gave a quick wave. She waved back with vigor, losing ash and grinning like a jack-o'-lantern.

"Hello!" Her voice was muffled through the closed window and she laughed and brought her hand to her forehead as if to say "What a dunce!" before she pulled it open. "Hello," she said again.

"Hello," the young man said and stood.

"You havin' problems, sweetie?"

"No."

"That's good."

She dragged on her cigarette and exhaled, but no smoke came out. Bewildered, she examined its tip. At the end was a quarter-inch of empty space, beyond which was loose-packed unlit tobacco. She let out a gasp and began to stamp at the floor. The room rattled with thunderous bangs and Mrs. Colman's body shook like a sack of potatoes beneath her loose pink housedress. Soon she gave the floor of final stomp and leaned halfway out the open window, smiling.

"Is everything all right?"

"It's fine, honey. I just lost the fire in my cigarette." She took a book of matches from her pocket, struck one on the windowsill and lit what remained of her cigarette.

"So, I see that you're mowin' this morning."

"I'm trying."

"Well, I was wondering if maybe you'd like to come over here when you're done over there and take a crack at my yard. I'll pay ya."

"You don't need to do that. I'll be over when I'm finished."

"Oh, thank you, dear. And I've got my own mower in the garage, so you can use that one. It might not be as new or as fancy as Edith's, but it gets the job done."

Mrs. Colman's yard was a mixture of crabgrass and thistles, with long dandelions interspersed throughout. The grass was brittle and its color was a muted off-green, like strained peas. It was much taller than Mrs. Parker's. The mower was in worse condition, too, so caked with rust the cylinder looked as though someone had run it through a pool of corrosive orange paint. The young man ran it grinding like stone up the length of the yard, but it did little more than flatten the grass and the weeds. He stopped and stared, uttering silent curses. The vegetation behind the house was even spottier. It had gone weeks without a trim. Here and there were mountainous hills of light brown sand, crusted and dried. There were pieces of trash and large rocks throughout. At the back of the house a window slid open.

"Mr. Peterson?" she sang.

"Yes, Mrs. Colman?"

"When you pass by the window I'll bring you a nice cold glass of water. How does that sound?"

"That sounds lovely."

She giggled and waved and closed the window.

The young man spat into the grass.

The furnishings at Mrs. Colman's house were blanketed with a thin layer of cat fur. It stuck to everything with a soft surface – rugs, furniture, drapery – and it hung in the air like dust, ready to attach itself to anything that remained still for more than three seconds. In the corners of the house were dusty clumps of it, as though someone had collected cobwebs and left them in a pile. Black and white strands of it floated in the young man's teacup. He did not drink.

"I wanna thank you so much for doin' my lawn today, sweetie. I don't know how long it's been."

"It was nothing."

"I mean it. Edith, you gotta keep him around as long as you can."

Mrs. Parker smiled and sipped gingerly from her cup. When she put it down she lifted her napkin and wiped her mouth, and opened it a fraction to scrape the fur off her tongue and front teeth. Mrs. Colman did not notice.

"Well. It sure looks a whole lot better than it did. But listen, you think it looks good now, you shoulda seen it a few years ago. Think your aunt's flowers look pretty? You shoulda seen the ones I used to have. They were really something, let me tell you. I had tulips with blooms the size of teacups. Roses like cabbages. You think I'm making all this up, but I'm not kidding. Edith, tell him I'm not kidding."

"They were very nice."

"You bet they were. They were the nicest flowers I ever saw, anyhow. They were so nice the paper a few towns over came 'round and took my picture – put it right on the front page, me in my gardening clothes, weeding the flowers, dirt up to my elbows, with the brightest smile you ever saw. 'A Green Thumb.' That was the headline. 'A Green Thumb.'"

"But you no longer grow them," the young man said.

"No I don't, and believe me when I tell you that I don't even miss it. I know you don't believe me, but it's true. I don't even miss it. And do you know why I gave it up?"

"Please tell me."

"It was all I was doing. Simple as that. You can't have flowers like the ones I grew, absolutely perfect flowers, without devoting simply all your time to them. I had so many other things I wanted to do, so I just said to myself, 'Look here, you've done better at growing flowers than anyone you've ever known, so now's your chance to get started on something else.' And that's just what I did."

She smiled and lifted her teacup. When she finished drinking she placed it with care back in the saucer. She said no more.

The young man scanned the walls of the room. The upper corners were marked with deep U-shaped water stains, and there were two faded stripes along the yellow-lined wallpaper where the beams of sunlight slowly worked their way across the room over the years. The room was sad. It looked like it belonged in an abandoned house.

A scratchy meow was heard and the young man looked down to find a large white cat with brownish patches rubbing against his leg.

"That's Muffins," Mrs. Colman said. "Muffins isn't sure about strangers."

The cat jumped into the young man's lap, where it turned three times before it curled into a ball and settled into purring sleep. Mrs. Colman lowered her gaze and spoke in a stony voice. "Muffins isn't sure about strangers."

With an embarrassed glance toward the women, the young man lifted the cat off his lap and set it on the floor. Upon waking, the cat looked up at him and meowed again. Mrs. Colman continued to stare until the young man shooed the cat away. As it passed her chair she leaned to the side and scooped it up with one arm and held it to her chest.

"It's okay, Muffins," she cooed. "Mommy's got you. Mommy's got her Muffins."

A long, pained whine escaped from the cat's throat.

"She's not been the same since her husband passed away," Mrs. Parker said as she and the young man prepared for dinner.

"What happened?"

"It isn't right for me to speak of it."

"I understand."

"They said it was a heart attack. But things like that don't stay secret for very long."

The young man nodded.

"It changed her. She doesn't have anyone now. They never had children. She only has those cats. And me, I suppose. I understand her little bit better than some people might." She glanced at her husband's photograph.

"For all the law is fulfilled in one word, even in this. Now shalt love thy neighbor as thyself."

The young man went to the dining room with a pair of clean plates, door swinging behind him. Mrs. Parker opened the oven and brought out the covered black roasting pan. She set it on the stove and lifted the lid. A heavy swath of steam poured forth and the room smelled warm and good. She poked the roast with the long, sharp two-pronged fork, squirting hot juice that popped and sizzled against the side of the pot. The young man pushed open the door and stood there and sniffed.

"I think it's ready," Mrs. Parker said.

"It smells delicious. Shall I carry it to the dining room?"

"No. I want it to sit a minute. You can finish setting the table."

With a smile, he entered the room and took two tall classes from the cupboard.

"Would you prefer milk or water tonight?"

"Milk, please."

The young man took the glasses to the dining room and returned for the milk. "Do you need anything else from the refrigerator?"

"I don't think so," she said and replaced the cover on the roasting pot. Next to it on the stove was a silver pan with a black handle half-filled with heavy, bubbling gravy. She dipped in with a big spoon and stirred the smooth tan mixture and scooped out a bit. She lifted it to her lips and blew, cooling it, before she took a tiny taste. It was good. Hearty and rich, without too much salt. She clanged the spoon against the side of the pan and turned off the burner. This task completed, she lifted the lid of the roasting pot and pulled apart the beef in large pieces with a fork and butter knife. The meat was so tender there was no need to cut it, and the air filled with steam as she transferred it from the roasting pan to a large white bowl. Also in the pan were chunks of tender cooked carrots and potatoes, the colors faded with a thin film of freckled brown, which she placed alongside the beef. The young man put what was left of the milk back in the refrigerator.

"Did you lay out the silverware?"

"I did."

"All right. Let's see, what else did we need?"

"I'll bring in the roast, and you can take the gravy and the..." His eyes darted to the photograph.

"Yes, that sounds like a plan."

"How does it taste?" Mrs. Parker asked after the young man had taken his first bite.

"It's excellent."

She smiled and lowered her eyes. "It was John's favorite."

"I can certainly see why."

"Any time I ever asked him what I should make for supper, this was always what he would pick. 'Could you make the roast, with the potatoes?' That's what he would ask for."

The young man sprinkled the lightest dusting of pepper onto his food. Mrs. Parker lifted the other shaker and poured. "Do you need salt?"

"No, thank you."

She put down the shaker. "I was a little bit worried. I haven't made it in so long."

"You needn't have. I don't see how you can improve on it." He took another bite and closed his eyes, chewing slow.

"I want to thank you for taking care of the lawn."

"Thank you for allowing me to. The wicked borroweth, and payeth not again."

"When we're finished eating, I have another chore you can take care of, if you don't mind."

"Of course not."

The young man approached Mrs. Colman's front door clutching a plate of food that was wrapped in a sheet of wax paper. It was smooth and slick against his skin. The sound of the river, the light through the trees. He stepped onto the porch and pressed the door bill, which emitted grinding buzz.

"I'm sorry about that bell," Mrs. Colman said as she opened the door. "It's been doin' that the past couple days."

"You should get it fixed. There could be a problem with the wiring."

"Would you know anything about that?"

"I'm afraid not."

"Could you take a look at it anyhow? I don't know a thing about that kinda stuff. Maybe it's somethin' easy. You could come tomorrow! You could come have tea again! Wasn't that fun today?"

The young man lifted the plate. "You don't want your food to get cold."

She gasped and her face broke into a maniacal grin. "Whatcha bring me?"

"It's roast beef with cooked carrots and potatoes."

She clapped her hands together and turned, walking at a rapid pace to the kitchen. "Goody-goody! Bring it inside! And close that door!"

The young man lagged behind. "You can keep the plate – Aunt Edith can pick it up tomorrow."

He stopped at the kitchen door. The room smelled like trash. On the counter was a bowl with old potato peels and bits of tomato heaped with used coffee grounds. Fruit flies clustered around it and others fluttered around his eyes and mouth. He sucked in his lips and blinked five times.

"No, no, no, no, no," Mrs. Colman said as she opened the cupboard. "I don't wanna do that." She grabbed a plate and flung it onto the counter, where it rattled on its sides. Then she looked to the young man and held out her hand, her fingers opening and shutting like a Venus fly trap. "Gimme."

The young man handed her the plate and stepped back to the edge of the kitchen. Mrs. Colman whisked off the wax paper and set it face-up on the kitchen floor. Standing up straight, she turned to the doorway and cupped a hand around the side of her mouth.

"Kids!"

A chaotic mass of heavy, rumbling thuds emerged from the corner of the house, building until the young man felt the large, soft bodies of the cats as they passed between and around his legs, and into the kitchen. They were utterly without grace, sliding on the tile as they made their way to the paper. The sound of their growling and their lapping tongues filled the room as they turned around and around the small sheet, fighting for each morsel they could get. Their movements were continuous, and so quick it was impossible to count them all.

"I hope Edith didn't want that back."

The young man shook his head. "I'm sure it's all right."

"Good." She leaned over the counter and dumped the food onto the empty plate with a great slurp. "It sure does smell good."

"It tastes good, too."

"You're lucky to be stayin' with her. She's a real good cook. Maybe it'll put a couple pounds on you – looks like you could use it."

She went to the sink and began to rinse Mrs. Parker's plate. She held it under the stream of hot water and rubbed it up and down with her empty palm.

"How long are you gonna be staying?"

"I'm not sure yet."

The young man's eyes were focused on the cats. The food was gone by this time, yet they continued to lick the paper as though they had not eaten in days. They looked to be about twenty pounds each.

"That's nice," Mrs. Colman said. "I know she gets real lonely."

"Oh?"

"Yeah. That son of hers never comes to visit. Not too often, anyway. And she's never gone more than a day at a time if she goes off to see him or do anything else. Hasn't since your uncle died. I don't know that she talks much on the phone with him, either. Your cousin, I mean. It feels like there's something goin' on there, but I make it a point to stay out of other people's business. Just the way I am. If they don't wanna say anything about anything, I'm sure not gonna ask them. Not me."

She turned off the water and wiped the plate with an old ragged dish towel, yellowstained and filled with holes.

"You don't know anything about it?"

The young man shook his head. "I'm like you. If they don't tell me, I don't ask."

"That's a good way to be," Mrs. Colman said and smiled.

"He that goeth about as a talebearer revealeth secrets."

"Don't I know it."

"Proverbs, chapter twenty."

Mrs. Colman rubbed the plate in slow circles.

"Have you ever come to visit your aunt before? I don't remember seein' you."

"We may not have met. It's been a long time. I've not been here since I was little boy."

"Didn't you come when your uncle passed?"

"I was unable to make it. By the time I learned what had happened the funeral was over."

"Oh, what a sad day that was. Your uncle was a good man."

The ratty towel scratched against the long-dried plate like nails on glass.

"Yes, he was. Of course, I didn't know him very well. We lived so far away."

Mrs. Colman stopped rubbing at the plate and held it against her stomach, the towel bunched in her palm, corners hanging loose like a tattered flag.

"He didn't say much. When he did it was always very pleasant. To the point. He was a listener. Very smart. He didn't show it off, though. To hear him talk you wouldn't know he was a doctor. He was that kind of man."

She held out the plate. The young man put his hand on it, but she did not loosen her grip. She just stood there and watched him and smiled.

"You're so much like him," she said.

The young man nodded. Both of them stayed very still. Finally, after fifteen seconds, she let go of the plate.

"I had better get going."

"Can't you stay just a little while longer?"

"I'm sorry."

"That's fine."

She took the food from the counter and brought it to the table. As she sat, the cats moved away from the paper and twisted, mewing, about her ankles.

"Don't worry about me," she said. "I'm never alone, thanks to my babies here. But you come tomorrow and take a look at my doorbell. Then you and your aunt and I can have a nice long talk."

The young man backed toward the door. Mrs. Colman continued to watch him well she shoveled forkful of roast into her mouth. "Yums!" she beamed.

Before the word was spoken, one of the cats jumped onto the table. Mrs. Colman shouted, spring out bits of beef, and smacked the cat with the back of her hand. It landed with a thump on its side and twisted into a standing position and stared dumbly as Mrs. Colman shook her index finger in its face.

"No, no, no! I told you before, no, no."

The cat sniffed her finger, thrust out its tongue and licked.

"I'll be going, then," the young man said.

Mrs. Colman looked from the cat to the young man and waved at him. "Okay, bye-bye! I'll see you tomorrow!"

The dining room was empty when the young man returned. Muffled noises came in through the kitchen, and soon Mrs. Parker appeared in the doorway.

"Mrs. Colman just called. She tells me you're going to fix her doorbell tomorrow?"

"She's mistaken."

The sun warmed the young man's back as he sauntered down the sidewalk. A soft wind carried the fresh scent of blooming lilacs and bits of fluff from Cottonwood trees hovered in the air like feathery snowflakes. The young man inhaled as long as he could, the bright orange ring at the end of the cigarette pulling hot and slow toward his lips. Breathing out, the wind neutralized the smoke, breaking it up as though he had taken nothing in. He inhaled once more and threw the butt into the street.

"Hey!"

The young man stopped moving. He glanced to the left to see Joe Nickles standing in a nearby yard at a rusted water spigot and clutching a green hose. "I know you!"

"Do you?"

It was more a declaration than a question. The young man fished out another cigarette and lit it before he stepped onto the damp lawn.

"Sure, you're that guy I keep seein' at the diner. See you there almost every day, seems like. You live here now?"

"For the time being." He slid the Zippo into his pocket and worked his thumb through one of his belt loops.

"Where you headed now?"

"I'm just taking a walk."

"Too late to go there today."

"I beg your pardon?"

"Diner. It's closed. Closes around three every day. Figured you'd know that. It's 'cause they can't get anybody to work there later, I imagine. Don't matter, anyhow, since I don't think nobody'd wanna eat supper there."

Nickles took off his stained brown cap and rubbed his forehead. Fat beads of water trickled from the hose and spattered down the front of his red and green flannel shirt.

"If you'll excuse me."

"Where you headed now?"

"That's none of your concern."

"I wanted to ask you. Why you been hangin' around the diner so much, anyway? Don't nobody like their food that much."

The young man shrugged, inhaling. "It's somewhere to go. You don't have many places like that in this town."

"No, I guess we don't. Not like your big cities, huh?" Nickles looped the hose around his forearm in a clumsy bundle. "I thought maybe it's 'cause of that waitress, that she's why you're always there. Don't see no other reason for it."

He dropped the hose in a heap at his feet. The young man made no reply.

"Nothin' wrong with that. I was your age, I tried to grab every bit of snatch I could get at. Don't tell my wife, though!"

He laughed and moved closer to the young man, stepping on the hose, which made a wet gurgle, and speaking at a rapid clip with no space for interruption.

"Go on, you can tell me. Is that to you're gonna see? You goin' off to find that bitch waitress? Like to slap her on the mouth, boy, the way she talks. Right on the goddamned mouth. Good body, though. She's got a nice ass. Firm, like a piece of fruit. You can tell that just by lookin' at it. That little dress she wears. I'd let her sit on my lap, you know what I mean? And lift that little dress. I'd give just about anything for the chance. I'd give my right nut. Just so I could screw it to her."

The young man put his hand on Nickles' shoulder. He stopped speaking. "And what kind of woman would ever let you fuck her?"

Nickles' smile fell. He opened his mouth to answer, but the young man continued.

"When I look at you," he said, "all I can see is a sad little dog that thinks it's a man. It yips a lot because it thinks it's smart. It thinks it's funny, and it thinks everyone enjoys listening to it yip. A couple of feeble steps on its stubby hind legs complete the illusion of humanity, but no matter how hard it tries, it's still just a stupid little dog that nobody likes. And once it's done yipping and hopping around on its legs, it'll go back to the corner once more, scratching at fleas and tonguing its asshole, nosing its sterile, shriveled testicles. So listen to me. The next time you see me anywhere, in the diner or on the street, keep your words to yourself. I don't much feel like listening to you yip."

The young man smiled and removed his hand from Nickles' shoulder. He gave it a playful bump with his fist and spat his cigarette in the grass before he walked away.

He arrived at Sarah's building to find her sprawled on the iron grating, cigarette protruding from her fingers. He cleared his throat. She turned her head and saw him standing below. She smirked and brought the cigarette to her lips, pulling slow. Exhaling, she dropped what was left through a space in the grating, and it fell to the ground and bounced with a spray of ash and sparks.

"Come on up."

The young man smiled.

The windows were open and the air was wet and warm and filled with the sound of a thousand buzzing cicadas, droning on and out like an engine winding down. The sky was a vast watercolor, with clouds of purple and blue against the shimmering backdrop of pink and orange and the pooling blood of the slowfading deep red sun. The lights were on in the sitting room, casting everything with a golden glow, like the sepia tones of an old photograph. On the sofa the young man held the Bible inches from his face and read with quiet intensity. He did not appear to blink but once or twice per page, as if he were afraid the words might disappear if he looked away for too long.

From her chair Mrs. Parker ran her pinky finger along the top edge of the picture frame and examined it for traces of dust. She blew a quick puff of air onto her finger and rubbed it against her thumb before she brushed them both against the soft fabric of her light purple dress. Taking the picture into her hands she removed a cloth from her right pocket and wrapped and slid it across each side of the frame. When she had finished she gathered the cloth in a loose bunch and pushed it in downward strokes against the glass. Holding the frame she gazed past the eyes of her husband into her own reflection. All she could focus on where the lines at the corners of her mouth and the two small folds of sagging skin that had formed on either side of the point of her chin. She blinked once. Then again.

The young man sighed and she looked up and watched him. He was entranced, unmoving. For him it seemed at this moment that the outside world did not exist. Mrs. Parker looked back to the picture, but raised her eyes so that she still could see him.

"I'm sorry."

The young man looked up. His face softened and he turned his body toward her.

"I'm sorry about the other night."

He closed his eyes in a long slow blink. "You have no reason to apologize."

"I do. I'm so ashamed for the way I behaved."

Mrs. Parker turned the frame facedown on her lap and stared at the floor. A dried flower petal, pale yellow with a pink border, had fallen between her chair and the coffee table and she moved her shoe, covering it.

The young man marked his page and closed the Bible. He set it on the table and rested his hands in his lap.

"Mrs. Parker, people live their entire lives feeling sorry for things over which they have no control. You did nothing but miss your husband. That is no reason to feel guilty."

She felt the smooth black stand of the picture frame.

"I never realized before how much I did miss him."

The young man nodded.

"I did. I didn't. You know what I mean."

"When did you first meet your husband?"

Mrs. Parker folded the cloth twice and slipped it back into her pocket. "I'm not even sure I can remember. I always knew him – we both grew up here, we went to the same church. He was a bit older than me, about five years. He was still in school when we were married."

She set the picture on the table and stared at it.

"Forgive me," the young man said.

"Why?"

"I didn't mean to pry. I know many people don't care to discuss their loved ones after they've passed on."

Turning away from her, he picked up his Bible and opening it began to read.

"Oh, that's all right. I'm fine."

The young man did not look at her. "I know so little about him that sometimes I feel the need to ask questions. But I've never been sure if you would be offended, or worse. I would never want to do anything that might hurt your feelings."

Mrs. Parker stood and walked to the sofa, where she sat in the spot right next to the young man.

"You haven't done anything wrong. If you have a question, you ask it. Don't be afraid."

She touched his shoulder and felt the bones shift as he closed the book once more. Neither of them moved. The sky had turned the color of grape jam and the clouds were no longer visible. The air now felt cool, but still moist, like morning dew. Mrs. Parker stood and closed the front window. She put her hands on the curtains and held them and stared.

"Thank you for everything, Mrs. Parker. You've been so kind to me."

She looked back at him and smiled. Releasing the curtains, she returned to her chair and sat. "I like this. Sitting here. When I'm by myself it's so empty. It's always better to be with someone, even if you're not doing anything but sit."

"Woe to him that is alone when he falleth; for he hath not another to help him up."

"I felt so alone. I didn't realize."

The young man looked as though he was about to speak. He frowned, eyebrows furrowed, and sat very still biting his lip.

"What is it?"

The young man raised his hand. He cocked his head and turned, pointing his ear toward the stairs. "Do you hear that?"

They listened in silence. Mrs. Parker strained to hear, but all she could make out was the sound of the refrigerator kicking on through the kitchen door.

"Mr. Peterson, what is it?"

"Be still. It's growing louder."

Soon she could hear it. A steady thump, thump of soft footsteps coming from the second floor. They fell at a slow pace, getting louder as they came near the top of the stairs and more quiet as they moved away again. Mrs. Parker let out a gasp, her eyes growing wide with fear.

"Is somebody upstairs?"

"Then you can hear it, too."

"Yes, of course I can."

The young man rose and crept toward the front of the darkened stairway, where he stopped and rested his hand on the banister.

"I heard it last night," he said in a soft voice. "I know I did. I wasn't sure if I was dreaming, but I swore I could hear it outside my door. It sounded much like this – very steady and quiet, as though someone were pacing back and forth in the hall. I'm not sure how long it lasted, but all of a sudden it stopped and everything was quiet again. Did you hear it, too?"

"I didn't. I certainly would have said something."

"I'm sorry I didn't, but I was afraid it might worry you."

Slowly Mrs. Parker got up from her chair and started toward the stairs. The young man heard her and let go of the banister. He stepped in front of her and held her by the arms. "What a second, Mrs. Parker, you don't know what's up there."

"Should I call the police?"

The young man looked at the ceiling as though he could see through it.

"What should I do? What do you think it is?"

The young man raised his hand and Mrs. Parker fell silent.

"Hello?" he called. "Is someone up there?"

The sounds showed no sign of abatement. The young man looked to Mrs. Parker. Her eyes fluttered and her face was pale. She gulped at her words when she spoke. "What do you think it is?"

The young man unbuttoned his sleeve and rolled it up just beyond his bony elbow. He bent his arm and held it straight. The scattered black hairs on it stuck out like the stiff bristles of a hairbrush and his white skin was covered with tiny bumps. "Are you cold, too?" he asked.

Mrs. Parker nodded. The young man clutched one of her hands. His skin was cool and clammy, like that of the corpse. She took a deep breath when she felt it. When she took another the cold reached her nose and the whole room smelled of frost. "It wasn't cold a minute ago," she said.

"That's because it isn't cold in here. It's summertime."

He glanced once more toward the stairs. "Wait here. I'm going to see what's up there."

"Be careful!"

She did not mean to shout. Her shrill voice cracked and she brought her hands to her mouth. Her shoulders heaved and her heart felt like it might explode.

"Are you all right?"

She nodded. She did not move her hands.

"Don't worry, Mrs. Parker. I'll be fine. I'll just go up for a second, to see if anything is there."

The young man rolled his sleeve back down as he approached the bottom of the stairs. He stood for a long while, and then began his cautious ascent. Although the footsteps had not changed in pace or volume, Mrs. Parker flinched each time she heard them, as if they were being caused by someone swinging a sledgehammer against a railroad track. The young man raised both hands before him, fingers spread wide like he was walking in pitch dark and trying to feel his way. Mrs. Parker saw the veins bursting in them like gross blue worms. He climbed as slow as he could, taking care not to make one sound as he was swallowed up by the shadows. When he reached the top he stopped moving.

"Hello?" His voice was wary, quiet, just above the sound of the footsteps.

"Can you see anything?" Mrs. Parker whispered.

The young man leaned over the railing and shook his head. Then, straightening himself, he took another step and peered into the hallway and cupped his eyes like a facemask, shielding them from the light downstairs. Mrs. Parker was afraid to breathe. She put one of her knuckles her mouth and bit into it until she broke the skin. Soon the young man lowered his arms and descended three steps, at which point he squatted and spoke to her in a hushed tone through the bars of the rail.

"I can't see anything."

"Do you want me to look?"

She did not move one centimeter.

"I'm not sure that anybody could see what's making noise," he said. "But I can sense a presence. It's strong, I can feel it. Something is definitely up there, Mrs. Parker, and it wants your attention."

"What would you want from me?" she sputtered.

The young man sighed. His head bent, he rose and came down the rest of the stairs. He stopped at the bottom and looked once more to the hallway above.

"What? What is it?"

The young man did not make eye contact when he answered.

"Did you not once tell me about your husband doing this type of thing? Of how you would wake in the night and hear him pacing in the hallway?"

128

Mrs. Parker's eyes were like glass, and her drunken blinks sent several scattered tears down her cheeks.

"Do you really think it might be him?"

"I can't be certain, but I do think it's a possibility."

"But he's been gone for such a long time. Why would he come back now, all of a sudden, after so much time has gone by? It doesn't make any sense."

"I'm afraid I have no answer."

Mrs. Parker wiped her face. "I didn't mean to get so upset," she sniffed. "Have you ever seen anything like this before?"

"Once."

"What happened?"

"In that case, someone was trying to speak from beyond the grave. They had a message for their loved ones which only I could deliver."

"What was the message?"

"I apologize, but I cannot tell you that. It is only the business of those to whom the message was given. What I can say is, I feel this may be a similar situation."

She shook her head. "But if this is my husband, why doesn't he just speak through you like he did before?"

"I cannot explain the motivations of the deceased. I can only interpret the signs."

Mrs. Parker flinched at the fall of each new footstep.

"What should I do?"

"Perhaps you should attempt to speak to him. Believe not every spirit, but try the spirits whether they are of God."

She took a breath. When she spoke it was as though she were being strangled.

"John?"

The footsteps showed no sign of stopping.

"Speak louder."

"John?" Her voice remained shaky.

"Louder still. You need to break through to him."

Mrs. Parker steeled herself and called once more.

"John!"

The entire house was quiet. The stillness was deafening.

"John, what do you want?"

No response was given. Turning, the young man trotted up the stairs and peered into the hallway. Mrs. Parker held her breath.

"It's empty. I can't feel anything. If it was your husband he's no longer here."

"May I come look?"

"Of course."

The young man held out his hand as Mrs. Parker climbed the stairs. His skin remained cold and she shuddered when she felt his fingers. Together they entered the hallway and looked. It was empty, and so dark that there were no visible shadows.

"Would you please turn the light on?" Mrs. Parker whispered.

The young man hit a switch, illuminating the empty space. Nothing differed from its usual appearance. Mrs. Parker took back her hand.

"What a relief. I don't know what I would've done if he'd been up here. My heart is just racing."

"How do you feel?"

"A bit nervous, but I'm fine." She took a few tentative steps forward. "I don't think I'll get any sleep at all tonight."

"I should think not."

Mrs. Parker walked the length of the hallway checking behind the doors. "I need to be sure," she said when she noticed the young man staring.

"Of course."

She closed the door to her bedroom. "I think I should be fine now."

"Shall we go back downstairs?"

"Yes, let's."

"I'll get the light."

It was impossible to see the sidewalk. There were no streetlamps and the light of the moon was masked by the harsh auburn of porch bulbs and the diffused glow of lamps through curtains and smudged glass. The yards were a mass of jagged lines of shadow that melted into deep black nothingness. If not for the steady crunch of pebbles beneath her flat hard-soled shoes, Sarah would have felt like she were floating, sailing through the empty void, invisible to everything. It was a pleasant thought.

The sun was not long down. Sarah enjoyed this time of day. She saw no one. She spoke to no one. It was as if the world belonged to her.

Up ahead was the sound of a motor that jangled like a clutch of tin cans tied to the end of a rope and swinging around and around like a lasso. Two pinpoints of light appeared at the end of the long empty street and Sarah stepped onto the grass behind a large beech tree. The light drew closer and the sound increased in volume until it was like an earsplitting avalanche of metal plates and nails shaking, grinding against each other. She moved round the tree as the car passed. It did not slow. When she could no longer hear it she went back to the sidewalk.

Sarah ran her hand along the skin of her arm and it was cool with dew. The air was like thick mist. You could eat it. You could feel it as you walked through. Wet fingertips. She brushed them on her clothes.

The glass shattered on the floor and the water spread out fast, people lifted their feet so their shoes would not get wet.

"You owe me for that," Leroy said. He lifted a French fry, dark and crisp, to his mouth and popped it inside. He chewed with his mouth open and made unconscious vocal sighing noises and after he had swallowed he licked each of his fingers and grabbed another fry.

"How much?"

"I don't know yet. I'll tell you when I do."

"Fire her!" Nickles shouted.

Leroy dropped the French fry on top of the heaping mound on his plate. "Why? You lookin' for a job?"

"Naw, I was just–"

"When I wanna know what you got rattlin' around in that big empty head of yours I'll ask you. Speaking of, you ever hear me ask you? Ever in your life? No. Didn't think so."

He picked up the fry and jammed it into his mouth. He spoke in a soft voice and Sarah could see the crunchy bits of potato break apart and stick to his tongue like wallpaper paste.

"Go get the mop, honey, and wipe it up before these assholes make it into an even bigger mess." He swallowed the fry and gulped a half-cup of coffee. "Uhmmmm..."

White clouds like thick paint against the clean blue of the sky and the sun beaming rays like melted butter. Sarah sat on the grating in the shade and puffed. The air was hot and sticky, and her skin prickled with quick-forming beads of sweat. She wiped her neck with a rag, which she draped over an iron bar to dry.

In the alley below three boys ran and screamed and pushed each other, punching, kicking, laughing. Their shrieks were like a steel spike through her skull and she closed her eyes and breathed the soothing smoke until her head felt light and good.

Still scrambling, the boys stumbled into a pair of trashcans sitting side by side against the brick wall of a nearby building, and all three of them shouted and continued to laugh. As they stood, two of them grabbed the lids of the cans and beat them together, holding them out like shields. The third boy found a long splintery pole and swung it at them and they squealed, laughing more until they could not breathe.

Sarah opened her eyes and watched them. Taking a last drag she aimed the butt and flicked it with her fingers so that it landed near whey played. They did not notice. She picked up the dampened rag and wiped it down her neck and across her forehead. She held the rag to the side of her head and gave a shrill whistle. "Hey! Boys!"

They stopped for a moment and stared at her. The biggest one of them guarded his eyes with a lid while the other two squinted against the sun. Their faces were marked with gray streaks of sweat and their hands were black with dirt. Another of the boys had a crusted green trail that led from his right nostril to the top of his lip, where it abruptly disappeared.

"Go play somewhere else!"

"You can't tell us what to do!" shouted the one with the lid above his head.

"Yeah!"

"You can't tell us!"

"Don't copy me!"

"Shut up, I didn't!"

"Boys! Would you please?"

The leader stuck out his tongue and blew, at which point his friends began once more to attack one another.

Sarah draped the rag and helped herself to another cigarette. She held it in her mouth but did not light it. "Come on..." she mumbled.

The boy with the stick began to wield his weapon left and right like a batter warming up on-deck and edged toward the others, swinging faster.

Sarah took out a match and held it as she watched.

Soon the stick connected with the knee of the biggest boy. He dropped the lid on its handle and fell to the ground, where he sat and hugged his leg. The lid rattled against the cement, all but drowned out by his screams. His eyes were shut and his mouth opened so wide Sarah thought he might unhinge his jaw.

The other boys stared as he continued to wail before, never speaking, they dropped their weapons and ran in opposite directions down the narrow alleyway. Sarah smirked and lit her cigarette. She tossed the blackened match at the remaining boy and it missed him by inches.

In a few seconds the boy quieted down and pulled the hem of his T-shirt to his face, brushing it roughly over his eyes, nose and mouth, and leaving an oily mix of sweat, tears and snot embedded into the material. When he let go of the shirt he blinked several times and looked around. "Fellas?" he called, standing.

One more sniff, long and wet like boots traipsing through thick mud, and he ran away without a limp.

Sarah inhaled and looked at the sky. "Fucking kids."

Nighttime had grown so slow in arriving.

After the sun went down she followed her usual route. She started early and walked it twice in a big loop. He legs were stiff from standing all day and her knees would pop and it felt good to walk. On her second time around she had a cigarette. The dusty flutter of moth wings zipping around the glow of the red light at the tip. The stillness and silence of the streets. People sitting behind windows and screen doors beneath hardburning electric lights, blind to the outside.

Vern stretched his elbow until it made a sound like tightstretched elastic mixed with the snapping of seven tiny twigs. He stretched again and again until he could move it in silence. "You hear that?"

"Uh-huh," Sarah said as she exhaled. "Does it hurt?"

"Kinda."

"It doesn't sound too good."

"Feels like my arms are filled with gravel."

"You should see somebody."

"Soon as my well comes in." He lit a cigarette and looked at the wall with a blank stare. He pulled a rolled-up newspaper from his back pocket and flattened it before he fanned it near his face and closed his eyes.

"Does that do any good?"

Vern did not open his eyes. "No, not really. Supposed to be even hotter today, you hear that?"

"Ugh, don't remind me."

"You're lucky. It's gettin' to be a goddamned Turkish bath in the kitchen. Keeps up, by the end of summer I'll be half the size I am now."

"You'll be two feet tall, then?"

"Funny."

She chuckled and stubbed out her cigarette. "Have you seen that cat around lately?"

"What cat?"

"You know, that cat that's always goin' through the trashcans back here, the one that meows until you take off the lids for him. That cat."

"What's he look like?"

"Like a scroungy old alley cat."

"Haven't seen him."

"That's too bad."

Vern took another drag.

"He's the only one I don't mind servin' around this place."

"Sorry. I really haven't seen him. I'd tell you."

Sarah took out a fresh cigarette and held it, making no move to strike a match.

"You know who I have seen? I wasn't gonna say anything."

"Maybe you shouldn't."

Vern dropped his cigarette against a yellowed clump of weeds growing from a crack in the pavement. "He talk to you?"

"Not in a while."

"Wanna hear what he told me?"

"Nope."

"Yeah." He leaned against the door. "Wish it would cool off a bit."

Sarah poked her cigarette in the air. "Poof. Didn't work. I tried." She put the matches in her pocket and slid the cigarette like a pencil behind her ear.

"It was about a week and a half ago."

"Vern, don't talk about my dad anymore."

"Sorry."

"I'm not his fucking maid."

He nodded. "I know. I'm sorry."

Sarah stood and he stepped to the side. The handle of the door was hot and she was quick about touching it and sucked in a sharp hiss of air when she made contact.

"Don't worry about it," she said.

She heard him before she saw him. The sound of Nickles' voice, cackling and crass, carried clear through the unopened picture window. As soon as she heard it her mouth felt like she had eaten a skunk. He looked in her direction as he spoke but he could not see her in the blanket of dark.

Kneeling, she found a big rock in the grass and held it in her palm. She tossed it and caught it and took it between her thumb and forefinger, aiming with cool precision, wondering where to throw – at the center of his waxy bald head or the zigzagging yellow peaks of his teeth. She stared for a long time. He remained where he was. It felt like he was taunting her.

As she drew back her arm he walked away. He did not return.

She dropped the rock, stood and walked the rest of the way to the house.

Sarah turned on the faucet and covered the orange with her hand. Her work clothes lay in a pile near the toilet. She dipped her free hand into the stream of water and waited for it to cool down. Then she closed her eyes and cupped both hands until they filled and she splashed her face once, and then again. Water still running, she opened her eyes and stared at her reflection. Clear droplets dappled the rim of the sink and then ribbons of wetness ran down her chin, curling across her neck, itching, tickling. She blinked. She smiled.

Mrs. Parker took down the small ceramic cardinal from its spot on the shelf and polished its dull finish with a clean dust rag before she placed it on the collapsible table at her side. Queuing in front and around the red bird were dozens of tiny animals and objects, each newly cleaned, awaiting their return to the cluttered shelf. She hummed as she worked and took special care to set each piece in the exact right position. Although they were packed as tight as sardines on the shelf she managed to touch a single piece at a time. Her movements were brisk and her hands did not shake.

The young man watched her, Bible lying open in his lap. She turned, holding now a clear glass rabbit the size of a fifty-cent piece. When she finished wiping it she set it on the table and reached back toward the shelf.

"Mrs. Parker, please wait one moment."

She stopped, her arm stiff above her shoulder, and gave him a curious look.

"I'm sorry. There is something I feel we should discuss. Please, come sit."

Mrs. Parker lowered her arm and folded the cloth, which she carried to her chair and put on the coffee table as she sat. The young man closed the Bible and set it near the rag. Leaning forward, he began to speak.

"Mrs. Parker, this has been going on for more than a week now. I think we need to try something new."

She did not reply.

"I think I may be able to put a stop to these noises, but to do so, I must ask that you promise me you will do whatever I request of you when the time comes. If this is your husband we've been hearing, I think I can speak to him and get him to tell me what he wants. But you must promise to trust me and listen to what I say. Can you do that?"

As she spoke, Mrs. Parker took the dust cloth from the table and refolded it with forced calm and stared at it as though she were reading words embroidered on its side.

"Will you ask me to go upstairs?"

The young man nodded. "I may have to. If I can at all avoid doing so, I will, but I can make you no assurances."

"I don't know," Mrs. Parker sighed. "This isn't so bad, really. I can get used to the noise – especially when I remember it stops. It always has. You've heard that yourself."

The young man rose and approached her chair. She looked up from the cloth as he knelt at her feet and stared at her with soft eyes. He placed his right hand on the arm of the chair and gripped it.

"Do you think that would be fair to your husband? It seems obvious he wants to tell you something, but for whatever reason he won't do it yet. Or more likely can't. Mrs. Parker, he needs to rest. You speak as though you could tolerate this for the rest of your life, but I would bet that you would begin to feel pretty guilty before long. It would not be fair to your husband if we were to take no action, nor would it be fair to you."

Mrs. Parker said nothing. She glanced down at his hand and saw his bulging veins grow fatter as he continued to hold the chair. He was so close to her that she could smell the sweet cologne he wore.

"And anyway," he continued, "I'm sure you're getting pretty tired of having me around the house." He removed his hand from the chair's arm and hid it behind his back. When he resumed speaking he tilted his head in a way that forced Mrs. Parker to look into his eyes.

"I can't stay here forever."

She felt sick. "What's going to happen to me?" Her hands flew to her mouth and her eyes widened. She shook her head and waved her arms as though she were shooing away a fly. "I'm sorry," she said.

On the porch the loud stomping of heavy footsteps could be heard through the door. The young man jolted up, stumbling back on his heels. Someone knocked on the door and Mrs. Parker rose. She avoided looking at her husband's photograph as she paused at the stand.

"Forget what I said," she told the young man. "Forget I said anything."

She cleared her throat and swallowed before she put her hand on the doorknob. It clinked like a loose coin and she held it for a moment and, looking down, took a breath. Then, head raised, she opened the door to reveal Pastor Gruber standing on the other side.

"Mrs. Parker." Although his tone was warm, his voice was thick and slurred as though he had been running. The air was not yet hot, but his collar was limp and soaked through, and his oiled hair had begun to wilt and there were moist patches at his temples. His hands were closed at his stomach and they made a sound like tacky adhesive when he opened them and spread his arms.

"What brings you by today, Pastor?"

"It's been some time since I paid you a visit, Mrs. Parker, and from what I understand you have a guest. So, as I was in the neighborhood, I thought I should stop in and say hello."

"I see."

"Have I caught you at a bad time?"

"No, excuse me. I'm sorry. Please come in."

"Thank you," he said and smiled, piggy eyes blinking slow as they adjusted from the sun. "Sometimes I seem to pick the exact wrong moment to visit the congregants. I like to do it once a month at least, but people can get so busy."

The young man approached the pair and stopped before the collapsible table.

"This is my nephew, Jacob Peterson."

"How do you do?" Pastor Gruber said and extended his hand. Smiling, the young man accepted it in silence. The pastor's skin was hot and his palm was sticky and moist as if it had just been licked by a large dog.

"Why don't we all sit down? Have a seat on the sofa."

"Thank you."

Pastor Gruber sat with a groaning sigh while the young man went to the other end of the sofa and Mrs. Parker to her chair. The pastor's cheeks were like ripe pink peaches as he smiled and breathed through his mouth.

"Is it very hot?"

"No, but it doesn't take much for it to get to me. I've always been that way. Since I was a boy." He wiped his hand across his greased scalp and it made a noise like someone chewing tapioca open-mouthed. "How is your son? Do you speak with him often?"

"Yes, at least once a week, usually more."

"And how is he?"

"He's fine. His family is fine. They're all doing quite well."

"It must be very rewarding to have such a nice family."

"It is."

"Speaking of which," Pastor Gruber said and shifted on the sofa, the springs pinging high and sharp beneath him like a tuning fork. "I don't believe we've met before."

The young man spoke for the first time.

"You are correct. We have not."

"What brings you to town?"

"I thought it would be nice if I paid a visit to my aunt Edith."

"That is nice. How long have you been here? I could have sworn I saw you here a while back – it must've been over a week ago. You were out in the yard cutting the grass."

"He's been here almost a month, maybe a little more than that."

Pastor Gruber turned his head between them like a spectator at a tennis match.

"Really. I would say that's more than an ordinary visit."

"He hasn't been here since he was a little boy."

"I see. Tell me, how long do you plan on staying?"

"That remains to be seen."

Pastor Gruber nodded, and his mouth hung open. His tongue made slippery sounds as he licked his back teeth.

"May I get you anything, Pastor?" Mrs. Parker asked.

"A glass of water might be nice."

"I'll get one for each of us."

The men stood when she left her chair and waited until she was out of the room to resume their seats.

"So, you've been here a whole month."

"I have."

"If I may ask, why haven't we seen you any of those four Sundays? I'm sure your aunt would enjoy it if you accompanied her."

"My aunt and I have an understanding. I keep the lord in my heart and in my life."

"I'm sure that's true. He will guide your eye with his. I would never want to pressure you into anything, I hope you know. We preach a very positive message of love and forgiveness."

"We."

"Well, I, yes."

"I see."

"Love worketh no ill to his neighbor: therefore love is the fulfilling of the law."

The young man smiled and nodded. "Let love be without dissimulation," he said.

"Good. That's very good. I think that's very nice."

The young man spoke at a steady pace without raising his voice.

"Abhor that which is evil; cleave to that which is good."

"Yes, yes."

"Diverse weights are an abomination to the Lord; and a false balance is not good."

"I agree–"

"It is joy to the just to do judgment: but destruction shall be to the workers of iniquity."

"May I please break in?"

"If thou do that which is evil, be afraid; for he bareth the sword not in vain."

Pastor Gruber said nothing.

"For he is the minister of God, a revenger to execute wrath upon him that doeth evil." The young man smiled and folded his arms.

"That's very impressive," the pastor said as he stuck a finger between his neck and his collar and pulled.

"Are you all right?"

"I'll be fine. Do you mind if I use...?" He pointed to the folded white cloth on the coffee table. The young man motioned toward it with an open palm and nodded.

"Thank you so much." Pastor Gruber held the cloth by one of its corners and let it fall open, after which he dabbed it against his neck and forehead, leaving splotchy mousebrown marks on his skin. Then he folded the cloth down the center and rubbed the back of his neck.

"I hate to impose," he said. "Especially when it isn't even hot out." He folded the cloth once more and put it in the front right pocket of his black trousers.

Mrs. Parker entered the room carrying a tray with three tall empty glasses and a big glass pitcher of iced tea with sliced sections of lemon bobbing at the top. The men stood as she approached the table and set the tray on it.

"I brewed this a few days ago so it should be nice and cold," she said and straightened the contents of the tray. "I thought it would be better than just plain water."

The word stuck in her throat when she caught a glimpse of the pastor and she gave a dry cough.

"Is something wrong?" he asked.

"What happened to your face?"

"My face?" He brought his hand to his squishy cheek and wiped it and looked at his fingers, now stained a rodential shade.

"Oh, no, was that the dust rag you used?" the young man asked. "I'm sorry, I had no idea."

Pastor Gruber stared at his hand and rubbed his fingers together. "It's fine," he said with a nod.

Stifling a smile, Mrs. Parker headed back to the kitchen.

"Let me get you a clean washcloth."

The pair continued to stand, silent. The young man shrugged.

"May I pour you some tea?" he asked.

"Why do you have to go?" Mrs. Parker said midway through dinner.

The young man set down his fork. "Someone else might need me."

"When this is all over, what happens? You leave. Is that it?"

"As soon as I receive another message."

"How long does that take, usually?"

"It varies, but it's never more than a few days."

Mrs. Parker pretended to wipe her mouth with her white cloth napkin. A half-kernel of corn lay next to her glass and she put it on the plate and rubbed its juice from the table.

"If I can, I'll return to visit you. Would you like that?"

"I would."

"Mrs. Parker, this has nothing to do with how I feel about you as a person. I hope you can understand that. I must do this for you and your husband. It is why the Lord sent me here. To fail to help you would be an insult to Him."

She nodded. "I understand."

"I knew you would. And I want to thank you for all that you've done. It's a debt I could never possibly repay."

"You don't have to. You've done so much for *me* – I wouldn't want anything else."

The young man smiled. "You're a good person," he said.

The young man retrieved his Bible hours before the sun went down and kept it close. The house was tense. Neither he nor Mrs. Parker ate dinner, opting instead to bide their time in the sitting room, where she started at each familiar snap in the floorboards, every ordinary rattle in the walls. The young man remained implacable. Quiet and relaxed, he sat with a patient look on his face, as if he were waiting to get his hair cut.

Time dragged. Mrs. Parker grew more anxious as each second passed. She refused to be three steps from her husband's photograph and repeatedly cleared her throat while she fiddled with her collar like it was constricting her supply of oxygen.

The wind picked up. A branch fell from a tree in the yard and brushed a window screen with a prickly scratch on its way to the ground and Mrs. Parker gasped and jumped from her chair. The young man turned his head, undisturbed, and watched her. Mrs. Parker's hands were clasped at her chest. Her shoulders heaved and her stomach bubbled and she squeaked out an embarrassed apology before she reclaimed her seat.

"I'm just so nervous."

"Do you think it would soothe your nerves if we talked?"

"It might."

"Is there anything in particular you would like to discuss?"

"I don't know. I'm not sure I could keep my head straight."

The young man crossed his legs. "You simply need something on which to focus. Perhaps you could try to tell me a story."

147

"What about?"

"Anything you like. Tell me something about your family."

"I don't know what I would tell you."

"Think of when your son was a boy. Was there anything you, he and your husband did together? Something you can remember really well. It could be an activity of some kind, or a trip. Is there anything that stands out in your memory?"

She thought a moment. "Sometimes on Saturdays – or on Sundays after church – we would go on a picnic."

"That's good. Tell me about that."

"There isn't much to tell. I don't know what I would say."

"Tell me whatever you can think of. And when you do, I want you to try and remember every possible detail. Close your eyes and when you speak, I want you to describe it to the extent that it appears before you."

Mrs. Parker shook her head and let out an exasperated sigh. "There's nothing to tell. We never did any more than what I said."

"You've told me that you went on picnics. That is all. I don't know where you went, nor what you ate or what you did."

"I'm sorry. This won't be very interesting for you."

"That is immaterial. This exercise is not for my benefit. Now. Close your eyes."

"Do I have to?"

"Yes. Please. And remember, when you speak I want you to give me as many details as possible. That is what I want to hear about."

She stared at him.

"Please," he said. "You'll be surprised at how well you can see it."

"Oh, all right..."

"Good. Now, close your eyes."

Mrs. Parker rose when the sun was nothing but a faint pinkish glow on the black edge of the horizon. John still was asleep. Nathan was sleeping, too. Mrs. Parker could hear his deep, steady breathing through the closed bedroom door when she passed by before she went downstairs to the kitchen to make sandwiches. A jar of strawberry jam, cold and fogged from the icebox, sat on the counter as she cut two slices from a loaf of fresh bread and spooned out juicy crimson dollops that quivered on the bread before she smoothed them. She spread a thick layer of peanut butter on two more slices of bread and set them on top of the jellied ones. She made sandwiches until the loaf was gone, with flaking chunks of turkey, crisp lettuce, thick tomato slices and dabs of yellow mustard. When the sandwiches were finished she wrapped them in brown paper, arranged them with care in the basket and started the coffee.

"Morning," John said and went to the cupboard, feet dragging. His hair was uncombed and he had not shaved. His thin brown shirt was buttoned halfway, revealing an old white T-shirt underneath.

"Good morning. I thought you might sleep a little while yet."

He took a white cup from the shelf and closed the door.

"I tried. Been up long?"

"No."

He kissed her cheek and shuffled over to the coffee pot.

"It's probably not as strong as you like."

"I'm sure it's fine, Edith."

He filled his cup and brought it to his face. Closing his eyes, he inhaled. "Smells good." He sipped as he walked to the table and sat with his head propped on his hand.

"How is it?"

"Very good."

"Are you sure? I can make some more if it isn't."

149

"It's fine. Can I help you with anything?"

"I don't think so. I've got the sandwiches all made, the soda pop is in the icebox, the potato chips are already in the basket. All that's left, really, is Nathan."

"You want me to get him?"

"No, let him sleep a little more. It's early yet. What time should we leave?"

"I wanna be on the road by eight."

"I'll start breakfast."

"It can wait a few minutes. Sit down with me, have some coffee."

She poured herself a cup and took the seat across from him.

"What's the matter? I don't bite."

"I know that." She lifted the cup, her senses filled with steam, and took a slurping sip.

"Why won't you sit next to me? What did I do?"

"Nothing. I just sat down. I didn't think about it all."

"You'll hurt my feelings if you stay over there."

"No I won't."

The right corner of John's mouth pointed up into a half-smile and he stood holding his coffee cup in the palm of his hand and walked slowly around the table, coming to a stop behind her chair. He set his cup beside hers and stooped until his face was resting between her neck and shoulder. He ran his hands along her sides and closed his eyes. Her skin was smooth and it smelled like soap.

"Are you going to shave this morning?"

"Tomorrow." He wrapped his right arm around her and began to kiss her neck. She placed her hand over his and patted it.

"I should really get a start on breakfast."

"It can wait."

"If it waits too long someone might come looking for you before we're ready to go."

"We won't answer the door."

"You wouldn't do that."

Groaning, he removed his hands and gave her one final kiss. He stood and straightened the front of his trousers.

"I'm sorry."

John finished his coffee in three big gulps. "It's all right," he said as he set down the cup. "Go ahead and get started. I guess I'll go and wake Nathan."

Slender blades of yellow-green prairie grass and tall weeds scratched against the rolling silver hubcaps as John turned the car off the highway and down the narrow dirt path. The car began to bounce like a horse-drawn wagon and Nathan leaned over to stabilize the bulging basket on the floor between the front and back seats.

"We won't be able to drink that pop for a while yet, will we?" Mrs. Parker said.

The car slowed as they reached the grove of trees, and John pulled to a flat shaded spot in the grass and killed the engine. The air was still and the sun flared over the tops of the trees.

"We made pretty good time," John said, checking his watch. "About an hour."

He popped open the windscreen before he pulled the keys from the ignition and turned in his seat. Mrs. Parker sat facing him and Nathan draped halfway over the backseat, his knees stretched to the seat behind him.

"All right," John said. "Who's carrying what?"

"I got the basket!"

"Are you sure you don't want to carry the blanket?"

"I carried it last time, Mom, remember? It ain't heavy."

"But with the plates and everything."

151

"He can carry it if he wants to. Only you've just gotta promise not to run with it. We don't want the sandwiches to get squished."

"Yes, sir. I won't."

Light broke through the trees painting brilliant patches on the ground and filling the air with a warm haze. The grass beneath the shelter of the branches was short and sparse, strewn with dry pine needles and fallen leaves. Nathan walked at a brisk pace ahead of his parents lugging the basket with both hands. Over one arm Mrs. Parker carried a folded blanket soft like fleece and blue with white and yellow stripes.

"You want me to take that?"

"No, that's all right."

Twigs snapped beneath their shoes as they continued to walk.

"Are you mad at me, Edith?"

She did not look at him. "Of course not."

Up ahead, Nathan reached the edge of the river. He set down the basket and shielded his eyes from the blinding glare of the slow-moving water. It seemed almost too bright beyond the trees and from the shade Mrs. Parker could scarcely see him standing in the sun in his blue shirt.

"Nathan, you'll wanna bring that basket back here a ways – at least until we eat. Don't want everything to get warm, do we?"

"Yes, sir!"

He hoisted the basket with a grunt and carried it back one-armed against his hip, legs spread out for balance, until he met the others.

"This should be fine," John said.

Nathan put down the basket and rubbed his ruddy palms together.

"Are you all right?"

"Yeah, Mom, I'm fine."

"Sure he is."

John reached out and grabbed him by the back of the neck and pulled him close. Mrs. Parker watched as he brought his hand up and rubbed it across the short-clipped sides of the boy's head. Then he mussed the part in his hair so that it fell into his eyes.

"Cut it out!" Nathan laughed and shoved him.

"So, what should we do first?"

"Let's see if any trees got knocked down by that storm a couple weeks ago!"

"I don't know if the storm made it up here, but we can sure take a look. Whaddayou think, Edith?"

"You two go on ahead. I'll lay out the things."

"That'll only take a few seconds – we can wait."

"Really, I don't mind."

"Come on, we'll wait for you."

"Yeah, Mom!"

With a sigh Mrs. Parker unfolded the blanket partway and held it by two of its corners. Spreading her arms she snapped the blanket in the air twice before it unfolded all the way, and spread it in the grass until it was free of creases.

"Let's go," she said.

Nathan ran flapping his arms and jumping in the air, punctuating his movements with bold shouts and roaring wails. His parents followed ten yards or so, not touching.

"Here's some! I knew it! I told you!"

"You find some trees?"

They gathered at the front of a great cottonwood tree with an enormous trunk and a vast network of forking branches. The tree was partway out of the ground, with half of its thick black roots showing, and its trunk was split with soft pulp exposed like an open gaping wound. The tree leaned at a forty-five degree angle against a giant oak.

"Look at it, Dad!"

"That's really somethin'."

John placed his hands on the base of the tree and leaned against it. Then he slammed into it with his shoulders like a football player. It did not budge, and he stood back with an admiring smile. "This is really somethin'."

"Can I climb it?"

"Give it a try."

"I'm not sure that's such a good idea."

"Aww, why not?"

"It's too dangerous. What if it falls over?"

"It won't, I promise!"

"It shouldn't. I couldn't move it, pushing on it. He's much smaller than I am."

"I don't know."

"Go on, let him try it. He's a boy – let him be one."

"Please, Mom?"

Mrs. Parker sighed. "All right. Just be careful."

John grabbed Nathan under his arms and lifted him giggling so he could reach the upturned side of the tree. "Can you make it?"

"Yeah."

Nathan swung his leg over the top and pulled himself up. John gave him a swat on the butt and he laughed and yelled and sat on the tree like a saddle, one leg on each side. Steadying himself with his hands he brought up his legs, trousers scraping off tiny bits of bark, and went into a crouching position before he stood. His movements were slow, and with careful steps he began to ascend the tree, arms spread like a tightrope walker. When he came to the first wide vee in the branches he turned and sat and waved to his parents.

"It's so high. I don't even want to look."

"He's fine. Tree's so big it didn't even wiggle." He cupped his hands around his mouth. "How is it up there?"

"Great! You should come up here, too, Dad!"

"No, I'm fine where I am!"

"Hi, Mom!"

She waved back, shielding her eyes.

"See, it's safe up here! I told ya!" He waved both hands in tight circles above his head.

"You stop that now! Keep one of your hands on that tree! I don't want you falling!"

"Oh, Edith, he's fine."

The boy. After he was born, that's when. That first time. Just fall. She faced her husband, eyes cold, lips tight.

"You told me you wouldn't do it again."

"What am I doing? I'm not doing anything?"

"Not now."

"Whaddayou mean?" He continued to stare at the top of the tree. Dark green leaves twirled in the low breeze and the sound of the river was like a faint whisper in the background.

"You know what I mean."

He turned to look at her. He waited to answer.

"You're mistaken."

"Dad! I can see some apple trees!"

John made a swoop with his arm. "Come on down, then, let's go pick some!"

Nathan turned and scooted until his back was to his parents. Then he got on his knees and crawled backwards down the length of the tree. Near the broken trunk he stood and jumped. He landed feet first on the soft ground.

"See Mom?" he said. "Nothin' bad happened!"

They threw their apple cores on the ground and watched as they bounced and scuttled against the grass, and started walking once more down the path. The dirt was fine like talcum powder, and they kicked up little puffs of it with each silent step. Nobody spoke. Nathan looked past the tops of the trees, his head raised in absent-minded wonder. The grown-ups looked at nothing. When they came back to the basket Mrs. Parker sat with her chin in her hand and picked a dandelion. John sat down, too, and put his hand on her knee. She did not move. Nathan kicked a dried-out stick end over end, and shoved his hands down his front trouser pockets.

"We're not gonna eat now, are we?"

"You hungry? You just had those apples."

"No, sir. But what're we gonna do? Are we just gonna sit here?"

"Your mother and I probably will. For a while. We don't need to eat lunch yet. You want a pop?"

"No, sir."

"There's nothing keepin' you here, then. If you have something you wanna do, you can go do it. We'll be here."

Mrs. Parker popped off the dandelion's head with her thumb, and it bounced face-up onto the blanket. She threw away the stem.

"Can I go swimmin'?"

"Ask your mother."

"Can I? Can I, Mom?" He knelt on the blanket in front of her and put his head close to her face. "Can I, please?"

Mrs. Parker put down her hand and straightened before she spoke. She did not look at him. "May I."

"May I, Mom? Please?"

With her free hand she brushed the hair from his eyes. "Yes you may. But stay where we can see you."

Before she had finished speaking, Nathan hugged her around the neck and gave her a kiss and bounded toward the water shedding clothes until they all lay strewn in a trail behind him. "Thank you!" he called over his shoulder.

Mrs. Parker shook her head and closed her eyes. "I should have told him to leave those here." She chuckled. "They'll probably all be grass-stained now."

"They woulda been either way," John grinned.

"I suppose you're right."

"You want me to get them?"

"They can wait a few minutes."

Nathan stopped at the river's edge and dipped one of his legs over the drop-off, testing the water. He brought it back up with a squeal and hugged himself.

"Cold?" John called.

"Just a little chilly!"

"Should be fine if you jump right into it!"

Nathan's arms fell to his sides and he stood very still. After a moment he threw his hands back, swung them forward again and jumped in. He shrieked so loud his voice cracked.

"How cold is it now?"

Nathan did not hear. He laughed and floated and splashed and clamored out of the water to jump in again.

"Must not be too bad," John said.

"Maybe he'll sleep a little on the drive home."

"It could happen."

Mrs. Parker picked up the head of the dandelion and ran her thumb over its petals until it was orange with pollen. Then she dropped it in the grass. John's hand remained on her knee.

"Edith–"

"I know."

"I'm sorry."

She brushed her stained thumb on the blanket. "I don't want to talk about it anymore. Please."

He nodded. "I better grab his clothes."

"Stay here," she said and put her hand over his. "You don't have to do it right now. Stay with me."

Nathan relaxed in the tall grass along the drop-off, feet dangling in the water, the sun drying his body. Mrs. Parker had emptied the basket. The sandwiches were set out on white cloth napkins with the soda nearby, and the potato chips. Some more apples lay in a lopsided stack in the grass. John reclined against a tree with his hands behind his head and watched his wife with a satisfied smile. Everything in place, she cupped a hand around her mouth and called out. "Nathan! Time for lunch!"

Nathan stood and trotted to the blanket, on the edge of which his discarded clothes were folded and stacked neat enough to be on a department store shelf. He picked up his shirt and pulled it on, followed by his drawers and his trousers.

"Are you hungry?"

"Yes, ma'am."

"John? Are you awake?"

"I'm comin'." He stood and stretched and walked to the blanket, knees popping.

"Does that hurt?"

"Just a little stiff." He squatted and his knees popped again. Sitting now, he crossed his legs and sighed.

"Mom?"

"Yes?"

"Do I hafta put my shoes back on?"

"Not if you don't want to. But when we leave you can't forget them. I'm not buying you another pair."

"Don't worry, I won't." He walked around the blanket and sat beside his father. John grabbed his shoulder and gave it a shake.

"Have a good swim?"

"Sure did. You shoulda come in with me, Dad."

"Maybe next time."

"Start eating, you two, before the ants get it."

John leaned forward and snatched two of the napkins and pulled the sandwiches closer. Nathan took one of them and bit into it.

"How is it?"

"Good, Mom. The jelly ain't even soaked through the bread."

"Isn't soaked through."

"Isn't soaked through."

"How about yours, John?"

"Just a second."

In his hands he held two soda pop bottle. With a metal opener he popped off one of the lids. It spritzed and a pale mist flowed out of the opening and he handed the bottle to his son.

"Thanks, Dad." Nathan gulped from the bottle with audible gurgling and John smacked him on the arm.

"Drink it right or you won't get any more."

"Yes, sir."

"Siddown, Edith, I'm sure you're hungry, too."

"I just want to make sure you've got everything you need."

"We have, and if we need anything else we can get it. Come on, you made these nice sandwiches, you should eat one."

Mrs. Parker knelt on the blanket and sat with her legs folded to the side. John slid his hand under a napkin with one turkey sandwich, and he lifted it and held it before her. Smiling, she took the sandwich and John draped the napkin over his forearm like a waiter. His nose curled like he smelled something and he lifted the napkin to find his arm was stained with a lumpy smear of mustard. He turned the napkin over and wiped his arm clean and took another soda bottle. When he popped off the lid its contents spewed forth like a geyser, drenching him. Fingers dripping, he threw the bottle against a tree and shook his arms with spray flying. Mrs. Parker clapped her hands over her mouth and laughed until it felt as though she could not breathe. John closed his eyes in disgust.

"Did we bring anything I could wipe off with?"

Mrs. Parker had trouble getting the words out. "Not apart from the napkins. I never thought of it."

Brown bubbling fizz dripped from John's skin like sweat. He eyed the water.

"You'll have to jump in!"

Nathan spat a mouthful of soda and dropped his bottle. The liquid poured out in a dark, syrupy stream across the blanket.

"It's not that funny – be careful!" John moved to smack him on the back of the head but Nathan stood and coughed and dug at his mouth with frantic fingers. "What's the matter with you?"

"A bee! In the bottle!" He began to hop from foot to foot, whimpering like a scared puppy. Hands on his knees he bent over and spat several times into the grass before he threw back his head and jammed his finger deep in his mouth. John reached over and grabbed him by the shoulders and tried to see.

"Where did it sting you? Did it sting you?"

Nathan spoke as if his mouth was crammed with balled-up newspaper. "Tongue – tongue!"

"You need to let me see."

Nathan whirled away from his father with a yelp. "It hurts!"

"I know, but you have to let me see." His voice was soothing as he grabbed hold of Nathan's arm and pulled him near. He caught him around the chest and held him. With his other hand he felt inside

Nathan's mouth, but the boy squirmed too much for proper examination. "Edith! I need your help."

Mrs. Parker had stopped laughing. She watched in a daze.

"Come on, Edith! I need your help now!"

She stood and trotted over to them. She turned Nathan around and held down his arms while John peered into his mouth.

"Do you see it? Do you see anything?"

"Right under his tongue."

"Can you get it out?"

"I've gotta scrape it out. Hold him still."

John took out his wallet and found a stiff business card. Holding Nathan's head he put the card in his mouth and began to move it slow and hard on the soft tissue. Mrs. Parker closed her eyes but still she could hear the wet scraping of the card and the choked gurgling sounds her boy made.

"Are you getting it?"

"I think I popped it out but I don't know how much good it did. It's swelling up bad."

Mrs. Parker was frantic. She held Nathan closer and kissed the back of his neck. "What can we do?" she said as she began to cry.

"We've gotta get him to the hospital."

"That's more than fifty miles away!"

"We're leaving now."

John took Nathan in his arms and sprinted back to the car. Mrs. Parker ran back to the blanket.

"Forget that shit! We have to go!"

She grabbed her handbag and followed them.

Minutes later, Mrs. Parker's hands clenched the steering wheel so hard she thought they would start to bleed. John and Nathan were in the seat behind her. Nathan was stretched out lengthwise, and John hovered over him telling him to relax.

The last time Mrs. Parker looked at them her son's face was like a melting rubber mask. She stared back at the road and listened to his labored breathing and whispered silently along with her husband that there was no need to worry. Everything would be all right.

A tear spilled out from Mrs. Parker's closed eyelid. Her cheek twitched three times before she wiped it away. "We never went back after that." She opened her eyes. The young man leaned close to her, his eyes glowing with intensity. His cheeks were warm and his lips hung in a shamefaced frown.

"I'm sorry. I didn't mean to upset you."

"You didn't. It's only that I hadn't thought of it in so long. In the beginning you do. After it happens, that's all you can think about. Your mind goes to the worst thing and you dwell on it for weeks after that. This could have happened, this could have happened, what would have happened. You blame yourself for everything. Once a little time passes, you might think about it, but after a while it feels like a dream. Then you don't think about it at all."

"It's a shame you couldn't remember more of what was said."

"When?"

"Any time. At the bottom of the tree. On the blanket. You told me what you did, and how happy you all were up to when your boy was stung by the bee, but you didn't mention what you said. Or your husband."

"It was a long time ago. I don't remember any of it."

"I understand. But you were very descriptive in what you could remember."

"I'm glad."

"And look how much time has passed. The sun is down."

162

Mrs. Parker blinked. The room was dark apart from the single burning lamp beside her chair. The light of it cast tall sinister shadows on the walls. It reminded her of the flickering light of a fire, except that it was still, painting everything in the same dim even glow. She stood and switched on the other lamps and stuck her arm in the dining room and turned on the light above the table. When she looked back to the sitting room she noticed that the young man had risen and his face was poised toward the top of the stairs.

"Listen," he whispered.

The familiar soft-thumping sound tapped through the ceiling and Mrs. Parker stood frozen in the doorframe, half-in, half-out of the room.

"Are you ready?"

She did not move.

"Mrs. Parker? Are you ready?"

Her body gave a sudden jerk as if she had been pushed and she stumbled toward him taking uneasy steps, trying to regain her balance.

"Is everything all right?"

"Yes. I'm fine. I'm sorry."

"Then we'll begin."

Carrying his Bible face-up in both hands, the young man walked slow and deliberate to the bottom of the staircase. Mrs. Parker brought her husband's photograph from beside her chair and joined the young man, stopping two feet behind him.

"Please fold your hands and kneel."

Nodding, she slipped the frame under arm and took the directed position. She closed her eyes and held her hands beneath her chin. She could feel the warm blasts of air from her nostrils and the softness against her knees as they sank into the rug.

"John Parker."

The young man spoke in such a loud forceful voice that Mrs. Parker jumped when she heard it, and felt it boom deep in her chest.

The footsteps stopped after he made his address, resuming a moment later, steady.

"John Parker. We need you to show yourself." The young man's voice dropped in volume as he continued. "Your wife has been waiting for you here each night, John Parker, waiting to hear what you have to tell her. We know you have something to tell her. What is it?"

The young man climbed one step. "You have returned to this house many times, John Parker, and we know the reason for this is that you need to speak to your wife." He raised his voice. "Speak to her now so that she may know you."

The footsteps grew louder, but maintained their same pace.

The young man climbed to the next step. "Dear Lord," he said, resuming his soft tone, "Heavenly Father, we pray to you. Please assist John Parker. He has come a very long way to find his wife and speak with her. We know he is here, he is very close. We can feel him in our presence, we can hear his footsteps." He raised his voice once more. "Lord, in your infinite wisdom, please assist the poor, tortured soul of John Parker, which is with us here this evening. Let him speak to his wife so and tell her what he has come to say."

The young man climbed two more steps. Just for a second, Mrs. Parker opened one eye a sliver and watched him through a thin veil of white lashes. Head bowed and shoulders back, he cast a long shadow down the stairs.

"John Parker," he intoned, "with the help of the lord our father, please speak. Please find the strength through him to communicate to your wife. She has waited so long, John Parker – for all these years. Please give her that closure she so needs. Hear her now, listen how she calls to you."

"John," she said in a shaky voice. "I'm right here, John. Please, speak to me, John."

The young man took two more steps.

"Listen to her, John Parker. Listen to how she needs you, to how much she longs to hear you speak just one more time. Please do no deny her that. Please find the strength through our lord to speak to her once again."

"Please, John. Please, John."

Mrs. Parker was crying. She did not realize it until the tears began to catch at the cleft in her upper lip. They dipped into her mouth, bitter like wet salt, but she did not wipe her face. It was as if her interlocked fingers had been soldered together and no amount of pressure or struggle could separate them.

The young man climbed another two steps as his voice reached a booming crescendo.

"John Parker, how can you deny this woman, your loving wife of so many years? Please put an end to her waiting now, right now as we stand here this night. Please, dear Lord, help John Parker to speak. Through your benevolent guidance, help him make his presence known to us."

He reached the very top of the stairs, and stopped there with the heels of his black shoes protruding over the top.

"Please, John Parker. Please. Come to us now."

"Please, John. Please, John."

The footsteps came to a sudden stop. A loud crash rang out from where the young man dropped his Bible and Mrs. Parker opened her eyes in time to see him falling backwards before he tumbled down to the landing in two complete somersaults. His bones smashed against the dense wood and his limbs flailed with limp dislocated ease. Mrs. Parker screamed and dropped the photograph, and stood as the young man fell at her feet in a broken heap. He was as quiet as a corpse and she knelt beside him repeating his name. She gathered up one of his hands and pleated at it and kissed his fingers and sobbed.

"Are you all right? Mr. Peterson, can you hear me?"

The young man's body jumped as though a heavy jolt of electricity had coursed through it. His eyes opened independent of one another and rolled lazily in their sockets. Then as they narrowed he spoke in a voice that was not altogether his own.

"Edith? What happened?"

"Mr. Peterson, you fell down the stairs. You fell down the stairs and–"

"Who?" he asked and shook his head. His fingers wriggled like drunken worms and his shoulder popped when he attempted to sit.

"Mr. Peterson–"

"Edith, what are you talking about?"

Mrs. Parker dropped his hand and it fell lifeless to the floor.

"John?" she whispered. "Is that you?"

"Of course it is. What happened?"

The young man smiled and stretched out beneath the massive oak tree. The thick bark was rough against his back so he removed his jacket and folded it twice, using it as a cushion. The day was bright and warm, almost hot, especially for April. It felt very peaceful to lay undisturbed and think.

There was still the matter of food. He had none, nor did he have any money. To be sure, he checked his pockets, but found only a business card that read, "Leland Edwards, Sales." At least the suit fit. It was a decent suit. Neither the jacket nor the trouser cuffs were frayed, and there were no stains on the loose white shirt, not even under the arms. He did not take the shoes. Although they were buffed and polished he found the soles had been lined with two layers of cardboard to protect from the holes. His own shoes had no holes.

He glanced at the sample case resting in the grass. Sitting up, he crossed his legs, took the case by its handle and pulled it toward himself. He set it on his knees and ran his fingers across it. Bound in cracking imitation leather, with holes worn into the corners and a handle so loose it made carrying difficult, the case looked like it had passed through a thresher. The young man flipped up the clasps on either side of the handle, causing one of them to pop off and it bounced into the grass. He smirked and opened the case. Inside were three sweat-yellowed undershirts, a greasy piece of waxed paper and an old Bible. Whatever Edwards had been selling, it was not here.

The young man frowned. He took out the Bible and pushed the case onto the ground. Standing, he brushed the grass off his trousers and wrapped the Bible in his jacket before he slid both under his arm. He checked his fingernails. Then he looked at the discarded case and thought a moment before he picked it up again.

He walked away from the road into the trees. His pace was steady despite the uneven slope of the land and the lack of trails. Save for the intermittent shafts of sunlight that pierced through the dense canopy of leaves overhead, it was dark among the trees, lending everything an air of unreality.

Soon he came upon a small clearing, where he found dozens of old rotting tree stumps with open cavities of muddy pulp. At the center of the clearing grew a tall withering apple tree. Only a few small shriveled apples sagged like tiny shrunken heads from its branches, and none hung low enough to pick. The young man set down his things and approached the trunk of the tree, placing his hands on it. He pushed, grunting, but the fruit was too high to absorb what little impact he made. He stepped back and squinted and frowned. He walked to his jacket and gathered it in his arms, revealing two large stones underneath. He dropped the bundle in the grass and picked up one of the stones. When he saw an apple that looked halfway edible he aimed and threw. The rock connected and the apple fell. The young man picked it up and ran his fingers along its dull green skin. Finding no soft spots or bruising he tossed the second stone away and bit into the apple. It was firm and tart, and juice dribbled down his chin as he chewed. Soon there was nothing left but the core. He threw it straight up in the air and kicked it with the tip of his shoe before it could hit the ground. The core arched in the air and banged against the splintered ridge of one of the stumps and rolled away.

The young man stopped. Not four inches from where the apple core lay was a cigarette butt smoldering a thin wisp of white smoke. The young man looked all around but saw nothing but an endless mass of vegetation. He walked to the cigarette and took it in his fingers. He smelled it before he took a long languorous drag. It had been days since his last cigarette and his head swam and he felt like laughing. Eyes closed, he exhaled slowly, making it last as long as he could. Opening his eyes again he took one final quick puff and flicked away the butt.

He approached a dried-out stump and sat, plucked a long blade of dead brown grass and twirled it in his fingers while he thought.

Soon he walked further into the trees, a chorus of crackling leaves and twigs snapping under his shoes. As he continued the branches began to thin and the trees grew sparse. Sunlight hit his face. The air smelled wet and soon he heard the sound of running water off in the distance. He quickened his pace.

The trees ended in a line when he reached the water, a narrow river whose current was steady, but slow. The water was clear and it shimmered in the golden hue of the late afternoon sun. At the edge of the trees the young man discovered a folded red-checked blanket and a large picnic basket. He dropped his things beside the basket and looked to the river, at the banks of which way two bundles of clothes. In the water swim a boy and a girl. They appeared to be about sixteen, seventeen at the oldest. They did not see him. They looked only at each other, always circling, faces close and hands unseen beneath the surface.

The young man smiled. Crouching low he edged toward the clothes, scooped them up and scrambled back into the woods, where he threw them away piece by piece so that they could not be found with ease. He took all the money in the boy's wallet, and the girl's pocketbook. It amounted to five dollars and forty-six cents. He did not look for any identification, and he did not take the set of keys he found.

Wrapping a purple robe about her shoulders Mrs. Parker crept silent and slow into the hallway toward the spare bedroom. The night was spent with her ear straining for sounds of pain, or worse, no sounds at all. She had not slept until after five, at which time she blinked and discovered her bedroom was filled with cool early morning light. The door to the young man's room was open a crack. The room smelled like him and she inhaled with closed eyes and put her hand on the door and pushed it open the rest of the way.

He was not there.

In a flash she rushed to the upstairs bathroom, also empty, before she raced down the steps and slipped on one and caught herself on the rail. Her spine cracked and she held herself there with her legs spread at different angles and her arms folded back like a scarecrow on a post. She struggled to breathe as she straightened her legs and loosened her grip until she could sit. She remained seated as she moved down the remaining stairs. When she reached the main floor she pushed off the steps and broke into a run through the dining room to the kitchen, where she pushed open the door and took one step forward.

She stopped moving when she saw the young man. Clad only in his pajamas, he was seated at the kitchen table. His top was halfway buttoned and she could see his chest. His feet were bare and spiderlegs of dark hair twirled out from under the navy blue cuff of his bottoms.

"Morning, Edith," he said with a welcoming smile.

The voice in which he spoke was not his own, and he had the carriage of a different man. He was relaxed, even jovial, with an easy smile and the air of someone with complete comfort in his surroundings.

"Good morning."

Mrs. Parker let go of the door and it swung back and nudged her side.

"Careful, now."

She moved aside and let the door swing shut. It bounced against her rump with a rattle on its return but she remained still.

"Careful," he repeated with a chuckle.

Mrs. Parker was bolted to the ground as she searched for something to say. "Did you have a good sleep?"

"Sure did. You?"

She shook her head. "No, I didn't – I kept waking up."

"That's too bad. I hope you get some tonight." The young man drummed his hands on the table. "I was wondering..."

"Yes?"

"The paper come today? It is Wednesday, isn't it? I checked the porch but I didn't see one out there. It is Wednesday – or am I wrong?"

"No. You're not wrong. It's just that the paper only comes out twice a month now."

"How long has that been goin' on?"

"A couple of years. I think it was getting to be too expensive for them to keep doing it the other way. It's just as well. They didn't always have enough news to print when it was a weekly, anyhow."

"That's the truth," he said and rubbed his eyes. "So, how's Nathan?"

"He's fine."

"And the family?"

"They are, too. Everyone is well. They have three children now."

"You see much of them?"

"No, I don't, but I do speak to him on the phone every week."

"That's good." He stared at her. "You all right? You look a little – I don't know – worried."

Mrs. Parker thought about how she had not combed her hair or brushed her teeth. She looked at the floor and saw that she had not put on her slippers and she placed one foot over the other as if to hide it.

"Don't do that. It's all right."

"I look awful."

"No you don't." He stood and moved toward her, and stopped a few feet away.

"You weren't upstairs. I didn't know – I was afraid."

The young man smiled. "You know I would never leave you, Edith."

"Listen," she said after she cleared her throat. "Why don't I go back upstairs and make myself a bit more presentable, and then I'll come fix you some breakfast. How would you like that?"

"You don't have to change. Lord knows I'm not formal."

"What would you like for breakfast?"

"You know what I like."

"Eggs. And bacon?"

"That's right. You know how I like 'em."

She nodded. She felt unsure of which way to move. "Okay. I'll go upstairs and get changed, and I'll be back down as soon as I can."

Before she could go the young man took her by the hands and lifted them to his face so he could kiss her fingers with gentle pecks. His lips were warm, and his breath, and the invisible stubble under his nose tickled her skin. She felt cold and the back of her neck began to tingle.

"You are so beautiful," he said between kisses. "You are so beautiful."

172

Mrs. Parker closed her eyes and let herself be kissed. She spread her fingers and rested them on his cheeks. His face was smooth and pink and she felt his parted lips press against her palm, warm and moist, and she opened her eyes and patted down his sleep-ruffled hair as he continued to hold her other hand to his face. He looked so young. She took her hand from the side of his head and tugged at the other, but he did not let go.

"I'll be right back. I just – I can't–"

He nodded. "I understand," he said and gave her hand a final kiss. He pulled a chair from the table and sat staring up at her.

"I'll be back," she said as she passed through the kitchen door, all the time watching as it swung open and shut. She could see him sitting there, returning her look, and it made her feel strange.

When the door stopped moving Mrs. Parker turned and walked through the dining room to the stairs. On the floor lay the photograph, facedown where she'd dropped it the previous night. Kneeling, she picked it up and examined it. The glass was unbroken and free of finger marks or streaks of tears. There was a single piece of green lint that clung to a spot near her husband's collar, and she plucked it off with her fingernails and blew it onto the rug. Then, carrying the frame, she stood and climbed the stairs and brought it to her bedroom, where she set it on her bedside table.

After she finished washing, Mrs. Parker put on a clean dress and clasped a delicate gold chain about her neck. She also applied a thin coat of rose red to her lips and gave her cheeks a light dusting of rouge. She felt silly upon seeing herself in the mirror and turned on the hot water. Hand still on the tap, she continued to stare as steam began to form on the glass. She twisted. The water ceased to flow.

In the kitchen she took the eggs and bacon from the refrigerator and the young man watched from the table as she fried them in an enormous black iron skillet. As she cooked, the young man would joke and she would laugh and look at him and smile until her cheeks hurt. It was easy to talk with him. When the food was finished she plated it and set it in front of him and watched as he ate with relish, spearing the yolks with the tines of his fork until his plate ran thick with coagulated yellow. He dipped his bacon in the warm ooze and chomped at it until the soupy mélange leaked from his mouth onto his lower lip. The bacon gone, he coated the eggs in a snowstorm of salt and pinch of pepper and happily chewed with dreamy half-closed eyes, punctuating swallows with loud declarations of "Boy, is that good!"

When he had finished eating he watched from behind as Mrs. Parker cleaned up, slumped in his chair with one hand on his flat stomach. His legs were spread wide with one foot flat on the floor and the other balanced on its heel. A satisfied smile played at his lips.

"Could use a nap now. You sure can cook."

"It's just bacon and eggs."

Standing, he threw back his head in a loud, protracted yawn and began to stretch. He stood on his toes and raised his arms, which lifted his pajama top so that Mrs. Parker could see the sparse trail of dark hairs that reached up toward his naval. He rubbed the back of his head and exhaled like a deflating tire through his nose. Then he pointed to the door with a jerk of his thumb.

"I'm gonna go upstairs and get cleaned up. There's dry towels?"

"Yes. In a stack in the cupboard above the clothes hamper."

"All right."

He began to move toward her and she froze. Watching her, he stopped and his head gave an almost imperceptible nod. "I'll be right back down," he said.

Mrs. Parker listened to his footsteps slap against the hardwood floor before they faded away, reemerging moments later as thuds from above. A door opened, closed. Muffled coughing. Running water.

She was waiting on the sofa when the young man returned. He wore a pair of gray slacks and a white shirt with the top two buttons undone and the sleeves rolled to his pointed elbows. His face was shaved and his hair was still damp, combed to the side. Without a word he sat down five inches from her on the sofa. He smelled of soap and Old Spice. Neither of them spoke. The young man folded his hands and let them slide between his knees. Mrs. Parker looked out the front window. The curtains were open and the shadow of the house spread across the lawn, darkening it, but the sun was strong and it blanched out the color of everything beyond the sidewalk.

He moved. She could feel him sitting right next to her, but she did not look. Fingers shaking, she lifted her hands and wrapped them around his arm. With a sigh, she laid her head on his shoulder.

"How long are you going to stay?"

"For as long as I can."

On impulse she lifted her head and leaned toward his face. She stopped an inch from his cheek. Then, pursing her lips, she put her head back down.

"What's wrong? Why did you stop?"

"I can't do it. I want to so badly, but I feel like – oh, I don't know. It's not the same. That's all."

The young man lifted his arm and held her, her face now nearer his chest. "I know," he said. "It'll be strange for a little while. It's strange for me, too, you know. But you'll soon get used to it. We both will."

"It just doesn't feel like you."

The young man smiled and began to rock her beneath his arm. "It's me. Only in a different form."

"What about Mr. Peterson? Where is he?"

"Don't you worry about him. He's still here. Think of it as if he's sleeping, and that he'll wake up again when I leave."

"I hope you don't ever leave."

The young man stopped rocking and with a tender smile took her face in his hands. Brushing an eyelash off her cheekbone he drew her to him and placed his lips at the center of her forehead and kissed.

"I love you," he said.

"I love you, too. But I do need some time to get used to this."

The young man held her again and they settled into the sofa cushions.

"Don't worry. I'm not leaving."

Mrs. Parker balanced the telephone receiver on her shoulder as she hooked her finger in the rotary.

"Who're you calling?"

"Mrs. Colman. I have tea with her around this time every day, so I'm going to tell her I can't make it."

"Why you doing that?"

"I want to stay with you."

"Aww, go on. I'll be here when you get back. Anyhow, I don't think you should change anything you're in the habit of doing. Might make her suspicious."

"I don't think so."

"No, not her. That'd never happen."

"I see your point, but can't you see mine, too?"

"Yes. But I think it would be better for me if we stuck to our daily routines. Is there anything this Peterson guy does when you're off having tea?"

"Usually he goes for a walk."

"Fine. That's what I'll do. And we'll both meet up here again this afternoon. You've gotta trust me. We'll be spending plenty of time together."

Mrs. Parker replaced the receiver.

"Whaddayou think?"

Next to Mrs. Colman on the table was a small plate with an enormous piece of yellow cake with white frosting thick as peanut butter. On her lap sat a cat with orange stripes that rubbed its wet pink nose on her chin and purred. On occasion she would pick off a crumb of cake and hold it under the cat's snout, and he would sniff at it a moment before he lapped it up, continuing to lick her palm long after any possible trace had been eaten.

"I beg your pardon?"

"I said, your nephew still hasn't fixed my doorbell. I'm surprised it doesn't zap you when you touch it, the way it buzzes now. And I have some heavy boxes I need brought down from the attic. You think he can help me with those?"

"I'll ask him, but I can't promise he'll know anything about wires."

"You'd think he was an invalid or something," Mrs. Colman snorted. "I haven't seen him in forever. Is he feelin' all right?"

"Yes, he's fine. He's keeping busy in his own way. He's working on some projects around the house. But I'll be sure to let him know you asked after him."

His warm breath. His lips, soft like the petals of a flower.

"I don't know that it'd do you any good."

Mrs. Colman cupped another bit of cake in her palm. The cat growled as it chewed, and once it had swallowed put its face back in her palm and bit.

"Ouch!" she screamed and slapped the cat to the floor. "That's it! No more! You don't get any more if you're gonna do that! No more!" Spreading her fingers and rotating her wrists she pushed her hands in the cat's face. "You lost your chance! No more! All gone!"

Unperturbed, the cat sat down and began to clean itself.

"You're ungrateful! If you're gonna act that way you can't sit on my lap no more! How do you like that, huh? Maybe I should just stop feeding you! Whaddayou think of that? You wanna starve to death?"

The cat continued to wash without troubling itself even to look at her.

"Ornery old thing," she spat with a shake of her head. She flipped her hand and prodded her fleshy palm. "It doesn't hurt so bad, at least. I'm not bleeding. I don't even think he broke the skin. But still."

Mrs. Parker cooled her tea. The raised pajama top exposing his dark hair, and the buttons undone so she could see his smooth chest.

"How long you tell me it's been since your nephew came around? A long time, right?"

Mrs. Parker twitched and spilled a splash of tea into her saucer. Taking a breath, she carefully set the cup and saucer on the table and slid them away. "Oh, yes. A long time."

"Did I ever see him then? Because I don't ever remember seein' him."

"It's been a very long time, as I told you," she said and forced a chuckle. "It's been a very long time. He wasn't very old. Ten, eleven. Just a boy."

"He's practically a boy now."

"It's possible you may not have even met him."

"I guess. He said the same thing."

Still near the table, the cat raised its paw and batted at Mrs. Colman's leg and mewed.

"What is it?"

The cat stood and mewed again.

"You gonna be good? Gonna be a good boy?" She relaxed her legs and the cat sprang onto her lap, where it circled and rubbed its head against her chin. "That's right. You be a good boy."

Mrs. Parker wiped her mouth with a pink napkin. The feel of his skin. When she looked up again she found Mrs. Colman was staring at her.

"You doin' okay?"

"Of course. Why do you ask?"

"No reason. Just seems like your head's someplace else."

"I see. I guess I must be tired."

The first floor of the house was empty. So was the stand by the door. It was the first time in years she had left it so.

"John?"

There was no answer and in a panic Mrs. Parker clambered up the stairs and into the hall, where the door to the young man's room stood half-open. She knocked and said his name again.

"Come in."

Mrs. Parker pushed open the door. Elbows bent and hands behind his head the young man lay in the bed on top of the covers. He smiled when he saw her.

"You don't need to knock, you know." He opened his arms as she approached the bed. "Come here, lay down with me."

She took hold of one of his hands. His skin was smooth and firm and he had long fingers that relaxed at her touch.

"I don't know."

Continuing to smile, the young man lifted his other hand and took her by the forearm and gave it a gentle pull. She acquiesced and faced him on the bed. She stared at his crystalline eyes and the curve of his young mouth. With her free hand she brushed back the hair on his head and then let her hand run down the side of his cheek.

"It's still me."

She nodded. She turned her hand and caressed his face with the backs of her fingers. His cheeks were flush and he smiled open-mouthed, exposing the straight rows of white teeth.

"I was worried," she said.

"I know."

He brought her hand to his chest and held it flat. The beating of his heart was strong, steady. The feel of it relaxed her. The young man gave a lazy sigh and nuzzled his face against the pillow. The bed was warm.

"What should I make you for supper?"

"Anything?"

"Yes, anything you want."

"Could you make the roast, Edith? With the potatoes?"

"Is that what you want?"

"Yeah. That's it."

"It takes a while to fix."

"I don't care. I've been waiting for it a long time." With a sudden frown, he raised his head. "You still know how to make it, don't you?"

"Of course I do. I would never forget anything like that."

He lay back down. "It's that important, huh?" he grinned.

She chuckled and gave him a soft kiss on the mouth. Blinking, she pulled back and rolled away from him on the mattress. A moment passed before she felt his hand grasp her arm and give it a squeeze.

"It's okay," he murmured.

She rolled back to him, eased against his body and buried her face in his chest. She tucked her arms under her chin, keeping them between herself and the young man. "I've missed you so much," she said. She began to cry. She kept her face against him so he could not see, but his shirt absorbed her tears like a cheap tissue.

"Shh..." He held her for the next hour until her tears subsided and she drifted into a peaceful, dreamless sleep.

The first thing Mrs. Parker did on waking forty-five minutes later was to rush downstairs and get started on dinner. The young man followed her to the kitchen and watched her from his place at the table. She moved like a young woman. It felt like a night had passed. It felt like spring.

The roast was perfect, juicy and rich without any dry spots, and the potatoes were soft and hot. The young man inhaled his food and Mrs. Parker spent so much time watching him eat that her plate had grown cold by the time she finished. As the young man drank the last of his milk the doorbell rang.

"You expecting anybody?"

"No."

"You want me to get it?"

Before he could leave his chair Mrs. Parker rose. Wiping her hands on her apron she went to the entrance of the dining room and said, "You keep eating." The bell rang again and she rushed to the front door and opened it without looking through the glass.

"Hi, Edith," Mrs. Colman said.

"Hello. Is something the matter?"

"Should there be?"

"No, it's just that I wasn't expecting you."

"I see. I wanna talk to your nephew. He around?"

"He's eating." Mrs. Parker did not move to let her in.

"Now?"

"I was late getting dinner started."

"I know how that goes. But can I see him anyways? I wanna talk to him."

"What about?"

"I thought I'd run by that idea I told you this afternoon. You tell him about it?"

"Of course I did."

"And? What'd he say? When's he gonna do it?"

"He didn't say, exactly. I don't know if he has plans or not the next few days."

"Let me in, then. I'll ask him myself."

"Ask me what?"

Startled, Mrs. Parker whipped her head around to see the young man standing at her side. She had not heard him approach and she let out a little cry when she heard he had reverted to his normal voice. Mrs. Colman smiled when she saw him, her face scrunched up like a pug dog's.

"You mean she didn't tell you?" she chided in a babyish tone. "You, I've got a score to settle with you, mister. Haven't seen you in so long – it almost feels like you're hiding from me. But listen, I've got a whole big bunch of boxes of stuff I wanna sort through, but they're all the way up in the attic and they're all so heavy. I was wondering maybe if you might be able to come over and fetch them down for me. I'll pay you."

"That is not necessary."

Mrs. Parker's eyes felt like they had been doused with acid.

"Oh, now," Mrs. Colman said. "I don't want you to feel like I'm takin' advantage of you or anything. I can sure pay you some money if you want me to."

"I don't. I'm sure it's not as big a job as all that. I don't need to be reimbursed in any way."

"You're such a sweetheart," she giggled.

"Bear ye another's burdens, and so fulfill the law of Christ. I can stop by tomorrow."

"Thank you, but can you do it now? If I don't have you do it now we'll both just wanna put it off. That's how people are, you know. If we put it off I'll never go through those things and they'll do nothing but collect more dust up in that old attic. You know how it is."

"Of course."

Mrs. Parker had stopped listening. She felt empty.

"I'll be back in a few minutes, then, Aunt Edith," the young man said as he approached the door. Sliding between Mrs. Parker and the doorframe, he lifted his hand to hers and gave her palm a feathery tickling flick with his middle finger. She looked into his eyes, startled. He winked.

"Be back soon, Edith," he whispered. "Promise."

She took a big gulp of air and caught her voice.

"It's not a problem. Take your time."

The young man had not closed the front door before Mrs. Parker wrapped her arms around his neck and covered his face with a flurry of staccato kisses. She did so without hesitation. "I was so worried," she kept saying.

"Don't be, Edith." He placed one hand on her back, the other on her side just above her waist. The feel of his hands made her self-conscious and she motioned toward the dining room.

"Do you want the rest of your supper? Your plate wasn't quite clear, so I put it in the refrigerator. I didn't know how long you'd be over there."

"It's okay if you still feel a little awkward, Edith. I'm getting used to it all myself."

"I'm fine," she said and took him by the hands. Then she let them go. "How about that roast, then?"

When the house was dark they stood across the hall from one another and said their goodnights. The light in the hall was not switched on and the bare bulb on the white ceiling of the young man's room left his face shrouded in shadow.

"I'll see you in the morning. Don't worry, I'll still be here."

She nodded. "I'm glad."

"Good night, then."

The young man remained where he was. Mrs. Parker did not move, either. Then, eyes downcast, she said good night, bounced into the hall and kissed him on the mouth. "I love you," she said before she went to her room and closed the door.

Sleep was impossible. She lay there for hours, thinking of him all the time. His hands, his thin, strong fingers. The taste of his lips. The doorknob turned and the door gave a slow creak as it pushed open. She could see him with ease as he stepped into the darkened room wearing blue and white striped pajamas of rough cotton. Once he was inside, he stopped moving. Mrs. Parker sat up, clutching the blanket in tense fists, afraid to speak, afraid even to breathe.

At a slow pace the young man crept to the bed. The whites of his eyes glowed bright like a pair of full moons as he approached. When he came within a few feet of her he stopped.

"Edith," he whispered.

The blanket shielded her mouth when she answered. "What is it, John?"

"I can't sleep."

"I can't, either."

"Do you wanna talk a little?"

"No."

He nodded. "I see."

"I want you to hold me. Like this afternoon. Like before. Like you used to. I've missed it."

The young man smiled and pulled back the covers and climbed into bed. Mrs. Parker scooted over to make room for him as he crawled under and lay down and opened his arms. She rested beside him and moved in as close as she could. It was as if she were trying to burrow into his body. He put his arms around her and Mrs. Parker placed her hands on his firm chest, feeling it through his pajama top and pressing her lips to his neck again and again.

"I love you so much," she whispered. "I love you, I love you."

"I love you, too, Edith."

She stopped at the sound of his voice and looked at him. She had wanted this from the start. She hesitated. Then he caressed her cheek and felt the side of her neck. She moved up in bed and kissed his lips, one hand bonded to his chest, the other traveling down below the waistband of his pajama bottoms.

"Are you sure–?"

"Yes," she hissed and stifled him with her lips.

Mrs. Parker slept better that night than she had in ten years. She awoke to the feel of the young man laying next to her, cradling her in his arms, his hot breath warming the back of her neck. He still was naked, she could tell through the thin material of her nightgown. As she wiped the yellow crumbs of crust from her eyes the first image that came into focus was that of her husband staring down on her from the photograph on the bedside table. Immediately she bolted from the bed and scrambled to the bathroom, where she slammed the door and knelt at the toilet before she released a gushing fountain of vomit.

Bitter, scalding tears streamed from her reddening eyes and she stood and flushed the toilet and went to the sink. Cupping her hands, she filled them with cold water and splashed her face. Skin dripping, water still running, she took a white paper Dixie cup and filled it. She swished the water in her mouth and spat, refilled the cup and did it again. She avoided her reflection in the mirror of the medicine cabinet. After she turned off the water she found a towel and dabbed at her face until it was dry. Her head ached and her empty stomach continued to churn as she looked out the window at the rising sun. With a scowl she ripped down the shade. The room now dark, she lowered the lid of the toilet and sat with her face buried in the towel and sobbed and wanted to die.

A tentative knock was heard on the door.

"Edith?" His voice was the same as it was the previous day. Mrs. Parker felt like throwing up again when she heard it. She crammed a

186

mittfull of the towel into her mouth and clamped her jaw onto it. The fabric was rough and it scratched and tickled against her tongue. She tried to swallow, but could only gag. Closing her eyes she prayed he would leave.

"Edith, you in there?" he asked and knocked once more. "Can I come in?"

When Mrs. Parker didn't answer, the doorknob rattled and began to turn. She lunged from the toilet seat to the door, towel dangling from her mouth, and pressed her fingers to the lock. It was too late. The door began to open and she thrust all her weight against it.

"Edith? You all right in there?" The young man's slender fingers snaked in, wriggling through the gap. "Edith? What's going on? What are you doing? Is everything okay?"

He knocked again and Mrs. Parker felt like screaming. The young man's fingers disappeared and she jammed the door shut and locked it. Twitching and shivering, she slid to the floor and held her stomach. The movement pulled the towel from her mouth and she closed her eyes and whispered, "God is punishing me."

"Edith. Open the door right now. I need to talk to you."

Mrs. Parker swallowed hard before she answered. "I'll be out in a minute," she gurgled. "Hold on just a minute and I'll be right out."

"Please let me in, Edith, this is important."

"Two more minutes. That's all I need."

"All right. I'll be back."

Her ear pressed firm against the door, Mrs. Parker heard the sound of his footsteps as the moved through the hall and down the stairs. When she could no longer hear him she closed her eyes with a sigh and rested her back against the door. Her lungs were like lead and it hurt to breathe.

The rim of the sink was cool from the water when she pulled herself onto her unsteady legs and looked in the mirror. Her cheeks and eyes were painted with bright red blotches, and the space beneath her nose looked like it was coated with egg whites. She brushed her teeth and rinsed out the sink, wiping it down with a dozen squares of toilet paper. As she threw the soggy mess in the wastebasket she again heard the young man outside the door.

"Edith?" he asked, his voice cloaked with concern. "Are you all right now? Will you please come out of there?"

She did not answer.

"I fixed you some tea."

Her stomach began to settle and she breathed easier. She unlocked the door and opened it. Outside, the young man stood in his pajamas holding a screwdriver.

"Is everything okay?"

She nodded.

The young man passed the screwdriver from hand to hand.

"I wasn't sure if I would need this. You remember how when Nathan was little he locked himself in there that one time? I still remember how to pop that lock open if I need to. That's one thing I still know how to do."

Mrs. Parker's cheeks felt cold and wet and she wiped them with her sleeve.

"Are you sure everything's fine?"

She nodded again. "Mm-hmm."

"You think you might need to talk about it, maybe?"

She shook her head.

"I was scared you might be mad at me."

"I was mad at myself."

"What for?"

"It isn't important. I'm not anymore."

The young man fumbled some more with the screwdriver.

"I made the tea just how you like it. A little sugar, a little milk. That's how I've seen you drink it, isn't it? Maybe I should've asked first."

"No. You did it just right. You always did."

Before he could reply, she came forward and embraced him. He put his hand on her back and she felt the cold metal point of the instrument and shivered. With a laugh, she stepped back and took it from him.

"Let's go downstairs," she said.

The tea was warm and sweet. Neither Mrs. Parker nor the young man changed from their sleepwear before they went to the kitchen, and they sat close to each other at the table. She watched him with a vague, puzzled expression as she took another sip.

"Is something wrong?"

"No," she said with a curious smile as she held her cup. "It's funny, but I think this may be the first time you ever had tea with me."

"I've fixed it for you often enough."

"That's certainly true. But you were always more of a coffee drinker. I don't believe you've ever had one cup of tea the entire time I've known you."

The young man set down his cup and rubbed his brow.

"I don't know about that. You're right about the coffee – I do like coffee. But I can't say as I never drank any tea."

"Not that I can remember."

"Hmm. Well, you know that they say – first time."

189

Edwards awoke in the dark with a wet stain spreading down the front of his trousers. Panicked, he jumped and knocked the empty candleholder off his lap and it rolled across the floor. He rubbed his fingers against the wetness and sniffed them.

"Fucking wine."

His candle was burnt out. The church was quiet. Through the windows shown the pale light of the moon and it was light enough for him to see his way out, and to walk to his car for his other pants. They were just like the ones he had on. The air was crisp and his legs stiffened as he changed into them on the empty street.

Back inside he paused, eyes adjusting, and felt his way to the storeroom. He found three more candles, one of which he lit. He carried them into the sanctuary and checked his fingers, now stained with a sticky purple. He licked them and dried them on the pews as he passed.

When he looked up again his heart nearly stopped beating. Sitting there quiet in his pew was a young man.

"Jesus!" Edwards shouted and fumbled with the candles.

The young man stood with upraised hands and fidgeted.

"I'm sorry, mister. I was going to say something when you were walking up the aisle. But then you weren't looking toward me and I thought that if I spoke it might frighten you."

"Boy, I'm sure glad you didn't say anything, then."

The young man looked like a guilty child. "I sure am sorry, mister."

"Yeah, yeah. Who are you, anyway? What the hell you doin' here?"

"My name is Charles Brandon, sir," the young man said and straightened his back. "I'm just looking for a warm, dry place to spend the night, much like yourself."

"You can just cut out that 'sir' bullshit, kid."

"I do apologize. If you like, I can leave. I can find somewhere else to go. It's just that when I saw you outside I thought you might need some type of assistance."

Edwards stared at the young man. His green zippered jacket was smeared with what looked like axle grease. The seams were split at the top of his shoulders and a corner of his too-large white shirt poked out like a handkerchief. The knees of his trousers looked as though he had crawled through a field of wet grass. His hands were clean and Edwards could see the pearl white of his nails by the dim light of the flickering candle.

"You look like shit, kid."

The young man stared at the floor.

"How old are you?"

"What does that matter?"

Edwards shrugged. "Doesn't, I guess, but you don't look like you belong out this late. You got a home to go back to?"

"Not anymore I haven't," he said and began to edge toward the door. "I don't want to burden you with any of my troubles. I can find somewhere else to go. I'm sorry to have disturbed you. I didn't mean to, truly."

Edwards set down the candle and walked toward him. "Hold on a second, you don't hafta do that." He put his hand on the young man's arm. It felt very small beneath the layers he wore and it shook like a frightened dog.

"It's all right, kid, you come on back and siddown."

"No, really, I don't want to bother you."

191

"There's no bother about it. It ain't my house." He ran his shoulders across the young man's slim shoulder and patted. "Come on, now." He guided him toward the pew. Still looking away, the young man fell into step. Edwards came to a sudden stop.

"You hear that?"

"What?"

"Not sure. I can't hear it now."

"What did it sound like?"

"I dunno. Water or somethin'. You hear it, too?"

"I didn't, but I'm fairly certain I know what it was."

"What's that?"

The young man opened his coat and pulled out a tall bottle, on which was pasted a white and black label with a gold border.

"Is that–?"

The young man nodded. "Would you care to drink some?"

"Sure, if you are. I don't want you to feel like I'm leachin' off you."

The men sat near each other on the pew, separated by some candles, two empty holders, Edwards' case and the young man's coat. The jug of wine sat between them on the floor.

"I'm glad you came. I can hardly stand that Communion shit."

The young man extended the bottle to Edwards who took it in his hands and held it like a delicate artifact.

"And it's full, too. Don't you wanna do the honors?"

"That's quite all right."

Edwards twisted off the cap with a crackling snap. "That's the most beautiful sound in the world, you know that? It's like your birthday when you're five, you know what I mean? It might not be better than sex – well, I guess it is, sometimes. But anyway, it's a beautiful sound."

"I prefer what comes after, myself."

"Now you're talkin'. Here, gimme your glass."

Edwards filled the candle holder and handed it back to the young man. Then he bent to fill his own. When he raised it, he saw the young man's was half-empty.

"Thirsty, are you?"

A warm red rose in the young man's cheeks. "I suppose I am."

"You'll wanna pace yourself, there, kid, this ain't soda pop. We got all night, you know. You don't have to prove anything to me."

"I'm sorry." He hung his head and set his glass on the case and slid his hands between his boney knees.

"Hey, it's all right with me. I remember what it's like to be a kid. You just need to take it easy, that's all. Keep goin' at that rate and you'll have it all gone before I get my first sip."

The young man nodded behind a shy smile.

"Come on, I'm just havin' some fun with you." He reached across the makeshift table and gave the young man's arm a playful sake.

"I know. I suppose I'm not in a joking mood. That's all."

Edwards drank; a hot tingling warmth down the back of his throat. "That's so good." He set down his glass. The young man continued to look away. "I understand, kid. But you know, sometimes bad things happen. You just can't let it get to you. Tonight's bad, sure, but things'll even out. Everybody has problems, you know?" He stopped speaking. "You don't know what'll happen tomorrow. I guess that's all I'm tryin' to say."

He emptied his glass, lifted the bottle and gave himself a refill. "You don't mind that I...?"

"No, take all you want."

"Thanks." He drank and held the Scotch burning in his mouth before he swallowed. "I just think you should–"

The young man looked at him with empty eyes and a sagging frown.

"Sorry," Edwards said. "I'll shut up now. You don't need some drunk asshole talking philosophical bullshit about how you shouldn't feel bad, like tomorrow's gonna be your lucky day or some shit. I'll just shut up."

The young man's glass was empty and he looked at the bottle, still clenched in Edwards' hand, and wore a self-conscious smile.

"Take it, kid, it's yours anyway. I won't say anything." He handed the bottle to the young man, who continued to smile as he filled his glass. Edwards sipped.

"May I ask you a question?" the young man asked as he capped the bottle and set it between them.

"Shoot."

"What are you doing here? Haven't you anyplace else to go?"

Edwards cocked his head and his face collapsed into a tipsy grin. "Who do you think I am?"

"I have no idea. You've not even told me your name."

"No, I mean do you think I'm some kinda bum or something?"

The young man did not answer.

"Well, I don't mind. I guess it's prob'ly what I look like." Trying to remain casual, he straightened his collar and crossed his arms. "I'm just spending the night. I'm on the road, selling. That's what I do. I'm a salesman."

"You're not selling anything now, though. Are you?"

"You playing guessing games?"

"No. It's just a feeling I had."

"Keep your feelings to yourself." He quickly downed what was left in his glass and watched the young man with narrowed eyes. "I'm not askin' you all kinds of questions, am I? Like maybe who you are or what you're doin' here?"

"I told you before, I was in need of a place to stay the night. Much like yourself."

"Leave me out of it."

194

The young man set down his glass and stood. "I'm sorry for having upset you," he said into his chest. "I can leave if you wish. You can keep the bottle."

Edwards sighed and attempted to catch the young man's line of vision. "Look, I'm sorry, all right? I'm sorry. I've got a lot on my mind, and – come on, just sit down. I'll stop bein' an asshole and we can both get nice and drunk, okay? How does that sound?"

The young man turned to the front of the sanctuary and bent his knees with impossible slowness until he was seated again. "I am sorry," he said, still looking away.

"Forget it."

The bottle was almost empty. Edwards loved to drink. It was one of the few things from which he derived real pleasure. His wife hated that, too. He had trouble standing and spoke as if his tongue were asleep. It did not take long. Although the young man matched him glass for glass he showed no discernible impairment. His voice was steady and clear and his movements were quick.

"You can sure put it away, can't you?"

"So can you."

"No, you know what I mean. Three drinks and I'm a slobbering idiot. But look at you. Hell, just – look at ya. You're really somethin'."

The young man smiled. He never made eye contact. When he spoke, it was to Edwards' shoulder or past his ear.

"Were you always able to knock it back like that?"

He nodded.

"How long you been at it?"

"Not so long."

"Well, it's a cinch I've had more practice than you and you're doin' better than I could ever hope to."

"It's one of my gifts, I suppose."

"But conversation isn't."

The young man stared into the dwindling light of the candles.

"Nothin' wrong with that," Edwards said and waved his hand. "Most people talk and talk and talk, and for all of it they don't say a goddamn thing. Like me, right? That's what you're thinkin', isn't it? I know it is." He shook the bottle and unscrewed the cap. "Other people, they just don't know how to talk. It's not in 'em. They can't do it. Nothin' wrong with that." He poured the remains of the bottle into the empty glasses. "You do what you're good at."

Edwards attempted to replace the cap but was unable to hold it or the bottle steady enough to make a connection, and he laughed and threw the cap and it clinked into the shadows. Then he tossed the bottle and it skidded across the wood and banged into a wall.

"No, you sure don't need to talk." He looked over to see the young man holding an empty glass. "Think you'll be okay?"

"I'm certain of it."

"I just can't get over that. What makes you do it?"

"You keep offering it to me."

Edwards collapsed into a fit of delirious laughter. "Boy, that's the story of my life! You get it! My wife could never understand that, but you sure do. I can hear her now, her and the kids. If she could see us here in this place. Ha! Bitch. Goddammit. Never come here without a fuckin' fight, you know?"

He emptied his glass and held it to his face, elbow pointed out, long after he swallowed. His legs were splayed and his other arm hung at his side. He felt like he could sleep for ten years. His eyes grew heavy and his raised arm began to jerk in the air. He took the glass and threw it against the well and shook his head and rubbed his face.

"So whaddayou do, anyhow? We know you can drink, it's one of your whaddayoucallits. Your gifts. Tell me, kid, what are your gifts? Because apart from what I've seen here I have no idea what it is you do. What is it that you do? Hmm?"

"I have no job at present. I'm looking for one, though."

"No, I mean what *can* you do. I could give a shit about what *do* you do."

The young man looked into Edwards' eyes for the first time. They were his strongest feature, a pure blue like ice that in the poor light made him appear almost blind.

"I can see things." His tone was grave, and his face.

Edwards forced a smile. "Whaddayou mean you can see things? Anybody with two eyes in their head can see things. One eye. Hell, I can see, there's no trick to it."

"I don't think that's true. You cannot see in the same way as I. Few people have that ability. I can see beyond what is merely visible."

"Don't give me that bullshit," Edwards groaned. He had seen all the tricks. Each hick town he ever visited had an old woman, a little boy with one arm, any old freak who claimed to have powers of sight, or of healing. They held court like some fairytale king from their homes or the pathetic little churches their followers had built for them, and suckers would come from all over to give them money for an answer or a touch. It was especially bad down South, but hell, even his own neighborhood had one. When he and his wife moved in, all they heard for the first five weeks was about the old man with flesh hooks for hands who could heal and who could sometimes even see. Edwards never asked how it happened, if he touched people with his hooks and it made them well again or if people kissed the hooks or caressed his forehead. Nor had he encountered one of the healed. The old man had not been seen outside for twenty years. Not since he had been laid up.

Edwards saw him once. It was after midnight as he stumbled home from the bar. The old man's family had brought him outside on a rickety wooden cart, which they pushed out the back of the house and into the middle of the yard so he could lie beneath the stars. Edwards could hear the man's agonized groans each time the cart hit a bump. The man's family watched Edwards as he passed by, their faces hard and suspicious.

"What you doin' out there?" one of them demanded.

"Just walkin'," Edwards said.

"You just keep on walkin', then. You wanna see him, you can come back tomorrow and pay like everybody else."

Edwards saw the old man only for a moment before his family crowded around and blocked the view. People were right when they described his hands as flesh hooks. His wrists were bent and his fingers were gnarled to the extent that they did not look like hands anymore. It was not just his hands, either, his whole body was hooked. His arms were twisted in awkward angles, like those of a praying mantis, and his back curved out and his shoulders pointed to the rear. His useless legs were folded under his broken body. He looked like a mannequin whose limbs went askew after someone knocked it to the floor. He needed to be in a hospital, Edwards thought, not to have every idiot within a hundred-mile radius feeling him all day long. It made him sick to realize that the one time the old man was ever allowed outdoors was after the sun went down and nobody could see him for free.

The young man blinked. "It's not – what you said."

"Bullshit. I said it's bullshit. It *is* bullshit."

"It's the truth."

"How drunk do you think I am?"

"Very. But I still am telling you the truth."

Edwards rolled his eyes. "So whaddayou want, then? You don't just say a thing like that and not expect anything. So what is it?

Money? You want some money? Want me to pay you for some kinda reading I didn't even ask for? Cold reading, that's what they call it. I know all about it, I worked the carnivals when I was a kid. How much do you want? I'll give it to you right now if you stop talking this bullshit."

"Please stop saying that word."

"Bullshit! Bullshit, bullshit! Bull! Shit!"

Everything went quiet.

"I do not want anything. What is it that you want?"

"I want you to shut up with this seeing things bullshit. Bullshit! You can't see anything. Nobody can." He grabbed the pew in front of him and stood. He swayed over the back of it and watched the young man with disgust. "You are so full of it. You've seen too many movies, that's your problem. Anybody who says they can see what isn't there is just – lying. There isn't anything there. It's all just – black."

The young man spoke in a quiet voice, his eyes growing more intense.

"I don't expect you to believe in something of which you have no concept. I don't fully understand it myself. Everything the lord gives us is mysterious in its own way, from the miracles of nature to the things that offer no explanation."

"All bullshit. Every bit of it. Sight, God, everything you wanna tell me. Bullshit."

"Please stop saying that–"

"Bullshit!" Edwards spat the word in the young man's face with such vehemence that he almost fell on top of him. He regained his balance and flung a hand to the head of the sanctuary. "You're just exactly like that guy who stands up there every Sunday and tells people how wrong they are. You're no better than him. You're no better than the goddamned pope."

The young man sat back. A faint smile crossed his lips.

199

"Tell me. Why is it you feel you must abandon your family? What have they done to you?"

"Don't talk about my family."

"Why are you leaving them?"

Edwards shook his head. "You know it all already. Why don't you just tell me?"

The young man continued to smile. "You feel they're stifling you. Your wife in particular. You're tired of hearing her ask you to do things – to go to church, or to stop drinking, for example. You're tired of your children. You don't even speak of them. You have a sense of guilt over abandoning them all, but it is far outweighed by the send of relief you feel for having done so."

"You go to hell."

"I am sorry, but I am only telling you what I see. You asked, so you can hardly blame me for acceding to your wishes."

"You go straight to hell."

Edwards rounded the pew and began to stumble toward the door.

"Sit down, now, you're in no condition to drive."

Edwards did not listen. He put his hands on the door and pushed.

"You've forgotten your case."

With a growl, Edwards turned and stormed down the side of the aisle back to the pew, approaching it from the young man's side. As he drew closer, he noticed a large puddle of golden liquid under the seat, into which fell the steady drip, drip, drip of liquor from the cushion above.

"You little shit. You lying little shit."

The young man smirked.

"You have anything to say, or are you just gonna sit there and grin like an asshole?"

As the young man's smile fell, the last of the candles burned out and the room went dark.

THREE

The young man did not snore, and he slept with his mouth closed. Mrs. Parker watched him with her head nestled in the crook of his arm. His pajama top was unbuttoned – he no longer wore the bottoms – and with her left hand she felt his warm stomach and twirled several of the long dark strands of hair that sprouted there with her finger. He blinked his eyes and smiled. Taking her hand in his, he brought it into the open and kissed her palm. Without speaking she sunk below the covers and pressed her lips to his chest and ran her nails along his sides.

They had been finished six minutes before either of them spoke.

"I'm so happy."

"Me, too."

"I never told you before – I never told anyone. I used to pray for you."

"That's nice."

"You don't understand. I prayed for you every night. Sometimes I would wake up in the middle of the night, and I would get out of bed and pray then, too. I thought about you every day. I wanted God to send me a sign that you were all right."

"What kind of a sign?"

"I don't know. I never thought that part through. Just something I would recognize. I kept all my focus on you. I left the rest up to God." She lifted her head. "Did you ever hear me?"

"I'm here, aren't I?"

"I'm glad you are," she said and kissed the corner of his jaw. She lay back down, and he felt her hair brush against his ear, tickling it. The young man lifted his head from the pillow to get a better view of her face. Her eyes were shut and she looked as if she would fall back to sleep.

"What time is it?"

"I don't know," she said, eyes still shut. "Seven-thirty."

"You'll be late for church."

She snaked her arm across his chest and kept it there.

"I'm not going."

"You always go to church."

"I won't be doing that anymore. I've decided."

The young man sat up a bit and rested his back against the polished headboard with his pillow as a buffer. His shoulder nudged Mrs. Parker and her eyes opened an annoyed few seconds and she placed her cheek on his chest.

"Well, gosh, Edith. You better think about this a little more before you decide to do anything one way or another."

"I have thought about it." He felt her lips rub gently on his skin as she spoke. "All that time I spent, all those prayers. They didn't amount to anything. Not until after Mr. Peterson came."

"What are you talkin' about?"

"He was the one who brought you here. It wasn't God at all."

"Why in the world would you think that?"

"Because it's true." She sat up and faced him and the blanket fell to her waist. The young man made no move to pull it over himself.

"Why didn't God answer me all those years? Tell me that. When I asked for a sign, why didn't he give me one? He didn't do a thing. He was content to let me sit down here and beg like a dog. He never had any intention of answering me. Ten years I prayed to him, and then Mr. Peterson comes and solves the whole problem in a few weeks."

"How do you know that? Maybe this is him doin' something now. Maybe God sent that kid here to answer your prayer. You think of that?"

"I don't care." Frowning, she laid her head back to his chest. His heart beat strong against her ear, and he ran his hand along her back. She did not pull the blanket over them again.

The young man waited to speak.

"I don't care," Mrs. Parker repeated. "I really don't. I'll think what I want to think."

"I guess you will," he yawned. "But I still say you should give it some more time. You shouldn't just jump into something like this. Think about it some more."

"I've been thinking about it for ten years. That's more than enough time." She gave him another kiss on the chest and set her chin on it. "You didn't always go to church, you know," she said, staring at him. "I never said anything to you about it."

He nodded. "You're right, but that isn't the same thing. You're not me."

She snuggled against him before she answered.

"It's too late. I've decided."

When she resumed kissing him he noticed a bare space on the bedside table.

"What'd you do with the picture?"

"It's gone."

"I can see that, but where did it go to?"

"It doesn't matter," she said between kisses. "I don't need it anymore."

The young man stood in the half-mowed back yard dressed in a white T-shirt and brown slacks and ran a faded red bandana across his neck. The handle of the mower stood propped against his side and he held it still with his arm when he returned the cloth to his back pocket, the end of it sticking out like a tail. With a sigh he grabbed the handle and once more began to push.

"Wait a second!" Mrs. Parker called through the kitchen window.

He did as she said, and watched as she emerged from the back door with a tall glass of water. She stared at the ground as she walked, and took care to avoid stepping in the damp dark mounds of fresh-cut grass.

"My goodness, it's humid. Don't you think you should finish up later?"

He shook his head and accepted the glass.

"If I put it off now, I'll put it off then. It won't take much longer."

Closing his eyes, he put back his head and drank with audible gulps.

"Not so fast, now. You'll get sick. What if Mrs. Colman wants you to do her lawn, too?"

"That I can put off," he said as he lowered the empty glass. "But I haven't seen her. I don't know if she's home or not."

"You should do it either way."

"Doesn't need to be today. It's near-dead, anyhow."

He held the glass toward her. She took it with both hands and snuck a feel of his bare arm with her fingers.

"You're sweating."

"It's humid," he said with a nod.

With a timid smile, she took one step back and watched him. She held the empty glass upright near her mouth, as if she were preparing to take a drink.

"You better get back in the house," he whispered.

She gave a slight nod and moved backward to the house, staining her shoes with green clumps of grass, as the young man raised the mower handle.

"When I'm done with this, I think I'm gonna putter around in the garage a little bit."

Mrs. Parker bumped into the corner of the open back door with her shoulder. "All right. Don't be too long, though, I'm going to fix you a snack pretty soon."

When the door was shut the young man began to mow, and dozens of tiny grasshoppers the color of dead twigs leaped out of the way of the rotating blades.

The garage was musty, and smelled of canvas and old wood. There were no electric lights, but windows stood in two of the walls, resulting in a crisscross of yellow sunbeams that intersected in the middle of the empty space and tinted everything surrounding them a warm shade of brown.

In the corner of the room was a table covered with a piece of heavy gray tarpaulin that reached the floor. The young man pulled the lower section, which was folded under the table, and freed a dozen fat crickets that scattered into the shadows. The young man put his hands on top of the table and grabbed the tarpaulin by its folds. The material was stiff and retained much of its shape when he heaved it to the floor, where it sat like a tent with no poles. He folded it down the middle and flattened it as best he could before he rolled it up like a sleeping bag and nudged it under the table with his shoe.

The table was bare apart from a red-colored press that was screwed into the side and a wrench and a handful of nails that were strewn across the top. It was covered in cobwebs, to which clung a thick layer of rust-colored dust. On the wall hung a brown piece of pegboard, with dull silver hooks sticking out in close configurations of twos and threes. Bulky wooden dowels. Above the pegboard was a white wooden cupboard. The young man opened it and found

207

haphazard rows of tools, worn and dull. Leaving the cupboard open, he put his face near it and blew, and sent a particulate brown cloud into the air. After he found a rag, he wiped down the table and took down the tools, cleaned them, too, before he hung them on the hooks. The last of these was a long heavy hammer, with claws like the wide fingers of a giant. He weighed it in his hand a moment before he hung it up, and left the garage.

Mrs. Parker was talking on the telephone when he entered the kitchen through the back door. She faced away from him, and she did not hear him come in.

"Yes. No, it's – I'm sorry, I've been very busy. I'm fine, I promise. How are you doing, how is everyone?"

The young man shut the door without a sound and crept into the kitchen and leaned on the counter as he watched her.

"That's wonderful. Oh, he is? And what about the others? That's sweet. Oh, I don't know. Well, I've been awfully busy. All sorts of things – it's been a very busy summer. I am sorry, really. I didn't mean – what? I don't know... For how long? I know I haven't, but – Listen, I have something on the stove. Can I call you back? This evening. Fine. All right, I'll speak to you then. I love you, too."

When she hung up the phone she folded her hands near her stomach and began to walk slowly into the dining room.

The young man coughed. "Edith?"

She looked toward him. Then she smiled.

"Who were you talkin' to?"

"It was just a phone call."

"I know that. Who was it?"

She stared at the floor as she returned to the kitchen.

"Nathan."

"How is he?"

"He's fine," she said as she continued toward the young man. His shirt was streaked with black and gray, and dust stuck to his arms and his neck. He was cleanest near his eyes and his mouth, which were surrounded by thin fingermarks.

Mrs. Parker extended her arms to him, but held off from making contact when she drew close. "You need a shower. Did you get a lot done?"

"Yeah, I did. But tell me, how is he really? How 'bout his wife, and the kids?"

"They're fine. They're all fine," she said and went to the refrigerator. "I wish I'd have known when you would be in. I could have gotten a start on that snack for you."

"I can wait."

"I'll get you something now."

"What'd he want?"

She brought out a covered white dish and set it on the table. "Do you want the rest of this pork?"

"Sure."

"Sit down at the table, then. I'll get you some silverware and something to drink. Would you like milk or water?"

"Either one."

He took a seat before the dish and watched as Mrs. Parker got the milk from the refrigerator and a glass from the cupboard. "Would you like some bread, too? I have some bread."

"No, thanks."

She set the glass of milk in front of him. "How is it? Oh – the silverware." She opened the drawer and got a knife and fork and brought them to the table. "Do you need anything else?"

"No. This is fine."

"All right. Dig in."

He picked up the silverware and began to slice the meat. "What did he want?"

"Oh, nothing," she said and took a seat next to him. "He wanted to chat, I suppose."

"Anything else?" he asked after swallowing.

"Not really."

"Seemed like he was askin' you to do something from what I could hear."

She waved her hand as if she were shooing away a fly. "He wanted me to go down there and stay with them for a few days."

"You should do it."

"What about you?"

"I'm a big boy. I can take care of myself. He doesn't know I'm here, anyway."

She shook her head. "I don't think so."

"Why don't you go? Seriously. I know you don't talk to him much. I'm sure you don't see him too often. I've never seen you write a letter to him."

"You haven't been here very long."

He shrugged. "Why won't you do it? Don't you wanna see the grandkids? Don't you wanna spend time with them?"

"It isn't about that."

"What is it about, then?"

Before she could answer someone knocked on the door. Mrs. Parker stared out of the kitchen and waited. There was another knock but she did not move.

"Aren't you gonna get it?"

"Yes," she said and stood. "Wait here."

Pastor Gruber stood on the porch looking like a man in a hospital waiting room. Lips pursed, he fidgeted and his hands twitched as though he had drunk five cups of coffee in ten minutes. When the door opened he gave a warm smile and put his hands behind his waist. His back went stiff and his legs were like stilts.

"Mrs. Parker – I'm so glad to see that it's you. When you didn't join us this morning I was afraid you might be under the weather."

"No, I'm fine."

"That's certainly good to know." He smiled so hard the corners of his eyes wrinkled. He laughed in choking gasps and took a small step to the threshold of the door.

Mrs. Parker stood anchored to her spot, nodding and smiling along with him.

"Is everything well? I don't mean to intrude, but why were you not with us this morning?"

"It's – my nephew – he was sick last night and I was up late caring for him."

Pastor Gruber began to sniff. "I see. Was it anything serious?"

"No, it was a bug. One of those things that sneaks up on you."

"He's feeling better, then?" He sniffed again and stretched his upper lip over his front teeth.

"Oh, yes."

Pastor Gruber brought his arms back and rubbed his hands together. He felt his pockets and frowned with embarrassment.

"I seem to have forgotten... Would you happen to have a handkerchief or something I could use...?"

"Are you getting a bug yourself?"

"No, ma'am. Only a tickle. Is there anything I could use? I don't mean to be an inconvenience, but it's driving me crazy. I can't scratch it. Not in the open."

Mrs. Parker lowered her eyes and nodded once. "Of course. Come in."

She held the door and he stumbled inside, tripping over his shoelaces.

"Be careful, now."

"I don't want to break my arm," he laughed.

She shut the door and motioned toward the sofa.

"I'll go find something for you to – I'll be back down in a minute."

As she went up the stairs, Pastor Gruber took a seat on the sofa and retied both his shoes. It was not long after that he snuck a look over his shoulders and shoved his thumbnail into his left nostril, twisting and itching, his eyes daring all the time. After he began to work his right nostril he glanced to the side and saw the young man standing over him. Startled, he let out a little cry and stood.

"Oh! Hello!" he said a bit too loud. "I didn't hear you come in."

"Evidently."

The pastor began to extend his hand, but soon withdrew it.

"Pardon me. Your aunt went upstairs to fetch me something to – I have an itch."

"I can see that. Are you certain you need something with which to wipe?"

"Yes."

"I have one in my pocket."

"Thank you, no. I remember the last time."

He opened his mouth to say something else, but no words came out. Instead, he ran his tongue along his bottom lip and grinned. "It looks like you used that rag yourself."

"I was cleaning the garage."

"I see," he chuckled. "You're feeling better, then?"

"I'm sorry?"

"Yes, your aunt told me you were sick last night."

"Sick?"

"Just a bug, she said."

The young man smiled. "I wasn't sick."

"No?"

"No."

Mrs. Parker called out as she came down the stairs and held a tattered white cloth before her.

"I found this for you. It doesn't look very nice but it was all I could find. You can keep it." She stopped when she saw them both. Neither of the men spoke. She lifted her hand. "Here."

"Thank you, Mrs. Parker." The pastor accepted the rag and tried to find the corners. It looked moth-eaten, and his fingers poked through the holes when he held it, and strings dangled off like the edges of a worn burlap sack. He folded it three times before he could no longer see through it. Then he put it to his nose and rubbed hard. "Thank you," he said as he put it in the pocket of his jacket.

The three of them stood, waiting. None of them did anything. Soon Mrs. Parker spoke.

"Thank you very much for stopping by, but we have some things to do yet this afternoon."

"Of course. Thank you, too, for the–" He patted his pocket. "And I expect I'll see you next week, Mrs. Parker, if not sooner."

"No." Her voice was flat. "I'm sorry, you can't expect that."

Pastor Gruber's smile fell. "I can't?"

"I'm afraid not."

"Are you going out of town?"

"No, I'll be here at home. I simply don't plan on coming to church. In fact, I think I should tell you that I won't be coming back. Not ever."

As she spoke, the young man moved to her side, one step behind her. He was silent, stoic, with the faintest hint of a smirk. His eyes laughed openly.

Pastor Gruber stared at her open-mouthed and twitched like an ant was crawling up his back. He squeaked a few unintelligible syllables before he was able to speak with clarity.

"You're doing it, too."

"I beg your pardon?"

"You must have noticed by now. Each week someone else drops off. A single person, a couple, a family. If this keeps up I'll be the only one left pretty soon. What is it? Why are you leaving? Is there something so wrong with who I am or what I say that you all can't stand to be in the same room with me?"

"I am sorry," she said, "but we do have to get some things done."

She went to the door and opened it. Pastor Gruber looked once more at the young man before he followed. He passed through the door without speaking and she closed it behind him. She watched as he skulked away, head lowered like a beaten dog.

"I hope you know what you're doin'," the young man said.

She answered without looking at him.

"I do, John."

Mrs. Parker's bedroom was neat to the point of sterility. The bed was made so the covers on either side of the mattress did not extend an unequal length toward the floor. Each small curio on each shelf or cabinet was placed with a slight skew to the right. The dresser drawers were closed and the closet door was shut. Everything smelled clean, like fresh rain. The single sign of irregularity in the entire room was the pale blue curtain, which wafted like a scarf in the breeze that passed through the open window. The young man got on his knees to check under the bed. The floor was as clean as a dinner plate, with no balls of dust or strands of hair. The entire floor was the same way, smooth like a polished stone. Standing, he walked to the dresser and opened one of the drawers, which gave a loud squeak. All he found were tidy stacks of clothes. Each drawer was the same, appearing as it would if it were under glass in a department store display case. When he opened the door to the closet he was met with a faint odor of mothballs. The clothes were arranged by color on the rack, beginning with whites and growing progressively darker. On the shelf above them was an assortment of hat boxes following this same pattern. Stepping inside, the young man reached up and pulled the long white string that was tied to the inch-long silver beaded chain next to the naked yellow light bulb on the ceiling. It was on one of the hat boxes that he saw it – the dark corner of the frame poking out over the top. He raised his long arm and nudged it with the tip of his middle finger before he hopped once and snatched it from its perch. He held the frame in his hands and stared into the eyes of John Parker in absolute silence. Continuing to stare, he turned off the light and stepped out of the dark enclosed space. Then he shut the door.

Sarah kept her money in a box at the bottom of the closet under a pile of yellowing Life magazines. The box was a sturdy cube that smelled like shoe polish. It was painted brown, and had a thick brass clasp on the front. Crouching, she pulled it from its place and snapped it open, and a fat pile of dollars emerged like rising bread dough in a hot oven. She dug into her pocket and took out the handful of coins, and they jangled when she tossed them in. She did not close the box. She rested her hands on her knees and stared.

Sitting now, she took the stack of bills in her hands. It gave beneath the pressure of her fingers as she squeezed it, soft and good, and she divided it by amount and set the little bundles in a line on the floor. She counted each, adding the total in her head. Then she collected the coins, weighed them in her hands, too, and tallied with a small smile. It would not be long.

When everything was back in the box she put it away. Her fingers were smeared gray with dirt, and they smelled like copper. She went to the bathroom and shed her uniform. Eyes shut, she felt her way to the sink and turned on the water.

Back in the room, she shuffled to the bed and lay down. She felt good. She sat up and opened the window and lay down again. The sounds of the birds and the breeze filled her ears. The air was warm and comforting, and breathing it in she closed her eyes and waited.

When she awoke eighty-seven minutes later the first thing she did was to reach for a cigarette. She lit it and puffed and opened her eyes. Alone. Upon standing she puffed again and went to the closet.

The store was nearly empty of people as Sarah traveled the aisles. She liked it that way. She grabbed a Wonder loaf and headed straight for the cans of soup that lined the shelves with bold stripes of red and white. Chicken noodle, tomato, vegetable beef. Scanning the names, she bumped into someone.

"Sorry–"

"Don't worry, dear, I wasn't looking, either."

It was Mrs. Parker. She smiled. An empty basket dangled from her arm and she patted Sarah on the shoulder.

"I have to be more careful. Sometimes I get so caught up in what I'm doing it's a wonder I don't hurt someone."

Sarah cleared her throat and juggled the items she was carrying, finally clutching them to her chest and stomach so they would not fall.

"Do you need a basket, dear? You can have mine – I can get another one."

"No, it's okay. I think I have everything. I just need to get it to the till."

"Let me help you."

"No, thank you, I'm fine."

"You might drop something."

"Nothing that'll break. I have it. Really. Thanks, though."

"If you insist," Mrs. Parker said with a shrug. "You have a nice day now, dear. It certainly is beautiful out, isn't it?"

"Yes," Sarah stuttered. "Thank you, you too."

She raised her head off the threadbare feather pillow and eyed the alarm clock. It was a few minutes past four. She lay back down. Sunlight flooded in through the window, blanketing the mattress with a warming glow. The sheet was clustered on the floor at the foot of the bed. She rested her hand on the young man's chest. He wore a bleach-white T-shirt, nothing else. The shirt was damp and it made Sarah's fingers feel clammy. She tickled his chest and felt him twitch beneath the fabric.

"Why don't you ever take that off?"

The young man opened his eyes and gave a few drowsy blinks. Upon seeing her hand, he lifted it by the pinky and tossed it aside like a rotten banana peel. He rubbed his face with both hands, his shirt sneaking up toward his navel. "Was I sleeping?" he asked, hands still at his face.

"I don't know. I just woke up myself. Maybe."

"What time is it?"

"Early."

"Be specific."

"Very early."

The young man put down his hands and glared at her as he scratched the inside of his thigh. Scooting up, he crossed his ankles and folded his hands behind his head.

Sarah frowned. "I feel bad."

He glanced toward her, but she had turned her head back the clock. He followed the indent of her spine with his eyes. Her skin was smooth and pink, but he made no move to feel it. Instead, he sat, silent.

"Don't you wanna know why I feel that way?"

"I could not be less interested," he said and rubbed his nose.

"You know, though, don't you?"

"I know it isn't about this."

"No."

He did not reply.

"Well?"

"What?" he sighed.

"What do you think?"

"Are you trying to annoy me?"

She wiped her eyes with the corner of the fitted sheet, which had been pulled from between the mattress and the box spring.

"I seem to remember that when I approached you with this idea any so-called moral concerns were non-existent. You were positively giddy – you could hardly wait to go through with it."

"I know."

The young man leaned over her and read the clock. "I suppose I'd better head back over there."

"I wish you wouldn't."

"Your wishes are immaterial," he said. He swung his legs over the side of the bed and stretched. "And anyway, nothing comes from wishing. It's like prayer."

The springs shook and Sarah felt his weight leave the bed. He cast a shadow across the bed when he stepped in front of the window and stared out. She shut her eyes and pushed her face deep into the pillow. The warm air blowing from her nostrils made her face grow hot. She thought she would choke but she did not move.

"Don't tell me you're crying now."

"I'm not," she said in a muffled voice. She felt the return of the sunlight and heard creaks from the ancient floorboards as he moved to the kitchen area, where he had stacked his clothes neatly folded on one of the chairs. He put one of his hands on its back to balance while he brushed the bottoms of his feet with the other.

"Do you ever sweep in here? It's like walking down a gravel path."

Sarah did not answer. She rolled over and watched him get dressed, raising her eyes from the bottom of his bare legs to his lower back. His T-shirt rose when he stretched again and she spied something hiding beneath it.

"What's that?"

"Where?"

"On your back."

"Don't concern yourself with it."

She propped herself up with her elbows. "Is it a tattoo?"

"No."

"What is it? Did you cut yourself?"

The young man pulled on his socks as Sarah approached him from behind. She slid her hands under his arms and felt his warm belly. She rested her mouth on his shoulder and held her breath and cupped his testicles with one hand.

"I told you I'm leaving."

"I know."

"So what is it that you want? Why won't you let me get ready?"

She let go of him and wandered toward the kitchen counter. She leaned against it, forehead resting on the cupboard, and kicked at the floor with one foot.

"Where are my shorts?"

"I dunno. I'm not your maid."

The young man grunted as he bent over and looked under the bed. Lying facedown on the rug, he reached under and fished them out. Before he stood again, Sarah turned and watched. She only saw his back for one second. On the lower left side was a thick, white rounded edge of irregular flesh that disappeared again when he tugged at his shirt. Sarah felt a chill.

"How much longer you think it'll be?"

"I have no way of supplying you with an answer to that question," the young man said as he hiked up his drawers. With a frown he returned to the chair and picked up his trousers and shook them. He did not zip the fly nor button them once he had pulled them on.

"If you could guess, how long would you say?"

"Aren't you going to get dressed?" he scowled.

Sarah cast her eyes to the floor, unable to look at him. She wanted to disappear.

"It's my apartment. I'll do what I fucking want."

The young man shrugged.

"But you think you can do it."

He zipped his fly. "I know I can."

"How?"

"You simply have to trust that I know what I'm talking about." He took his light green long-sleeved shirt from the chair and put it on. He flapped the sides three times before he began to do up the buttons.

"Don't worry, I do trust you." She forced herself to smile. He did not notice. "I know you know what you're doin'. I can tell you wouldn't stat somethin' if you didn't know how to finish it." She could not help but chuckle. "You're too much of a tight-ass."

"Do you seriously intend to continue to stand around like that? I didn't come here to ogle you."

"Didn't mind it so much an hour ago."

He looked around for his belt.

"After a few weeks with her I'd think you'd wanna look at me as much as you could. You never told me – did it say in his obituary how she likes to get fucked?"

"Do you mind?"

"Well, you got so much from it, clearly."

The young man stood with his hands on his hips.

"Belt's under the table, Einstein."

He got on his hands and knees and retrieved it. Then he stood and slid it into the first loop. Sarah pulled out the other chair and sat. The young man shook his head.

"Maybe you could read up on her neighbor's husband, find out how to service her, too."

He dropped his belt and it dangled from his waist by its buckle. Sarah put her chin in her hands and smiled with closed eyes. Glaring, the young man grabbed the belt and slid it through his hand.

"Have I made you angry?" Sarah asked. "Are you insulted?"

"You are disgusting," he said, still holding the belt.

"It's mutual. At least I'm not lying to her."

The young man pushed the belt through the next loop. "Apart from the notion of transference, I've told no lies about her husband."

She stretched her arms across the table and rested her head on them. Three red apples sat nearby and rolled in different directions when her hands bumped them. One fell to the floor with a hollow thud.

"So they were able to cram all that bullshit you spout into three lines of a newspaper, huh? I should start readin' more."

He spoke with studied patience as he slipped his belt through the remaining loops. "It has been my experience that most of the time, people will tell you what you want to know without realizing it. If you fail to obtain the information from them, you seek out other sources. That is, friends, neighbors, the occasional obituary. However, most of the time people are stupid enough to tell you what you want to hear, and stupid enough to be amazed when you repeat it back to them. If people want to believe you, they will, regardless of what you tell them. Most of the time they just hear what they want to, anyhow. If someone tells you they can see things others are incapable of seeing, or that there's a reason behind everything, that person is lying. You must never forget that."

"Sure thing, professor."

He buckled his belt. "I'm dressed now. I'm leaving." He went to the door.

"Forgetting something?"

"No," he said as he turned the knob.

"How about your hat?"

He looked at her and saw she was sitting back in her chair with her feet on the table. Perched at a jaunty angle on her head was his hat. Face clouding, he stomped to the table and held out his hand. "Don't be stupid. Give it."

She flung the hat onto the table and he brushed it and put it on his head. "You don't hafta be such an asshole all the time."

"How would you prefer I behave?" He did not raise his voice. His tone was quick, polite. "Be forceful in your personal life if you want, if you feel that it can make up for how you're treated when you leave this apartment. But, do not play games with me. Has my behavior changed in such a way that it's become a problem for you? Am I not paying you enough attention? Do you want me to slobber all over you like some high school boy in the back seat of a car? I have seen nudity before. I am not impressed. I told you when we embarked upon this that you must do what I want, when I want you to do it. That includes not acting like a child. For all intents and purposes, I own you right now. I am making it work your while, so if you insist on continuing this little girl act of yours, please do it after I have left the room. Watching you do it makes me want to throw up." He turned to the door. "So long."

In a rage, Sarah scooped the fallen apple off the floor and hurled it at the young man's head. It thumped against his skull and bounced into a corner, and he turned in time to see her rushing toward him. Without a change in expression he swiftly brought up his hands and gave a forceful shove to her shoulders. She stumbled, lost her balance and fell, landing on her back, although she felt no pain. The young man straddled her chest, pinning her shoulders to the floor with his knees.

"Can you not hear me?" he asked. "If you do anything like this again, you will regret it. I have no patience for this childishness."

Sarah grunted as she tried to push him off, and banged her hands against the floor.

The young man put his face close to hers. "Stop it," he snarled in a voice like fire.

She stopped kicking and glared back at him.

"This is not going to work if you disobey me," he said. His voice returned to normal. "You are ridiculous. Do you understand? It's a joke the way you are with your little nest egg and your sticker on the mirror. Look at you. So pathetic. And what is this nonsense about feeling bad? A few weeks ago you despised her, remember? How tough you were. What a farce." He smiled for a second. "Actions have consequences. Do you not know that? If you were unprepared to deal with them you should never have agreed to take part."

She waited to speak. "Fine. I'm sorry."

"I want one thing from you. I want you to promise that you will stop this foolishness. Do what I ask and be rewarded. Defy me and pay the penalty. Do you understand?"

"Yes. I understand."

"Promise me."

"Yes, I promise," she sighed. "I'll do anything you say."

The land was brown and dead, and still. There was very little air, and the brutal heat made it difficult to breathe. Standing on the side of the rutted dirt road, the young man wiped his brow with a crusty sweat-stained handkerchief and looked into the sky, which was grayed with gathering storm clouds. Putting the cloth to his mouth, he coughed once. Nothing came up. His lungs felt tight, like wet rawhide, and he was sure that any second he would be overcome by dizziness. He cleared his throat and spat a long, clean stream of saliva before bunching the handkerchief into a ball and jamming it into his pocket. Panting, he continued on his way on wobbly legs. It felt too hot to move and he walked with his sleeves rolled up and his cap clamped low on his forehead.

The road was empty, and although the fields were tilled, they stood lifeless and bare from weeks of blinding sunlight and punishing heat. Under the sunless sky they acquired a look of eerie desolation. As he passed them, the young man thought the fields must look like the surface of the moon, or the detonation site of a bomb. The arid appearance of the land reminded him of how thirsty he felt, and began anew the internal debate as to when he would find a source of water.

An ominous clap of thunder was heard. The young man would have welcomed rain. He would like to take off his shirt and let it all pour over him in a cool burst. He would like to open his mouth and let the drops trickle in, soothing and welcome and fresh. But the prolonged roll of thunder implied something more powerful than a passing shower. If he did not seek shelter soon, he thought, he might find himself on the receiving end of a thunderstorm or tornado, if he did not first die of dehydration.

Far in the distance he spotted a small grove of bare trees. It was the fourth such cluster he had come upon that afternoon, which was the primary reason the sight did nothing to raise his hopes. In the first instance, the trees surrounded a tiny house, toward which the young man ran in a steady trot, only to discover as he came closer that it was abandoned. The disappointment weighed heavy on his spirit, a burden that was magnified on finding each consecutive group of trees was nothing more than what it appeared to be – just trees.

He kept his pace slow as he made his way toward them, trying to focus on his destination, an objective that grew more difficult by the second. His head was light, his vision fuzzy. With each step the young man felt further removed from reality, as though he were floating rather than walking. He felt like vomiting, but there was nothing in his stomach. His fingers began to twitch and he lost all feeling in his legs, but still he moved forward, on toward the trees, and the relief that might be waiting beneath them.

The young man raised his head as he got closer. Nothing. Just like the other spots. He exhaled an anguished breath and felt stabbing pains in his stomach and chest.

The trees looked like death. They were tall and slender, removed of all bark. Their white, smooth branches reached toward the sky with ragged claws, like arms begging mercy from an unseen master. The young man stumbled toward the tallest of the trees and collapsed beneath it. He tried to speak, but his voice was gone. He could not even groan. Another thunderclap sounded as he rolled onto his back and stared wide-eyed into the murky sky until he blacked out.

The young man woke to see the dried grass passing in front of his face, as if he were being swung from a rope by his ankles. He soon realized he was being carried on a man's broad, thick shoulders, like the carcass of a deer. A pair of strong arms held him in place, one over his back, the other over his legs. The young man mumbled a few incoherent syllables, causing the man transporting him to jump. The man jostled him and gave an order in a rough voice, although the young man was unsure of what was said. He tried to sit up, and the man shook him again and yelled. The young man stopped moving, and his limbs dangled and shook with the up and down motion of the unseen man's footsteps.

Before long, the young man felt a sharp pain in his back and he opened his eyes to find he had been swung onto the splintered wooden flatbed of an old truck. He heard what he took to be another command, followed by the rattling of a poorly-maintained engine. He felt vibrations in the rough surface on which he lay, and soon everything jerked forward, and he knew they were driving. He closed his eyes and tried to concentrate on the rock inside a tin can sound of the engine and the bumps of the road. Soon he felt a pinprick on his forehead. Then one on his arm. Another on his lips. He opened his mouth and a raindrop hit his tongue. It was like pure frost, like an ice shaving. He gasped, greedy for more, opening wider. Seconds later, the rain poured with a force so strong the young man nearly choked in trying to swallow it all. Delirious with joy, he unfastened the top buttons of his shirt and let the rain spray his aching chest. He brought his hands to his face, massaging, soothing.

Then the rain stopped. The young man opened his eyes. He tried to sit but he was too tired to move, so all he could do was lie there and stare at the passing sky, willing it to gush down on him again. He closed his eyes and repeated his silent pleas as the truck continued on its way down the road.

Then the young man heard a loud pop next to his head and felt a wet blast of cold matter against his cheek. He opened his eyes to see the squished hailstone inches from his face. It was just smaller than a golf ball. Before he could react he felt a sharp, frigid blow to his sternum. It made an awful sound, like that of someone hitting a watermelon with a large wooden club, and the young man brought his knees up in an involuntary spasm, part defense, part sheer pain. Another stone hit his left shin, shattering on impact, and one more hit his right shoulder. The young man shielded his face with his arms as the stones began to fall with greater frequency, belting him in heavy, agonizing thumps. He rolled onto his stomach and curled into a ball, arms sheltering his skull, legs tucked beneath his torso. The truck continued to move forward, albeit at a much slower pace.

"Drive faster!" the young man tried to yell, but the words would not come. Neither would any conscious thought – only the recognition of the constant, unbearable blows and the sickening sound his body made as it absorbed them.

When he came to, the young man found himself lying on a bed for which he was too big. His head was pressed against the wall at an awkward angle and his feet dangled off the edge of the mattress. He tried to sit up but it hurt to move. His arms and legs were stiff and he was covered in welts the size of baseballs. He opened his eyes fully and gazed in confusion at his new surroundings. The room was small. The walls were bare and gray and there were no furnishings apart from the bed. The air was stale, like a sickroom. Near the foot of the bed was a closed door and on another wall was a tiny window. The window was open and the scent of wet air filled the room. Shifting under the blankets, the young man felt the scratchy fabric rub against his skin and he realized he was naked. He glanced at the floor beside the bed. He did not see his clothes.

Soon the young man heard footsteps, which grew louder until they stopped for a moment, replaced by the sound of a rusty key turning in an old lock. The door opened and a woman looked inside. She was large – more than two hundred pounds – but she was not fat. She was tall and she was strong. When she saw the young man was awake she smiled and came inside. She approached the bed on quiet footsteps, carrying a pitcher of water and a glass, which she set on the floor near the window. The woman's face was kind and her voice was soft.

"Hello," she all but whispered.

The young man opened his mouth to speak, but the woman shushed him. "Don't talk," she said and walked back to the door and brought in an old folding chair with thin slats of wood that lined its back and seat. She continued to smile as she closed the door and returned to the bed. She down set the chair near the young man's shoulder and sat before she picked up the pitcher and filled the glass halfway.

"You're very pale. I think you could be dehydrated, so I want you to drink some."

She curled her arm around the back of the young man's head, cradling it. It was like being cuddled by a football player. She put the glass to his lips. He slurped at the water. Soon he began to cough and sprayed down his chin.

"No big gulps," the woman said and stroked his arm. "Little sips, little sips."

The young man sipped until the glass was empty.

"I'll give you some more in a little bit. If you drink too much right away you could get sick, and you need your strength." She removed her arm from his neck and shoulder and guided his head back to the soft pillow. "Are you comfortable?"

The young man nodded.

"My husband brought you here. You should be glad he saw you."

He nodded again.

"He told me he thought you might be dead when he found you. He's gone outside. He's checking to see if everything made it through the storm." She looked at one of his hands, bulging now with a swollen purple egg.

"Are you bruised like this everyplace?"

The young man opened his mouth and gave a weak shrug.

"Don't try to say anything. It's all right." She took the edge of the blankets in her hands and pulled them down, just below the young man's navel. His body was a mass of blue and purple blotches, very swollen and very tender. The woman flinched when she looked at him and whistled through her teeth. "Oh my. It must be so painful for you."

The young man tried to avoid looking at his injuries. He looked instead into her eyes, which seemed to hold a mix of both sympathy and embarrassment. The woman broke free of his gaze and cleared her throat. "What about...?" she began.

The young man remained immobile.

"Lower?"

Just as he was preparing to motion a response, the woman pulled the blanket down further. The young man closed his eyes. The room was silent for a very long time.

Then the woman spoke.

"I'm sure you're relieved."

The young man kept his eyes shut tight.

"But your poor legs, though. They're covered with such awful welts. Do you think any of your bones might be cracked?"

Eyes still closed, the young man shook his head.

"How about here?" the woman said and felt his shin. The pain was intense, the spot raw and sore. Although she put no pressure on the wound, a small cry escaped the young man's lips when she touched it.

"I'm so sorry. What does this one feel like?" she asked, moving her hands to one of the discolored lumps on his chest.

"Hurts," the young man whispered.

"Are they very painful?"

"Yes."

A smile creeping across her face, the woman moved one hand to his stomach, which was free of bruises. She rubbed her hand on it in a slow circular motion. "How does this feel?" she asked as she twirled her index finger in the sparse hairs that grew there.

The young man tilted his head and stared at her with a bewildered expression.

"This doesn't hurt. Does it."

The young man concentrated on breathing as the woman trailed down to the inside of his thigh.

"Or this?"

The young man grasped the blankets in an attempt to cover himself, but the woman held them fast.

"No," she said. "I want to look at you."

She stared at him with a look of clinical detachment. She continued to look at him until the sound of footsteps was heard outside the room, at which point she tossed the blankets over him and stood glowering over his bed, hands balled into fists at her sides.

Soon there appeared a man so enormous he almost filled the doorframe. His face was dark with hate, and his voice was choked with a constant, simmering rage.

"How is he?" the large man asked.

"Well, he's sick," the woman answered with sudden bitterness. "I don't know when the idiot drank last, he can barely talk. Looks like he'll have to stay with us a few days."

"Goddammit. Lord help us." The large man punched the wall with such force it made the whole room rattle.

The young man lay still.

The woman addressed the young man as though she were speaking to a dog. "This is my husband," she enunciated in loud, slow syllables.

The husband lumbered into the room like a bull. He bent inches from the young man's face and shouted, "Soon as you're on your feet again, you're payin' us back, you got it? You're not stayin' here free, this ain't no hotel. You're gonna work off everything we give you, understand? You'll do the Christian thing, or may God have mercy on your miserable life."

The young man's ears rang and his eye gave an involuntary twitch.

"Can he understand?"

"Yeah, but I'm not sure it makes a whole ton of difference," the woman said sourly. "Might as well just let him rest now."

The husband grabbed the woman by the shoulders and flung her toward the door. "I know that! Go fix the coffee!"

The woman stumbled and cracked her head against the wall. She braced herself with one hand on the doorframe and pushed her hair back with the other. She turned around and glared at her husband, who was again staring at the young man. Despite the growing red patch on her forehead, the woman smiled once more at the young man before she left. Her husband did not notice. He snorted.

"You stay away from my wife," he growled into the young man's ear.

Dinner was not pleasant. For the young man, it consisted of one half-raw boiled potato and a glass of warm milk – not worth the trip down the narrow stairway slung over the husband's shoulder. Peterson. That was his name. Jacob Peterson. The wife's name was unclear, as it was never used when he addressed her. Peterson's dinner was more substantial: One large cut of meat, the origin of which was undetermined, three boiled potatoes and bread. He drank water. "Milk's for women and liquor is the devil's work," he had said. The woman did not eat.

"You're lucky I give you one of my potatoes," Peterson said. "The sluggard's craving will be the death of him because his hands

233

refuse to work." He shook his head. "Just wait until you work it off, you'll be sorry you ever barged in here."

"Ungrateful," the woman said from behind her husband's chair, where she stood, tall and stoic.

Peterson mumbled in agreement.

The young man ate in silence and avoided looking either of them in the face. He had been given an old nightshirt to wear while his clothes were drying. It was too large for his body and it hung over his frame like a huge deflated balloon.

"I hate to see it, a young man like yourself drifting from place to place, depending on the kindness of others to get him through life's travails and turmoil," Peterson said.

"Shame," the woman said.

"Where do you think you'd be if it weren't for me? You'd be dead out in a field and nobody'd know, nobody'd care. That's where you'd be. You think that's the kinda plan God had in mind for you? Do you think it makes Him happy to see you taking advantage of the kindness of others, such as my wife and myself?"

"Never," the woman said.

"Shut up," Peterson snapped.

The young man found it impossible to eat. He stared at what remained of his potato.

"Are you finished?" Peterson asked.

The young man said nothing.

"Will you please answer me? I said are you finished."

"I'm sorry," the young man said. "My stomach–"

"Won't even take what's given him," Peterson said.

"It's disgraceful," the woman said.

"Don't think just because you didn't finish what we have so generously provided that you won't have to work it off in the end. You might not feel real good, but we're still out a potato thanks to you."

"And milk," the woman said.

"And milk," Peterson repeated with contempt. "I just wonder what you think's going to happen here," he went on. "Do you think we'll just forget that you owe us and then let you go? No."

"Never," the woman said.

"You've made a promise, and we're both going to make sure you keep to it."

"Yes, sir," the young man said. "I'm sorry, sir."

"Obey your masters with deep respect and fear," Peterson said. "Serve them sincerely as you would Christ. Try to please them all the time, not just when they are watching you."

"Amen," the woman said.

"Shut up," Peterson said and turned to swipe at her with his gigantic hand.

The young man picked up his fork with quivering fingers and took another bite of his potato, which had all the flavor and consistency of old glue.

"Good," Peterson said with a nod. He crossed his arms. "What do you think?"

"Sir?" the young man said.

"When do you think you might be ready to begin your work? We're not gonna stand for you living here too long without paying your keep."

"I-I think maybe," the young man stuttered, "maybe in two days?"

Peterson smiled. "Two days. I'll hold you to that."

"Yes, sir."

"I won't let you make yourself out to be a liar, I can guarantee that, believe me."

The young man nodded.

"You wanna know what you'll hafta do?"

The young man raised his head, but kept his eyes downcast when he answered. "What is that?"

"You're gonna dig. Gonna dig me a great big hole. Think you can do that?"

"Yes, sir."

"Let's hope so. Two days. Promise me."

"I promise."

"Look at me when you say that. I can't trust a man says he'll do something for you when he won't even look you in the eye."

The young man looked up. Peterson fixed him with a cold glare. The woman smiled as she had in the upstairs room. Although her forehead was a bit swollen, it had returned to its normal color.

"I promise you," the young man said.

"In Jesus' name."

"In Jesus' name, I promise you."

"Amen," the woman said.

"Goddammit!" Peterson shouted. He stood and grabbed her by the throat. He slapped her hard across the face and threw her to the floor. "When I say shut up, I want you to shut up!" he shouted. The woman lay inert, her hands in no way shielding herself, her face upturned toward her husband. He slapped her once more before he moved away from her body. She made no sound of pain or discomfort. She remained in the same position until her husband had resumed his seat. Then she stood, brushed herself off, and once more took her place behind his chair.

"Don't ever ask when you can leave here," Peterson said in a tone that implied nothing out of the ordinary had transpired. "I will tell you when your work is finished. I will know when it is paid off, and then I will tell you."

The young man nodded. "Yes, sir."

"You got anything else to say?"

236

The young man looked at him. He felt small and helpless in his giant white shroud. Peterson looked at him with a gaze of entitled expectation.

"Thank you," the young man said.

Peterson nodded.

The night passed slowly as the young man lay in bed and contemplated his situation. His initial plan – to escape that first night, despite the continuing pain that made swift motion impossible – had been put asunder by a number of circumstances. First, his door remained locked at all times. Second, the lone window in the room in which he was staying was far too small to accommodate his passage, despite his slim frame. Most important, however, was that the woman had taken his nightshirt, leaving him once again naked. She stood on the opposite side of the door as he disrobed, one waiting arm extended into the room, hand open, fingers wriggling.

"I'm sure your clothes are dry," she said. "I'll bring them up to you."

She never returned, and after more than twenty minutes of waiting the young man heaved a sigh, switched off the light and got into bed.

Night crept into day, and by six o'clock the young man was roused from his fitful sleep by the sound of his door being unlocked. He opened his tired eyes and rubbed them. He tried to sit, but his muscles were so tense it hurt to move, so he lay there, defenseless like a turtle on its back.

The woman poked her head into the room. Despite the limited sunlight, the young man could see that she was smiling. "You're awake," she said in a soft voice.

The young man nodded.

"Did you have a good sleep?" She stepped inside and closed the door. She was dressed in a nightshirt and her thick brown hair hung in one long, ropelike braid.

The young man shook his head.

"How are you feeling?" the woman asked as she approached him.

The young man tried again to sit, but could not. "Sore," he whispered.

"I should think so," the woman said and sat on the bed with her back to the door. "You had quite an ordeal yesterday." She stroked his cheek with the back of her hand, and he gave an involuntary twitch. "Do you feel any better?" She held her hand to his face with tenderness.

"I think my back is a bit stiff. A bit more than yesterday, I'm afraid."

"Well, once my husband heads outside, I'll run you a nice hot bath, and you can have a good soak. That should help a little bit, don't you think?"

The woman still was smiling. It struck the young man as odd. It was not a smile that seemed in any way flirtatious, or even happy. It was fixed, blank, and it made him nervous.

"Thank you," he said. "That should help."

"Yes." The woman slid her hand from his face to his chest. The young man kept the blankets tucked tight beneath his chin, to prevent any actual contact.

"I was wondering," he said, "would you be able to bring me my clothes?"

"Of course." The woman did not move.

"When?"

"After breakfast. My husband says he's not going to carry you around the house anymore, so you'll have to eat up here. And I can help you down the stairs when it's time for your bath."

The young man nodded. A feeling of dread crept over him. "Thank you for everything. You have both been so kind in all that you've done for me."

The woman nodded once. Her voice was grave. "It's the right thing to do."

Peterson's voice rang out in the hall. "How is he today?"

"The twerp said he's even stiffer than yesterday," the woman yelled back and rose from the bed.

Peterson kicked open the door, which banged against the empty wall. He was dressed in overalls, boots and a work shirt, all of which were stained with what looked like dried clay.

"I don't care how you feel the day after tomorrow, you're going to start work if I have to tie you to a tree so you can stand."

"You might just have to," the woman spat.

Peterson shook his head with disgust.

"Work hard and be a leader; be lazy and never succeed."

"Praise Jesus," the woman said and folded her hands.

"Get my breakfast, dammit."

The woman left the room and her husband remained, staring at the young man.

"You got anything to say?"

The young man found it difficult to speak.

"I was just telling your wife how grateful I am for everything—"

"You damn well better be. You think you'll be ready to work the day after tomorrow?"

"Yes. Absolutely."

Peterson's mouth wrinkled into an ugly scowl.

"If a man will not work, he shall not eat," he said, and closed the door. The key turned hard in the lock.

239

About an hour later, the woman returned fully dressed, carrying a tray of food: Eggs, toast and coffee. She sat in the chair beside the bed and balanced the tray in her lap. With quick movements, she cut a piece off of one of the eggs and held the fork before the young man's face.

"You don't need to do this," he said. "I think I can manage all right."

"You just lie back and let me help," the woman said as she brought the fork to his mouth.

The young man chewed. The egg was runny, but good. The woman held out a piece of toast and the young man bit into it.

"Jacob just went out."

"Does he always start this early?"

The woman nodded and held out the cup of coffee. The young man blew, cooling it, and sipped.

"He's a hard worker. He always has been. Are you a hard worker, too?"

"Yes, I think so."

"I'm glad. I'm glad you're here. I'm glad you're able to help us."

"Pardon my asking, but what will I be helping you with? I know your husband said that I would be doing some digging, but what is it for? Is there some kind of project he's working on?"

The woman pursed her lips and fed him some more egg.

"I promised Jacob I wouldn't say."

"It's not anything bad, is it?" the young man asked after swallowing.

"I can't tell you," the woman said and pushed the toast toward him. "He told me I couldn't tell you. He made me promise. I can't break a promise."

"That's fine," the young man said as she put the toast in his mouth. "I don't expect you to do something like that." He began to cough on the last word as the crumbs began to tickle against his throat.

The woman's smile returned.

"You're hungry, aren't you?"

The young man nodded, chewing.

"I knew you would be."

Soon the plate was empty. The woman took the tray with both hands and stood.

"Okay," she said. "I'll go put these dishes away, and I'll be right back to help you downstairs." She turned to go.

"Wait–"

The woman stopped, and looked back at him.

"Would you be able to bring that nightshirt I wore yesterday? Just for when we go downstairs?"

The woman smiled and nodded. "Of course I will," she said, and left the room.

When the woman returned ten minutes later, her hands were empty.

"The tub is full, and the water is hot, so let's get you down there."

"But the nightshirt–" the young man began.

The woman shook her head. "You don't need it. We'll just be going downstairs. No one will see you." She walked to the bed and unceremoniously pulled back the covers. The young man's bruises had darkened, making them appear even more painful than before, and the woman clicked her tongue and shook her head. "You poor man," she said.

The young man covered himself with his hands and, flinching, swung his legs to the side of the bed. His muscles ached and he gave a sharp gasp when he moved, pausing a moment before letting his feet touch the floor.

"Let me help you," the woman said. She approached him, placing her hands on his shoulders. "When I count to three, try and stand," she said. "One, two, three –"

The young man groaned when he stood. The woman held him tight.

"Now put your arm around my shoulder."

The young man complied, keeping his other hand cupped over his genitals. The woman placed one hand over the arm that was draped across her shoulder, and wrapped the other around his side, holding her palm flat against his stomach.

"Okay, now," the woman said, "let's take a step."

She stepped forward, and the young man hopped on one leg after her.

"Good. Now the other one."

Again they each took one halting step and rested a moment.

"How does it feel?"

"Painful."

The woman nodded. "You'll feel better after your bath."

Descending the stairs was a complicated process which took three minutes to complete, with the young man gasping and wincing with each jolt forward and the woman's strong arms supporting him. When they reached the bathroom the woman opened the door and a wall of steam poured out.

"I hope it's hot enough," the woman said. "I thought it would be good for you. The hotter, the better."

"Yes. Thank you."

They were blanketed by the heat as they entered the room. They approached the tub and the man lifted his leg and placed it in the hot water. He closed his eyes and grunted.

"Is it too hot?"

"No. I just have to get used to it."

He stood there for a moment and took some deep breaths.

"All right, let's get your other leg in there."

The young man balanced himself on her thick shoulders and brought his other leg into the tub. He sighed, and remained standing. Soon he removed his hands from the woman's shoulders, and placed them onto the rim of the tub, and lowered himself with slow satisfaction into the water. He closed his eyes and cupped his hands, filling them, and rubbed his face. He had long since forgotten to hide himself.

"There," the woman said. "I'm sure that's better."

"It is. Thank you."

The woman smiled. "I'll be back in later to check on you."

The water was wonderful. It was the first real bath the young man had taken in more than a week, and it felt good just to lay there and let his tired muscles absorb the dense heat. He stretched out and sank down to his chin, keeping still and thinking of nothing. Every so often he brought his hands out of the water and wiped them across his face in a backward motion, but soon he ceased to even do this, and just stayed still, submerged and content.

When he opened his eyes again, he saw that he was not alone.

"You fell asleep," said the woman, who was watching him from the closed lid of the toilet.

His body limbered from its sustained period of palliation, the young man sat partway in the tub, hiding himself with his hands.

"Don't worry," the woman said in a soothing tone. Rising, she took a bar of soap from the sink and brought it to the tub. The young man remained in the same protective position. The woman kneeled beside him and dipped the soap into the cooling water, and began to roll it in her hands.

"Sit up a little," she said.

The young man didn't budge. He stared at her, unsure of what to do.

"Sit up, I said. I want to help clean you off." When he still refused to move, she added, "It's all right. My husband won't be back inside for at least two more hours yet."

With suspicion, the young man sat, still guarding his penis. The woman pulled the bar of soap from the water and continued to spin it in her hands. When she had worked it into a thick lather, she set the soap on the floor at her side and rubbed her hands together. She smiled as she brought her hands to the young man's chest and began to scrub it up and down. Her hands were large, and their skin was thick like leather. Neither of them spoke. The young man looked away from her. She began to hum. The sound of it echoed off the bare walls. Then she stopped.

"Lift your arms," she ordered.

The young man looked at her.

"Lift your arms."

"Why?"

"I want to wash under them."

"You don't have to. I can do it."

"Don't argue with me." Her smile fell and her tone grew dark. "Now lift your arms."

The young man obeyed, hooking them in right angles at the elbows as water drip-dropped off, and into the tub. He focused on the peeling white paint that coated the ceiling, and the smell of the soap.

"Keep them just like that," the woman said brightly as she grabbed the soap and worked it some more in her hands. After a few twirls in her fingers, she let it drop into the water and brought her hands to his sides. She slid them in slow strokes along his ribcage, lingering over the injured areas.

"How does it feel?"

"Fine."

"Did you crack any of them?"

"I don't think so. They're just bruised."

The woman dipped her hands in the water and rinsed the soap off the young man's torso. She submerged them a second time, and held them there as she shifted and looked into his eyes.

"Okay, that's enough," the young man said.

"Shh," the woman said and moved her hand. "Just relax."

Peterson had just opened the front door of the house when his wife and the young man emerged from the bathroom. Still naked, the young man gasped in alarm, but the woman acted as if nothing was out of the ordinary and continued helping him to the stairs.

"How is he?"

"Whinin' all the time," the woman said with a look of revulsion. "He can't even get up and down the stairs without my help."

Peterson made a face. "You wouldn't be much to look at, even without all them bruises. Puny, puny. You sure you can help me out here?"

"Yes," the young man sputtered. He tried to hop toward the stairs, but the woman held him still.

"Are you really sure? This is real work. It's hard, physical. Man's work. We aren't gonna be plantin' daisies, I can assure you of that."

"Yes," the young man said. "Honestly I can."

"You better. Cursed is the one who trusts in man, who depends on flesh for his strength."

"Amen," the woman said.

"Get that fool upstairs so you can get back down here and fix me something to eat."

The trip up the stairs, while still painful, was easier than the hobbling voyage down. Back in the small room, the woman helped the young man get in bed, and then turned to leave.

"Wait," the young man said.

The woman turned and looked at him.

"Could you by any chance give me my clothes? I would like to be able to put something on."

The woman paused before she answered.

"No. You won't be going anywhere until the day after tomorrow, and besides, it'll be another hot one today. You just stay as you are."

She smiled before leaving, and locked the door after she closed it.

Night fell. The young man did not leave the room again for the rest of the day, and after spending the majority of it in a reclined position he found sleep impossible. The bed grew more uncomfortable by the hour. At the foot of the mattress was a hole, out of which protruded the end of a spring. No matter how the young man positioned himself, he could not avoid touching it. He sat up and looked at the moon through the window. Careful not to make noise, he stepped onto the floor and stretched. He walked to the window and pressed his face to the glass and looked out on the spread. There wasn't much to be seen: A barn, two or three small sheds and the old pickup, all colored a pale, watery blue by the moon.

The young man walked to the door and kneeled, eyeing the keyhole. He knew he was locked in, as he had heard the key turn when the woman left after she fed him dinner.

He stood and walked to the bed and pulled up the sheet, exposing the curved end of the spring. Brushing aside some clumps of excelsior, he grabbed it with both hands and began to work the spring back and forth, continuing as the metal grew flimsy and eventually broke off.

Returning to the door, the young man inserted the end of the spring and twisted. The lock popped and he put his hand on the doorknob, turned it and stepped outside. He left the spring sticking out of the keyhole.

It was not easy to see in the hall. All the doors were closed, and the only light that showed was leaking up from the stairway. The young man heard snoring from what he assumed was Peterson and the woman's room. It sounded like it came from a pair of animals. He crept down the hall toward the stairs, pausing before he began his descent. The stairs were old, and his previous assisted trips up and down them were noisy, creaking affairs. Spreading his legs, he placed his right foot on the first step as close to the wall as possible. Slowly, carefully, he shifted his weight as he stepped down with his left foot, which he kept close to the other wall. It took him a total of five minutes, but he made it to the first floor in total silence. His heart pounded and his stomach bubbled. His body still was sore, but he did not care. There was not much time.

The young man searched room by room for his clothes, but his efforts were futile. He failed even to find a bed sheet or a large towel with which to cover himself. The entire floor was devoid of small towels or handkerchiefs, as if every scrap of cloth had been hidden to prevent his early departure. The young man returned to the bottom of the stairs and gazed up at the awaiting darkness. He sat on the floor a moment with his chin resting on his knees and tried to convince himself to go back up.

Ten minutes later, he closed the bedroom door, turned the piece of bedspring and clicked the lock shut. He carried the spring with him to the mattress and sat down.

The bed was not empty.

"Shh," the woman whispered. "Don't make any noise."

The young man jumped and took a step back. "What are you doing in here?" he whispered as he squinted and tried to see her.

"Be quiet. I don't want my husband to hear you."

The young man remained standing as his eyes adjusted. He could see the vague shape of the woman huddled under the blankets. It was easier to see her white nightgown, the top buttons of which were unfastened.

"Please go back to your own room," the young man whispered.

"No. I won't leave until you get in bed with me."

The young man did not move. He tried to think of some threat, but the notion died as soon as he tried to verbalize it.

"Get in bed," the woman ordered. "If you don't, I'll tell my husband you tried to escape."

The young man stared at her.

"I'm not asking you again."

With a sigh, the young man climbed back onto the bed and stretched out beside the woman.

"Get under the covers," she said.

The young man obeyed, and the woman pulled him close, covering his face with wet kisses. Her breath was foul and her hands gripped him too tight. Panting, she took him by the ears and pulled his head to her chest and he thought he would be smothered by the weighty globes of her flesh. She giggled and cooed and tickled his sides before she wrapped her arms around his body and flung him on top of herself.

"All right," she said as she cinched her nightshirt midway up her belly. "You know what to do."

The next morning it was decided that since the young man could walk well enough without assistance, he would begin to pay off his debt. After breakfast, Peterson commanded the young man to follow him outside, where they walked to one of the sheds, a hand-built structure with a thin coat of light brown paint. Peterson slid open the door, reached inside, pulled out a shovel and handed it to the young man.

"Come on," he said, motioning with one arm.

They made their way to a grove of trees behind the house. Still smarting from his injuries, the young man struggled to keep up with Peterson's long strides. He said nothing, as every word he spoke seemed to infuriate the man.

"Hurry it up," Peterson barked when he noticed the young man lagging behind. "You got a lot to do today."

"Yes, sir. I'm sorry, sir."

"Don't talk to me."

The young man scanned the landscape as he walked. The brief rains had not been enough to rejuvenate the grass and the trees, and everything was the same sickly brown it had been two days previous.

Peterson stopped at the edge of the trees.

"All right, here we are," he said. "Start diggin'."

The young man cleared his throat.

"Sir?"

"I told you not to talk to me. If you have something to say, you think about it first, and then if you still think you need to say it, you raise your hand. If I wanna hear what you have to say, I'll call on you. Have you been to school?"

"Yes, sir."

"I said don't talk," Peterson said with rising anger. "Pay attention and listen to the sayings of the wise. Now, if I ask you a question that you can say yes or no to, just nod, you got that?"

The young man nodded.

"Good. Do you still have somethin' to say?"

The young man nodded again.

Peterson rolled his eyes. "All right, what is it?"

"When you say dig, how do you want me to go about it? Are there specific dimensions you want me to go follow?"

"You ever seen a grave?"

The young man paused. With some hesitation, he nodded.

"Dig me one of those. Make it deep, too. It ain't of no use to me if it isn't deep enough."

The young man stood and thought for a bit, shovel in hand, before Peterson spoke again.

"Start it now!" he shouted. "Come on!"

With quick, frantic movements, the young man broke ground. Peterson watched him dig several shovelfuls, a look of dull, suspicious hatred on his face. The young man avoided staring back, keeping all of his focus on his work.

"I'll be back," Peterson said. His voice caused the young man to jump. "I got something to do. You keep at it."

The young man watched him as he walked to one of the sheds. The urge to flee grew strong inside him. He knew it was impossible, though. Even without the body aches, the young man doubted his ability to outrun Peterson, and he had the added disadvantage of being unfamiliar with the terrain around the house. Grunting, he pushed the shovel through the turf and then swung the clods of dirt and dead grass over his shoulder.

"Be careful where you throw that stuff!" Peterson shouted from the open door of the shed. "You're gonna have to gather it all up when you fill the hole again!"

The young man felt a sense of relief when he heard these words. He scooped another shovelful and deposited its contents in a pile at his side. The sun was hot. He began to sweat through his shirt, which soon plastered itself to his back. Before long the hole was finished, and the young man heard the sound of Peterson's plodding footsteps, which slowed as he drew nearer.

"Okay, you can sit down a minute."

The young man set the shovel beside the hole and walked a few steps to the shade, where he turned and saw Peterson staring at him. They both stayed that way for some time, motionless, watching each other.

"I told you to sit. It'll be your last chance for a while."

The young man sat with his hands on the ground and his knees bent, ready to spring up again as fast as possible.

Jacob remained standing and staring. He frowned and crossed his arms.

"I heard all about it."

Startled, the young man held his breath before he responded.

"What do you mean?"

Peterson kicked the shovel and sent it bouncing into the hole.

"Did I say you could talk?" he shouted. "Did you hear me give you permission to say one word?"

The young man shook his head. His stomach felt as though it weighed one hundred pounds and he tasted a sour tingling beneath his tongue.

"Through insolence comes nothing but strife," Peterson said. He took a deep breath, and tried to control his rage. "My wife told me what you tried to do. She told me that yesterday when she bathed you, you tried to force yourself upon her. And again last night before she locked the door, how you tried to encourage her to partake in impure acts." His face broke into a disgusted grimace. "We saved your life, gave you food and shelter, and this is how you choose to repay that service?"

The young man's upper lip began to twitch uncontrollably.

"Everyone who looks at a woman with lustful intent has already committed adultery with her in his heart."

"I didn't–" the young man began.

"I did not give you permission to speak!" Peterson shouted. He leaped over the hole and rushed the young man. "Speak unless I say that you can, just do me that one honor. You've betrayed me in every other way, so just listen to me now."

"But I swear I didn't–"

"So you're accusing my wife of lying? My wife is a liar, is that what you're telling me?" He held out his giant hands and flexed the fingers slowly, his eyes simmering.

The young man kept quiet.

Peterson took one step back. "I don't know what I'm going to do about this," he said. "But something must be done. You give me little choice."

The young man listened, his insides churning.

"But right now I need you to assist me. We'll decide what to do with you when we're finished." He turned around and began walking. "Follow me," he ordered.

The young man scrambled to his feet and walked several paces behind. Peterson swung his arms and clenched his fists and the young man thought they looked like a pair of great stones. When they arrived at the shed Peterson stopped at the door.

"You first," he said.

Swallowing, the young man went inside the small building. Upon entering, he was knocked back by the thick stench of death. He covered his mouth and struggled to breathe as Peterson entered behind him.

"That's it," Peterson said and pointed to an object in the corner that looked like a heap of rags under a white sheet. He pushed past the young man and grabbed the sheet at one end, bunching it in both hands like the end of a sack, before motioning for the young man to join him at the opposite side. He was careful as he copied Peterson's handling of the sheet. He was not sure what it contained, but he knew he did not want to spill its contents.

"Okay, now lift," Peterson said.

The young man complied with a grunt. The horrible smell made inhalation torturous. It was like kissing garbage.

"Start walkin'," Peterson said.

The young man moved out the door. He took several deep breaths when the sunlight hit him, but it did little good. The odor was so strong and so close that it felt like he had bathed in it. He stumbled, but kept moving.

"Be careful!" Peterson shouted. "That's my mother you almost dropped! You show some respect!"

The young man nodded. His nostrils remained clogged with the stink. It was difficult to walk. It was difficult to think.

"It wouldn't surprise me one bit if you had dropped her, either. Seems exactly like some fool stupid thing you would do. Stupid, worthless animal. It would just fit with the picture I got of you. She dies the day you come here, and you drop her when it comes time to bury her. Yeah, that would fit just right, I'd say."

The young man focused on walking.

"Died that morning. Just brought the doctor back to town when I found your sorry carcass, then I brought you home and put you in her bed. Shame I ever picked you up, too, if you ask me. Thought I was doin' such a good thing, too. That's what I get for it. That is what I get."

The men panted in the heat. The slick scratches of dead prairie grass scuttled beneath their shoes with each step, and the leaves on the trees crackled as the wind blew through them. After what seemed like years, they reached the hole. They stopped walking.

"Set her down before we put her in."

They put the bundle at the edge of the hole and rested.

"Shoot, it's hot," Peterson said as he wiped the back of his neck. He took the shovel out of the hole and tossed it away. He looked down at the misshapen lump at his feet and folded his hands. Without prompting, the young man did likewise. Peterson spoke quickly, devoid of emotion, his words flowing together like those of an auctioneer: "The Lord is my shepherd, I shall not want. He maketh me to lie down in green pastures, He leadeth me beside the still waters. He restoreth my soul; He leadeth me in the paths of righteousness for his name's sake. Yes, though I walk through the valley of the shadow of death, I will fear no evil; for thou art with me; thy rod and thy staff they comfort me."

The young man was surprised to find himself mouthing the words in silence.

"Thou preparest a table before me in the presence of mine enemies; thou anointest my head with oil; my cup runneth over. Surely goodness and mercy follow me all the days of my life; and I will dwell in the house of the Lord forever. Amen."

Peterson opened his eyes and stared at the hole. "All right, let's put her in there." The men eased the body into the grave and stood watching it for a time before Peterson spoke again.

"Cover it up." Turning to go, he added, "I'll come get you when you're through."

The young man used careful movements as he covered the body with dirt. He watched Peterson as he worked. Peterson had returned to the shed, where he found another shovel and began to dig a shallow, circular hole near its entrance. The young man tried to remain calm. He watched as Peterson leaned the shovel against the shed and gathered a makeshift bundle dry grass and twigs, and some large pieces of wood. He squatted at the hole. First he put in the grass and smaller sticks. Then he brought out a book of matches and lit the little pile. Flames flared up and he put a sizeable log on the top. The young man continued to fill the grave, taking his time, watching. Bitter white smoke streamed from the pile and drifted to the gravesite like fog. The young man's nose burned. Peterson waited until the log was fully engulfed, and then stood and waited for it to burn down. The young man was finishing his work when Peterson turned from the fire and began to walk back to him.

"All right, come with me," he said upon arriving.

The young man took his shovel and followed.

"I suppose you're wonderin' when you'll get to leave."

The young man nodded.

"Let's take a look at this. It's the third day now that you been with us, so you owe us three days right there. We fed you and gave you shelter, so you have to pay us for that. We kept you clean and allowed you to regain your health, so you have to pay us for that. So, I figure you owe us about two weeks' work."

The young man nodded again.

Peterson stopped walking and jabbed the young man's chest with his meaty index finger. "But you tried to take advantage of my wife, and when I called you on it, you denied it ever happened. As far as I can tell, there's no payin' back for somethin' like that. You follow me?"

The young man did not move. Peterson placed his hand on the young man's shoulder and gripped it.

"You belong to us now."

With that, he punched the young man on the side of the head and knocked him cold.

The first thing of which the young man became aware when he regained consciousness was that his wrists and ankles were bound with scratchy yellow rope and his arms were stretched to the ceiling of the barn and his legs were spread apart. He felt the tickling of a fly walking around his navel and realized that his shirt was off. Another fly buzzed past his pubic hair and he found his pants were pulled to his knees as low as they could go. He heard a snorting sound, and he jerked his head to see a tall brown horse watching nearby. The horse flared its wide nostrils and shook its head up and down and threw its long black mane. The young man began to struggle, but soon Peterson appeared, and he stopped.

"That's right. You just stay still while I get this ready."

"What are you going to do?" The young man was seized with panic when he realized he had not been given permission to speak.

Peterson arched an eyebrow. "You're our property now. Understand? That means you live out here in the barn. You behave like an animal, and that's just the way we'll treat you."

"You can't leave me tied up like this."

"I'll cut you loose when we're finished," Peterson said as he turned to leave.

"Where you going? What are you going to do?"

Near the barn door was a workbench, above which hung an array of tools off bulky wooden dowels. Approaching it, Peterson reached out and pulled down one of the tools. He shielded it from the young man's view as he made his way back. Stopping three feet from him, Peterson lifted his arm and held the tool close to the young man's face.

"Know what this is?"

The tool glimmered in the limited light. It had long handles that spread like a pair of pliers, with a ratchet jutting out from the bottom of one and a rounded clamp on the top. An emasculator. Peterson twirled it in his hand like a cowboy with a six-shooter.

The young man began to struggle, but the knots binding his wrists and legs only increased in tightness. His back began to spasm, and he felt like he had to defecate. He stopped moving, and tried to think. His stomach muscles twitched, along with his eyes. His ears rang, and although he did not realize it, he had begun to whimper. The horse watched him with a nervous look, shifting its weight on its front legs.

"Stop that, now, you're spookin' the horse!"

The young man paid no attention and pulled at the ropes until it felt like his shoulders would dislocate themselves.

"I can't do this when you're squirmin' around like that. Keep it up and I'll cut the whole thing off."

The young man grunted and pulled until Peterson eased the emasculator through one of his belt loops. He shook his head and lifted one finger before he left the barn again. The young man put all his strength into pulling on the ropes that held his arms, but it did no good. His eyes began to water and he leaned back and stared at the high ceiling, where there was a window, and the sun poked through in a solid shaft of orange.

When Peterson returned he was carrying a long branding iron, the end of which was a circle with an X through it, like the crosshairs in the scope of a rifle. The iron glowed red and the young man could see the waves of heat as they rose off of it. He could smell the heat, too, and his mouth went dry. He began to sputter but Peterson held up his free hand.

"Don't bother," he said. "I've made a decision and you can't talk me out of it." He began to walk toward the young man. "It didn't have to happen this way, you know? If you had just behaved like a decent Christian we wouldn't be here right now. I'm sure you don't believe me, but it pains me to have to do this." He crossed behind the young man and stopped. "You are now my slave, and I place this mark upon you as a labeling of my property, but also as punishment. Every sin that a man doeth is without the body; but he that committeth fornication sinneth against his own body. You brought this on yourself."

At that moment the young man felt a scalding, blinding pain unequal to anything he had known before. He could hear the small of his back as it sizzled against the iron and he smelled the smoke that arose as his flesh cooked. Writhing against his restraints, he tried to scream, but it died in his throat. It felt like all the air had left his body and he could do nothing but shake and choke and try to breathe. He could feel nothing but the iron. Peterson stepped back and set the iron on the ground before he walked to the horse – which had reared up and begun to scream – and attempted to calm it. "It's all right," the young man heard him say. "Nothin' to worry about. Nothin' worth gettin' all upset about."

The young man awoke lying face-down on the straw-covered floor of the barn. He was wet. The water was cold and it sent piercing stabs into his back when it reached his wound. He found he could scream again, but he had trouble moving. Somebody set a bucket on the ground several inches from his head, and he rolled his eyes to see Peterson standing over him.

"You awake now, slave?"

The young man moaned. His arms lay lifeless at his sides. His thumb rested against his naked hip and he snaked it over his leg and began to feel and cup.

"Yeah, they're still there. I want you to be awake for that one. Wide awake. Now listen. I want you to go out by the shed and put that fire out. Just cover it up with the dirt that's sitting there. I left the shovel nearby."

The young man began to inch his arms toward his chest so he could push himself up from the ground. It hurt to move very fast, and he heard Peterson groan with impatience.

"Come on. Get out there and get busy, I still got more for you to do before the day's over."

The young man's arms shook as he tried to get to his feet. His legs were like noodles and the slightest motion made it feel as though his back would split down the center.

"I said get up!" Peterson shouted, and tramped over to where the young man lay. He picked him up by the shoulders and set him in a standing position. The young man began to cry.

"You knock that off right now. And don't you go blamin' me for anything that's happened here. Don't have no more sense than a dog."

The young man almost collapsed again when Peterson let him go. His vision was blurred, but he knew he was being watched. He thought this may have been what was keeping him upright.

"Now pull up your britches and get to work."

The young man looked down and saw that he was still exposed. He hooked his useless fingers in the waistband of his trousers and pulled, gasping at the feel of the material against his skin. Shaking, he zipped up and fastened the snap.

"Get out there. I'm not tellin' you again."

The young man wandered into the sunlight. Nothing felt real. He saw the smoke from the fire pit and began to move to it in faltering forward lurches.

"That's right," Peterson said. "Get on over there, slave."

The young man shuddered.

"Wait a minute, slave."

He stopped.

"Turn and look at me when I talk to you," Peterson said.

With slow, excruciating movements, the young man turned toward him. Peterson smiled, hands on his hips. "I'm just gonna go on into the barn here and take care of somethin', but I'll be back soon. All right?"

The young man nodded.

"Have any idea what I'm workin' on?"

He shook his head.

"I got an old table and a couple of straps, and I'm gonna jerry-rig something that'll keep you tied down. You get me?"

The young man nodded again.

"Good," Peterson said. "Now get on over there."

The young man looked to the fire pit and started to move once more. He wished for a gun, to shoot himself. Or a knife to stab himself with. The wound on his back pulsed and oozed. The wind beat against it, and he let loose a series of ragged gasps. It felt like cold water on a cavity. He continued toward the hole, his eye on the shovel. When he reached the hole, he squatted and the skin of his back felt tight enough to tear. He grabbed the shovel and held it, deep in thought.

By the time Peterson emerged from the barn, flaming patches dotted the grass where the young man had deposited the hot coals.

"Slave!" he shouted. "Where are you?"

He ran toward the spreading fire and began to stomp at it with his boots, but it did no good. The grass was like hay, and each stomp served only to spread the fire, which was in turn fed by the wind. Peterson whirled around to the shed to find another shovel, and when he did he saw stars.

The last thing he saw was the figure of the young man holding the shovel in his hands like a club. He brought the handle down with repeated blows against Peterson's head, and wore a detached smile as Peterson felt the flames envelop his body.

The young man opened the door and stepped inside the house. The sitting room was empty and quiet. His Bible lay facedown on the sofa next to a pair of Mrs. Parker's white cotton gloves, which were folded against each other like a nesting bird. He went to the first-floor bathroom and washed himself with soap and hot water. When he left the room he heard the sound of footsteps upstairs and began to climb, silent and slow, hands at his sides. When he reached the top he entered the hallway. He peered into Nathan's room, where Mrs. Parker was busy adjusting the top blanket on the bed. Her back was to him as she pulled it down an inch on the side so that no part of it extended lower than any other. When it was as even as she could get it, she stood and moved around the bed to compare.

"Doesn't have to be perfect, you know," he said as he entered the room.

Mrs. Parker jumped and pulled the blanket to her face. Then she threw it to the floor with a scowl.

"Look what you made me do!"

"Sorry, I thought you heard me."

"I most certainly did not."

Bending over, she took the blanket by its corner and picked it up. After she spread it over the mattress in a haphazard way she walked to the foot of the bed and began to smooth the blanket where it had been tucked under.

The young man went to the desk and sat in the chair. "Whatcha doin'?"

"Making the bed, can't you see? I washed the sheets and now I'm making the bed." She knelt to make a closer examination of it.

"Why?"

"I didn't think you would be using it again."

"I see."

She put down her hands and cast a glance over her shoulder. "You won't be, will you?"

"Course not," he said with a chuckle.

She grinned and went back to her work. When the end of the blanket was as smooth as a sheet of paper she went back to the side of the bed and began adjusting once more.

The young man turned in his chair and looked at the desk. It was a smooth light brown with a heavy canvas protector on top. A row of books with olive green covers were lined on it against the wall. They were, most of them, Rover Boys titles or Tom Swift, with a few Penrods thrown in. He put his hand on one of the drawers close to his knee and pulled but it did not budge. Elbow on the desk he put his head in his hand and watched Mrs. Parker as she stood and eyed the covers on the bed.

"It looks fine from here," he said.

"It has to be right."

"It looks right."

"Men don't know about these things," she said without looking his way.

"Could be," he shrugged.

"Did you have a nice walk?"

"Yep."

"Where did you go?"

"Usual places."

"Where do you go?"

"Just around. You can walk clear across town without getting tired."

"Do you meet anyone?" Her eyes remained focused on the blankets, to which she gave miniscule tugs.

"Nope. I walk by myself."

"You know what I mean." Her tone was no different than if she were asking him the time of day.

He sat up straight and crossed his arms. "I don't think I do."

Mrs. Parker put down her hands. She continued to face forward. "I thought that was why you came back. To apologize."

"I don't know what–"

Her head whipped to the side and her eyes narrowed. "Gloria. I know all about it. I know enough. I know it wasn't just her. We both know I do. Don't we."

The young man's mouth hung open as if he were about to speak.

"Why did you come back?"

He sighed. "It's you and Nathan. I had to tell you. You're throwing it away. When was the last time you saw him more than a few hours? And the grandkids – this is it. You get a chance to see them, I don't. Kids are wrong sometimes, that's the way it is. You hafta just let it go. You don't even like talkin' about him. That's crazy. That's what I had to tell you. Keep it up and you'll regret it. I know you will, you gotta believe that."

Mrs. Parker sat on the rug and curled her legs to the side. Her eyes scanned the floor and she pretended to adjust one of her hairpins. The young man got off the chair and crawled toward her. Floorboards creaked when he sat beside her, an inch from touching. She did not look at him. Tears began to form in her eyes and she broke the silence with a series of wet, sloppy sniffs.

"I'm sorry, Edith. It's gone on for too long."

When he reached out to feel her arm she slapped his hand away. Before he could react she fell into him and he felt the wetness of her tears and the slimy discharge from her nose as it soaked into his shirt near his stomach. With a shudder, he wrapped his arms around her as she began to sob.

"Shh. It'll be fine."

"You're leaving, then, aren't you?" she blubbered.

"I am. But listen, once I'm gone you won't be alone. You'll have Nathan back. You'll have his wife, you'll have the kids."

"But I won't have–" The word caught in her throat.

"Hey, you'll see me again. I know it."

Mrs. Parker did not respond. Instead, she felt his pockets until she found a handkerchief, which she pulled out and rubbed across her eyes and nose as if they were clogged with sand. When her face was dry she dropped the cloth and it came to rest on the young man's knee. She picked it up again and tossed it away and placed her hand where it had been. She never wanted to remove it.

"I am sorry, Edith. I'm sorry for everything. I know that doesn't help much, but I do mean it."

When he finished speaking she lunged for him, her lips pressed firm against his, and began to undo his buttons.

An hour later Mrs. Parker, still laying on top of him, snored like a dog as a slick trickle of saliva dripped from her open mouth and pooled on his chest. Bringing his fingers together in a point, he jabbed her in the side before he dropped his arm and closed his eyes. Snorting, she raised her head and gave a few sleepy blinks. "What is it?"

The young man brought his hand to his mouth and mimicked a yawn. "Hmm?"

"Look what I did," Mrs. Parker said and wiped his chest with her hand and brushed her chin against his shoulder.

"What? What is it?"

"I slobbered all over you."

"That's all right."

She put her head back down. "When are you leaving?"

"Friday night."

"Do you really have to?"

"Yes."

She did not move. A few seconds passed and the young man shifted beneath the weight of his body.

"I'm sorry," he said. "My back."

"Oh," she said, sitting, and pulled her skirt below her knees. "Does it hurt?"

"It's just sore, a little stiff."

He stood and buttoned his shirt. His trousers were gathered about his ankles. Mrs. Parker said nothing, and reached out to run her hand along his shin and up his thigh. When his shirt was buttoned he put his hands on his hips and waited. She withdrew her hand and blushed when she noticed the overly patient expression on his face.

"Excuse me," she said.

The young man grinned and bent over, grabbing his trousers and drawers, Mrs. Parker reached under the bed and grabbed her underpants and pulled them halfway up her legs. Putting one hand on the floor and the other on the mattress, she pushed, struggling to stand.

"Help me up."

"Say please."

"Please, before I fall."

The young man grabbed her under the arms and lifted with a grunt. When she was standing he tickled her and she swatted him on the arm. Then she pulled up her underpants the rest of the way. Glancing back, she surveyed the blankets on the bed and she sighed and knelt and began to straighten them. The young man crossed his arms and cleared his throat.

"I know," Mrs. Parker said. "I'll get started on supper in a minute. I just need to finish this."

The dining room was warm with the smell of steak fried in butter, and sweet caramelized onions limp and brown. There were baked potatoes polka-dotted with four-puncture marks stacked on a small white plate, and a little bowl with smooth dollops of sour cream and a dish with spoonfuls of milky yellow butter. When the young man and Mrs. Parker opened their eyes and unfolded their hands it was as if they were unable to touch any of it, that the evening would be of perfect contentment if they could simply sit and inhale.

At last the young man stood and lifted the big flat plate with the steaks and held it before Mrs. Parker.

"Which one do you want?" she asked.

"It doesn't matter, they're both about the same size. Take whichever one looks best to you."

"I can't do that. Which one do you want?"

"I already said, they're both fine. Now take one before my arm gives out."

Standing partway, she took the smaller of the two and put it on her plate. It was crisp and charred, and when she pulled out her fork the juice began to flow. The young man took his steak and sat and picked up a potato and tossed it onto his plate, flicking his hand in the air and whistling.

"Is it hot?"

"No, not at all," he answered before he blew into his hand. He lifted the plate with the other potato and held it to her. She speared the potato with her fork and dropped it onto her plate.

"Eat now, before it gets cold," she said.

He rubbed his hands together. "I want it to last."

"I can always make more."

"No. I want to remember this. Every second."

He picked up his silverware and cut into the meat. He brought his fork to his mouth and closed his eyes when he chewed. The outside was crispy and salty and warm, and the inside was soft and red like velvet. The blood spread onto the plate, soaking into the potato.

"How is it?"

"Absolutely perfect. You sure can cook."

Mrs. Parker smiled and dredged her food with salt. The young man cut his potato down the center and dipped his spoon into the butter, which he plopped into the slit. He did the same with the sour cream and the two melted and mixed in with the blood. Then he sprinkled some pepper over all of it and took another bite of steak.

"Do you really like it?"

"Already said so, didn't I?" he asked as he scooped into the potato with his fork, butter and cream drizzling off. He groaned with pleasure as he swallowed.

"I'm glad."

"How's yours taste?"

"It's good."

"It's not good. It's great."

Table clear and dishes washed they retired to the sitting room, where she nestled in close on the sofa. Her warm breath dampened his shirt and every few minutes she would lift her hand and brush his hair or caress his cheek. Her fingers were coated in a thin layer of grease-like sweat, as if she had been handling fried chicken. He twitched at her touch and his eye spasmed in a series of rapid, uncontrollable blinks.

"What time's Nathan coming tomorrow?" he asked as he took her hand and held it against his knee.

"Around ten, he said."

"He's the only one coming?"

"Yes. Why do you ask?"

"Just wondered."

The young man felt her fingers contract as she tried to release herself from his grip. She soon gave up and he smiled and closed his eyes.

"John?"

"Hmm?"

"What's it like?"

"What's what like?"

"You know..."

He opened his eyes and cocked his head. "Can't you say it?"

She shook her head. "I couldn't even ask before now."

"Why not?"

"I don't know. I was afraid."

The warmth of her body against his made him drowsy and he closed his eyes once more.

"So, what is it like?"

"I can't really say," he mumbled, on the verge of sleep. "I can't describe it. It's just – it's too... It's not that different, really."

His breathing deepened and became more regular as he relaxed. Mrs. Parker was silent for a long time.

"John?"

"Hmm?"

"I'm not afraid anymore."

He said one word before he went under. "Good."

When the young man awoke he was alone. The room was dark, apart from a single faded ray of orange light that pointed down the stars from the hallway. Above his head he heard the sound of objects hitting the floor and quick pacing footsteps, as if someone were perpetually stumbling, grabbing at whatever was available to hold them up.

He stood, slow and quiet, and waited as the noises continued. He brushed at his clothes and headed for the stairs. Placing his hand on the rail he began to climb. When he reached the bedroom he found Mrs. Parker on her knees in the closet. Most of the clothes were pulled from their hangers, and the shelves were bare. The entire room was in disarray. Drawers were pulled open, with clothes unfolded and hanging over the tops. The floor was littered with bric-a-brac scattered everywhere like colorful pebbles.

Mrs. Parker did not hear him. Her redstreaked face was wet and her lips flapped as she breathed through her open mouth and clutched an old shirt and pleated at it with her hands.

"Whatsamatter, Edith?"

Her head jerked toward him. She did not look at his face and when she answered her words came tumbling out so fast she was all but unintelligible.

"Where is it?"

"Where's what? Edith, what are you doing?"

"The picture! Where is the picture?"

"What picture? The one of me?"

"Where is it?"

"I couldn't tell you, Edith, you put it away, remember? I don't know where you put it."

Her eyes focused on him, sharp like cold steel. She said nothing.

"Anyway, you told me you didn't need it anymore. Remember, Edith?"

"I remember."

"So what's...?" His voice trailed off.

Mrs. Parker let go of the shirt and kicked it aside as she stood. She approached him with care, as if she were walking on shattered glass. The young man was rooted to his spot, breathing easy under her relentless stare, a dull, puzzled look on his face.

When she reached him Mrs. Parker held up her hands and felt his cheeks. His skin was warm and smooth. He did not speak, and she stared hard into his eyes. A long black eyelash stuck to her cheekbone, but he did not brush it away. She nodded.

"I don't need it anymore," she said with a forceful voice.

The young man nodded, too, and she stood on her toes and brought his face to hers and kissed him on the lips. She let him go and he resumed his full height. The she brought back her hand and slapped him as hard as she could. He saw a yellowy flash of white, and staggered as he held his prickling skin. It felt like hot blood.

Mrs. Parker wore a tiny smile and nodded her head once more. Then she went back to the closet and pushed the clothes away from the door with her foot.

"Let's go to bed," she said, and slammed the door.

The young man stared at the workbench. It was free of dust and cobwebs, and the tools hung on the wall behind it in a uniform fashion, straight up and down without the slightest skewing to the left or right. He heard the sound of a vehicle pull in front of the house and he crouched and edged toward the windows. When the motor shut off and the car door closed he poked up his head to see Nathan walking across the lawn to the porch. He was of average height, but he appeared to be short – inches taller than Mrs. Parker. It was his legs. They were like two fat cigars below an overlong torso. He climbed the porch steps and knocked and held his hands in front of his stomach, pulling fingers. Soon Mrs. Parker appeared. They stood and talked with quiet smiles and soft eyes. Then they went inside. Standing, the young man lit a cigarette and looked at the house. A ghostgray cloud gathered around his head like a smoggy crown before he crossed back to the workbench. He entered the house through the back door, slinking along like a tomcat. Cool breeze like fresh water licked the skin of his face and neck as he passed open windows. Before he left the kitchen he dismantled the telephone. In the sitting room he could hear them murmuring to each other. Their words remained indistinct even as he entered the sitting room and found Nathan on the sofa, Mrs. Parker in her chair. The front door was shut. Neither of them saw him until he had come around the sofa, and brought down the hammer full force on Nathan's knee. The crack was like a musket blast. Nathan opened his mouth but all that emerged was a choked gurgle, and the young man hit the same spot once more before Nathan fell to the floor grasping his leg. Mrs. Parker sprung from her chair clucking like a terrified chicken and grabbed at her son's shoulders as the young man folded his arms and waited for them to quiet down.

The swimmers stood kissing waist-deep in the water when the young man returned a few minutes later. The boy cradled the back of the girl's head in one of his hands as the other made clumsy passes from her rear to her breasts, squeezing and kneading them like bulging lumps of dough. She was motionless, nervous, with wide eyes, opening her mouth only when the boy's tongue darted past her lips.

Eyeing the pair, the young man returned to the picnic basket. Lifting it, he opened one of the flaps and looked inside. There were two egg salad sandwiches wrapped in wax paper, an unopened bag of potato chips, a pair of shiny ripe red apples, salt and pepper shakers, a handful of moist chocolate chip cookies, a bottle opener, some napkins, a bottle of lukewarm Royal Crown Cola and three chilled bottles of Grain Belt Beer. He grabbed a beer and the bottle opener and laid the basket at his feet. The bottle hissed when he popped off the cap, which he tossed into the open basket along with the opener. The beer was good, not yet too warm to give off a sour taste. When the bottle was half-empty he glanced back to the swimmers and saw the girl clamoring onto the shore.

The young man stepped behind a tree.

The girl collapsed in the grass, laughing with abandon as her chest rose and fell. Her hair was brown, medium in length, and her skin was flush from the cold water. She bounced when she spoke and the young man could see bits of dried brown grass clinging to her wet thighs. He downed what was left of the beer.

Water dripping from his arms and legs, the boy knelt next to the girl and placed his hand on her bare stomach. He sat, leaning in close to kiss her, hand sneaking between her legs as he whispered in her ear.

"No!" The girl yelped as though she had been nipped by a dog. She swatted away the boy's hand and gave his chest a playful shove before she devolved into a fit of high-pitched giggling.

The boy eased his face close to her ear and began to purr into it. His voice was faint and the only words that could be heard with clarity were "please," "you" and the repeated "love."

"That's right, tell her what she wants to hear," the young man muttered.

The girl let out a cackle. "No, I don't wanna do that."

The young man leaned toward the picnic basket and fished out the bottle opener and another Grain Belt. He opened it quietly and took a long slow drink, savoring the taste and the feel of the bubbles as they fizzed down the back of his throat. After he swallowed he returned the cap and the bottle opener to the basket.

The boy and the girl stopped speaking. His hand was again between her legs and she sat very still. Then with a sudden lurch forward she hugged him around the neck and gave him a kiss on the cheek. "Please," she said. The boy said nothing and the girl let go of him and turned her attention to the water. She wore the expression of a person standing in an elevator.

The young man finished his beer and sat down with his back against the tree. He smiled.

Eyes still averted, the girl grabbed the boy's hand and he gave a lascivious grin. Then, grunting, he stood and his erection bobbed before him in the air. He put his hands on his hips and took a step forward but the girl did not look.

"Touch it."

The girl turned her head and stared a while before she reached out her hand and felt him gingerly with the tip of her pinky finger. "It's warm!" she shrieked and pulled away her hand.

"Well, what did you think it would feel like?" he laughed.

"I don't know. I don't know what I thought."

"It's not s'posed to feel like a Popsicle or anything."

"I know that." She frowned and arched her legs so she could rest her chin on her knees.

"Put your legs back down."

"Why?"

"I wanna see you."

"You have seen me."

"I wanna see you again."

"Why?"

"Because you're beautiful."

She closed her eyes and smiled. "I am not."

"Sure you are. Why d'you think I asked you out here?" He kicked at the grass. "Come on. Please?"

The girl opened her eyes and put down her legs. She looked up at his face and blushed.

"There you go. See?"

The girl said nothing.

"Touch it again."

"I don't know."

"Go on, touch it. It won't bite." He wore a drunken smile, with squinting eyes and parted lips. He gave a sharp intake of breath when the girl placed her finger at the tip of his glans. She held it there as though she were trying to stop it from falling off. The boy soon exhaled. Stretching he rubbed the back of his head and scratched his neck and stood on the tips of his toes. "Why don't you hold it? With your whole hand?"

"Do I have to?"

274

"I want you to."

"How?"

"Like this." The boy pointed his index finger in the air and curled his other hand around it. "Nothin' to it," he said and rubbed his flat stomach.

"I'm not sure."

"Try it. You'll like it. Trust me."

"All right," she sighed. The boy closed his eyes and shuddered as she raised her arm and wrapped her fingers around him. Without warning he groaned and bucked his hips and ejaculated all over her wrist and hand.

"What the heck?" she shouted angrily as she released him and shook her hand like a kitten that has stepped in snow. "Why didn't you tell me you were going to do that?"

She whirled toward the young man. He was sitting in plain view but he did not move and he was not seen. The girl's reddening face scrunched up and her eyes were closed. A second passed before she began to whine and grunt. Like a pig, the young man thought.

"I didn't mean to," the boy said in an irritated voice. "I didn't know it was gonna happen 'til it happened. Otherwise I'dve said something, honest." He reached down and gave himself a few tugs while her back was turned.

The girl wiped her eyes with her clean hand and grimaced with humiliation. She stared at the ground and panted as if she were ready to run.

The boy was gentler when he spoke again. "Hey, I'm sorry." He squatted and placed his hand on her back. "I shoulda told you that might happen, but I guess I got caught up in it a little bit. I didn't mean to surprise you or make you mad or nothin'. Nothin' like that. Honest I didn't."

"I need to wash. I need to do it right now."

275

After she gave her hand some cursory wipes on the grass, she and the boy walked back to the water. She did not let him touch her. She bent her knees and plunged her hands beneath the surface while the boy stood at her side and made halting apologies.

"I'm really, really–"

"Aren't you going to wash yourself off? How can you just stand there like that? And can't you make it go down?"

The young man looked to the picnic basket and took out a sandwich. He heard a splash as he unwrapped it. He folded the paper in an even square and put it in the basket. He took a bite. The eggs were fresh and cold, with just the right amount of pepper and salt. When the sandwich was gone he cleaned his fingers on the blanket.

When he looked up, the young man found he had been discovered. The boy, standing on the shore, saw him first. When the girl saw him she shrieked and clung to the boy, whimpering with her face buried in his shoulder.

"Stay here," he said and approached the young man in long strides, hands clenched and swinging his shoulders and his arms.

The young man stood and waited, his hands folded behind his back.

"Whaddayou think you're doin'?" the boy barked.

"Please stop."

"Or what?" The boy raised his arms but before he could do anything the young man hit him on the top of his head with one of the empty bottles. It made a hollow gong sound on impact and the young man hit him again, whereupon the bottle cracked in half. The boy fell back into a sitting position as the blood began to flow and oozed like red ink into his eyes.

The girl screamed and ran to him. She crouched behind him and held him tight as she repeated his name and began to sob.

"I told you to stop." The young man held what remained of the bottle and examined the clean gleam of the broken edge.

276

"Please don't hurt him. Please don't hurt him again."

In a daze the boy pawed at his face in an attempt to clear the blood from his sight. He blinked repeatedly and shook his head, all the while muttering confused syllables. "What–? What did he–?"

"It's okay," the girl cried and grasped for his hands. "You're going to be okay."

"Stop crying," the young man in a tone that was never anything less than civil. "I want you to listen to me."

The boy freed his hands and blinked some more and rubbed his fingers together. He looked toward the young man and lunged at him with an animalistic roar. As he approached, the young man drew back his leg and kicked him square in the testicles. The boy groaned in agony, stepped back and fell to his knees, and began to vomit in thick orange heaves until his stomach was empty. Urine spilled from his penis and his scrotum turned purple and swelled to the size of a grapefruit. Curling into a ball, he began to shiver and coated himself in vomit and urine and clutched at his hemorrhaging testicles.

The girl screamed and threw herself on top of him, folding her arms about his chest. She tried to rock him as he rolled to his side and she sputtered through her mouth and nose like a tractor motor. "We're going to be okay," she whimpered and kissed the back of his neck. "Everything's going to be okay."

"Please be quiet," the young man said. "I need you to stop crying so you can hear what I have to say."

The girl's eyes were shut and she continued to blather. Taking the bottle, the young man gouged two fresh holes in the boy's scalp, from which more blood flowed dark and thick.

"Stop!" she screamed and clung closer to the boy. "Please stop!"

"I directed you to be quiet. Please do so. If you will not stop yourself from making these noises I cannot be held responsible for what happens."

The girl sniveled and wiped her nose with the back of her hand, which was now smeared with the boy's blood. It left a smear like cherry pie filling across her face. She watched the young man with bleary eyes and sucked in a haggard breath through her open mouth every so often.

The young man nudged the boy with his shoe. "When you came running up here I asked you to stop. Have you any memory of that?"

The boy did not answer.

"Of course you do. You refused to listen, which is why I was forced to stop you. If you continue to disregard my requests, I will be forced to stop you again. Do you understand?"

The boy was incapable of speech. He let out an anguished moan and shook as if he were freezing.

"We understand," the girl said. "We understand, both of us. We both understand."

"My hearing is not damaged. One answer is sufficient."

"I'm sorry."

"Please be quiet until I speak to you again."

"Don't hurt her," the boy choked out. His blind eyes rolled in their sockets and his head would jerk at the slightest sound. The girl held him close and kissed the side of his face, further staining her lips a slick shade of magenta.

"Don't interrupt me," the young man said in a pained voice.

"Just don't hurt her. Just let her go."

The young man bent over and spoke into the boy's face. "I am not going to tell you again. If you speak without prompting just one more time you will wish you hadn't." He held the broken end of the bottle to the boy's cheek. The boy jumped the girl whimpered and put her hand over his face.

"Do you feel this?" the young man asked.

The boy lay there, silent and shaking.

"You have my permission to speak. I am asking you a question now. Do you feel this?" he clinked the body of the bottle with his fingernail.

"Yes. Yes, I can feel it."

"If you do not listen to me and do as I ask, I will twist this bottle. Do you understand?"

"Yes."

The young man withdrew. The girl touched the spot where the bottle had rested, and kissed his head.

"I have a proposition for you. I've scattered your clothes all around the woods here, but if one of you is able to go into the trees and find everything you put on when you got dressed this morning, I won't kill the other one. How does that sound?"

Nathan clutched his shattered knee with a feeble groan as Mrs. Parker held him and kissed his forehead. His words spilled out fast and half-formed like a man speaking in tongues.

"Let me go, let me go, let me go, please, I don't want to move."

She pulled back but kept her fingers tight in the folds of sleeve. Still wielding the hammer, the young man pulled one of the pillows off the sofa and tossed it to Nathan. "Bite this," he said.

Nathan sunk his teeth deep into the fabric until he could hear them puncture through and he felt the snow white goose down tickle his gums, and the prickly scrapings of the feather pins like little fish bones. The sound that escaped his throat was like the lazy growling of an old hunting dog.

Mrs. Parker watched as the young man dragged the heavy coffee table away from the sofa with a deafening scrape. The legs of it left scratches on the wood, the smooth brown seen when bark is pulled off a healthy tree branch. It was as if Mrs. Parker was staring through a film of clear, colorless gel. Before he sat on the table the young man took the crystal bowls off of it and lined them in a neat row beside Mrs. Parker's chair.

"You can stretch out if you wish," he told Nathan. When there was no reply when he slid the hammer handle-up between his knees and exhaled. "Well. Here we are. I would like to say first of all that I've taken the liberty of dismantling your telephone. However, even if it was in working order I would be far, far away by the time anyone arrived to provide you with assistance."

He looked at Nathan's leg, which was bent at the knee, and pointed to it with the hammer.

"I do recommend, sir, that you straighten that. The more time you allow to pass, the more difficult it will become."

Nathan's heel already was dug into the floor, and it stayed there as he slowly clawed his way back, pillow in his mouth, and Mrs. Parker helped him along. Every inch was excruciating. When his leg was straight it was clear the knee had begun to swell, and the foot bent out at an odd angle as if someone had tried to twist it off.

The young man snapped his fingers. "You love your son."

Mrs. Parker said nothing.

"You may speak when I ask you a direct question. You love your son, do you not?"

Her voice trembled. "Yes."

"You don't want him to die, do you?"

"No." She did not wipe her tears.

"Then you must do one thing for me." He grinned. "How much do you think you could withdraw from your bank account without attracting attention?"

"I don't know."

"Well, figure it out, because after you get ready, you're going to the bank and you're going to make a withdrawal."

"How much?"

"However much you can. However much you think it's worth. Then you'll bring it back to me."

"And then?"

"I'll leave."

Mrs. Parker's eyes drifted toward her son's leg. It had expanded at the knee to the size of a melon, pressing against the material of his gray trousers.

"If you don't do it," the young man said, "your son is as good as dead. As are you."

She looked back at him. "I don't believe you would – I can't."

He took out a cigarette and lit it. "Don't test me," he said with a trail of smoke aimed in her direction.

"I'm a good person."

"Are you." He ashed into one of the bowls. "It's true you will feed and clothe a complete stranger for months at a time, along with–"

Mrs. Parker cut into the air with her hands as she stood. "All right, I'll do it, I'll go."

"Excellent."

Nathan pulled the pillow from his mouth and spat saturated balls of white down his chin. "No, Mom, don't do it, just run and get help."

"Mrs. Parker," the young man said. "Your son is not aware of what he is saying. If you listen to him I promise I can make things quite unpleasant for both of you. If he insists on voicing his opinion I'm given no option other than to quiet him. Please do it for me so I will not be force to hurt him."

He held the hammer by its handle and knelt at Nathan's side and put the claw to his knee.

"Mom, listen to me–"

Before he could finish Mrs. Parker grabbed the pillow and forced it into her son's mouth. "I'm sorry. I love you," she whispered. She pushed his sandy hair to the side and gave him a kiss. "Please, just do as he says. Let me do this for you." She looked to the young man. "If I do what you want, you'll leave, won't you?"

He nodded once.

"Mom," Nathan began through his gag.

"Be quiet," she said. "I have to do this."

The young man took the hammer handle from Nathan's knee, which now was so swollen the stitches in his trouser leg looked ready to pop. Mrs. Parker blinked and went to the stand by the door, where her pocketbook lay. She picked it up and ran her hand along the top, lingering there.

"Just one moment," the young man said.

She turned, looked at him.

"Go wash your face. You look terrible."

She let the cold water run a long time before she cupped her hands and splashed some on her cheeks. Her mind and her face were blank. She did not feel the urge to cry. She did not feel anything. Face dripping, she turned off the after and picked up a towel and dried herself. She did not look in the mirror. She was the stupidest person in the world.

The young man stood on the other side of the door, hammer dangling. He was calm, quiet, with relaxed shoulders.

"Who are you?"

Smirking, he itched his upper lip with his index finger. "That may be the least important question you could ask."

"Then why are you doing this?"

"You're letting me."

"Why did–?"

"No. That is the answer to everything."

She nodded. "I had better get going, then."

The young man stepped to the side and let her pass. He spoke as he followed her down the stairs. "If you do anything inadvisable, I cannot be held responsible for the consequences."

Mrs. Parker stopped by the door and listened.

"Therefore, I will give you fifteen minutes. If you do not return within that time, well... Can you make it?"

"Yes."

"Let's hope that you do, if only for his sake," the young man said and indicated Nathan with the claw of the hammer.

Mrs. Parker looked at her son as he lay on the floor. His chest rose and fell with rapid fluttering movements as he continued to gnaw at the pillow. "I love you," she told him. "I'll be back soon."

Then she opened the door and stepped outside. A screechy voice like the cry of a seagull called out just before she reached her car.

"Edith!"

Mrs. Parker shot the young man a panic-stricken look and he stepped onto the porch and shut the door with one hand and used the other to slide the hammer into his back pocket. Soon Mrs. Colman was huffing and puffing her way to the car. As she approached, the young man thought how much she resembled an enormous candy apple.

"How are you both this morning?"

"Very well, thank you," the young man said.

"Who does that belong to?" Mrs. Colman asked with an arm thrown toward the maroon Ford Coupe parked at the curb.

Mrs. Parker hesitated. "It's Nathan's."

"Oh, is he here?" Mrs. Colman smiled.

"He arrived this morning."

"That's so nice. He staying long?"

The young man stepped forward. "That all depends. Aunt Edith has to perform an errand right now. The time at which she arrives home will be a determining factor in how much longer he's with us." He pulled the hammer from his pocket and played with it. "Isn't that right, Aunt Edith?"

"Yes. That's right."

"Which means she must be on her way."

Mrs. Parker climbed into her car and started it. As she moved to put it in gear, Mrs. Colman spoke.

"Can I go and say hello? It's been ages since I've seen him."

"Go right ahead," the young man said.

Mrs. Parker rolled down her window. The young man looked at her over his shoulder and smiled while Mrs. Colman made her way to the house. When she placed her foot on the first step the young man called to her.

"Wait a minute, Mrs. Colman." She stopped, turned back to look at him. He did not take his eyes from Mrs. Parker. "I don't think Nathan is feeling too well. Aunt Edith is running out to get him some medicine."

"That's right," Mrs. Parker said and stuck her head out the window. "He got sick right after he came. It looks like he might have some kind of stomach bug. You don't want to catch it."

Mrs. Colman shook her head furiously and started back down the walk. "You'd better believe I don't. I'm so glad you told me. If I'da gotten sick, who'd take care of my babies?" She stopped near the young man. "Whenever I get sick they worry so much, you can see it in their faces. Just breaks your heart. And then that gets me worried and it takes me that much longer to get better."

"I'm sure it does," the young man said, all of his attention still focused on Mrs. Parker. "You had better run along now, Aunt Edith, so you can get back soon."

"I'm going."

The young man came closer and leaned in the driver's side window. "He that diligently seeketh good procureth favor. But he that seeketh mischief, it shall come unto him. Remember that." He straightened himself and waved the hammer in the air. "Hurry back!"

Mrs. Parker did not allow herself to think as she drove the speed limit to the town's main street. She could see the bank, now just three blocks away. Her heart beat so hard she could hear it. Her mouth was like sand and she could not swallow. She stopped at the sign and waited for a car to pull through. Then she drove to the next sign. A boy in a white T-shirt and faded blue jeans used the crosswalk and smiled as he passed but she did not see. When he stepped onto the curb she drove to the next intersection. The bank was not twenty feet from the car. She stared at it. There were no cars, no pedestrians. There was nothing to slow her. She did not move. The bank sat just up ahead to her right.

"Mrs. Parker!"

She looked to her left through the still-open window to spy Pastor Gruber's bulky frame trotting toward her. She pulled the gearshift into park.

"Good morning!" he wheezed.

She gave a polite nod.

"It's wonderful out, isn't it?"

"Yes."

He twisted his body back and forth and held his arm for a few uncomfortable seconds.

"Mrs. Parker – I wanted to tell you that I'm sorry." He heaved a small sigh through his clenched grin. "You're not the first one, you know. I told you that. They're still dropping off, it's ridiculous. I don't know." He glanced to the rear of the car to make sure there was no oncoming traffic. "It's me. That much I do know. I just don't know why."

Mrs. Parker gripped the steering wheel, her skin scraping against the vinyl.

"You have to go. I'm taking up your time, I realize that. But I'm trying to change. I'm trying to be the man you all want for me to be. Anyhow, I just wanted to tell you that, and to tell you I apologize."

She swallowed. "You don't have to."

He cocked his head as if he was going to ask a question, but he said nothing.

"You don't have to apologize," she said. "You don't have to change."

The pastor's lips twitched in an attempt to smile. He nodded.

"Thank you."

"I have to go now," Mrs. Parker said.

"Yes. Yes. Thank you."

She turned her head back toward the street.

"Wait!"

"Yes?"

"Does this mean you might be joining us again this Sunday?"

She paused. "I don't think so."

"I understand," he said, nodding. "But listen, if you feel the church has let you down in some way, I want you to remember that God hasn't. He is–"

"I do have to go now."

"Of course. Have a pleasant day."

"You, too," she said as she pulled away. "Goodbye, now."

Pastor Gruber raised his hand up straight, palm front, and held it still.

Mrs. Parker drove past the bank. At the end of the block she turned and began the trip back to her house. The sun was bright, warm through the windshield, and there was a slight breeze. Dancing leaves, tall grass swaying. The air was like cool water on a hot day, and she sucked it into her lungs. There was a clean taste in her mouth and her arms and legs felt so light it was as if they had disappeared. She felt young. She felt alive. It was a beautiful day.

The young man stood when she came in the front door. "You've made it just in time," he said as he approached her. "Tell me, how much did you get?"

She closed the door. "Nothing."

The young man stopped. He did not speak.

"The bank is closed."

Sarah dropped the ticket on the table next to Nickles' empty plate, which she picked up and carried to the kitchen.

"I want more coffee!" he called.

She set the plate in the order window and called to Vern and went to the coffee pot, one-quarter full.

"No, no. Don't gimme that – it'd taste like a skunk's asshole it's been sittin' there so long. Make me some fresh."

She picked up the pot and approached his table. "It's five to three. Drink this or get out – I'm lockin' the door."

"I said make me some fresh."

"You're the only one here. I'm not making a new pot just for your sorry ass."

"You better watch it, now. You don't get your attitude in line I'll put in a complaint, get you kicked out into the street."

"Good. Do it. I'm leavin' soon, anyway."

"No you ain't. You'll be here tomorrow, and the next day and the day after that. You ain't goin' nowhere."

"You want this coffee or not?"

"No. I want fresh. I want free coffee for life."

"You aren't getting' either. Not from me."

"Yeah, you sure got yourself a bad attitude. What's your beef? Don't you like men?"

She turned to leave. "When I see one I'll let you know."

He muttered a single word, just loud enough for her to hear. "Bitch."

288

Before he could stand and fish out his money, Sarah whirled around and smashed the coffee pot over his head. It shattered like a dropped light bulb, lukewarm black liquid spilling around his face with crystal shards raining on the table or collecting on the bill of his cap. Vern stood frozen in the door to the kitchen, staring, and Sarah towered over Nickles' table, the black handle of the pot still clenched in her hand. With careful movements, Nickles raised his hands and felt around his head for cuts. His mouth hung open like that of a dead fish, and his eyes rolled slow to the spot where she stood, as if a quick movement would elicit another attack. Sarah breathed hard through her nostrils like a bull and threw the handle onto the table. It bounced and landed on the floor in a clatter.

"Get out," she said in a sharp whisper.

Without speaking Nickles rose and bolted out the door. He did not pay and he did not look back. Sarah did not move. Soon Vern went to the door and locked it. From where she stood she could see him watch Nickles as he walked away. Soon he turned back and leaned against the door. His teeth showed and it was unclear if he were on the verge of smiling or throwing up.

"I have to go," Sarah said at last. "I'm not coming back. I wanted to save more but I just can't stay here."

He nodded, still silent.

"I'm sorry about the mess. I have to go." She wore a half-smile. "I'll miss you."

Sarah avoided eye contact with everyone she passed on the way back to her apartment. When she arrived she found the front door hanging open. She pushed her way in and called but no one answered. The place was empty.

She went to the closet and pulled out her suitcase, a hard forest green body with strips of brown leather along the edges, and laid it open on the floor and started dropping in clothes. When it was about full she went to the bathroom and got her toothbrush and some Colgate, and put them in the case, too.

Closet door still open, she stepped out of her uniform. Taking it in both hands she ripped it down the back until it was in two pieces, which she threw with glee to opposite sides of the room. She then pulled on a pair of loose tan slacks and a red shirt.

She glared around the room with disgust. She shook her head. She knelt on the floor and reached for the box in the closet. As soon as she touched it, she knew something was wrong. It was empty. That was obvious. Her fingers shook as she unsnapped the clasp and threw open the box. Nothing. Not even a note. She looked at the window.

Outside the air was warm. Sarah felt hot as she held her suitcase in front of her building. She looked one way up the street, then the other. Her pulse had slowed and she felt tired, weak. She took a step, then stopped. She dropped the case on the curb. She sat. She thought for a long time.

"Fuck it."

As she prepared to stand once more she felt something rub against her back. It was small and pointed like the tip of a shoe. Turning, she was met with the face of a graystriped cat. One of its green eyes was crusted shut with lumps of brown matter. Sarah could hear it purr and purr as it rubbed her with its nose and head. She bent toward it and scratched it behind the ear and it went rigid and closed its good eye. Its ears smelled like stale dung, and its nose. She took back her hand and the cat opened its eye and mewed and rubbed against her again.

Standing, Sarah took the cat in one arm and stared up the street. Then she picked up her suitcase. And waited.

EPILOGUE

It was night, and cloudless. The biting chill of the late October wind permeated everything. The fact that the car's heater was broken did not help. Every few minutes the young man would remove a hand from the icy steering wheel and blow into it. He looked out the driver's side window at the vast barren landscape, dotted every few miles with the dim orange lights of tiny farm houses. He turned the radio dial back and forth but heard nothing but crackling, groaning static.

The Chevy's gas gauge had moved beyond the E about ten minutes earlier. He continued looking out the windows for a place to turn off, but none presented itself. He wondered how long it would be before the engine would give out. He thought maybe the car would keep moving for a while – there was a slight downhill grade. He might be able to go another mile, maybe two. He did not have much in the way of supplies: A shovel in the trunk, an old brown army blanket in the back seat and a half-eaten Hershey bar in his pocket.

He had not forgotten anything. He switched on the dome light and checked under his fingernails for the fourth time. They were still clean. He turned off the light and stared out into the road.

Soon the car's engine began to whine. He shifted into neutral and let it glide into a long slow stop on the shoulder of the road. When the car stopped moving, he turned the key and took it from the ignition. He wondered if he should start walking, but soon thought better of it. It was too cold. And anyway, he was not sure where he was. He would start walking in the morning. It would be warmer then. He stuck a hand inside his jacket and felt around. He was out of cigarettes. The money – what was left of it – was still there.

He locked the doors.

He reached over the seat and grabbed the scratchy blanket. Shifting his body, he stretched out, draping it over him. He pulled the blanket tight around himself, tucking it under his legs and under his shoulders. He sighed, and watched as his warm breath fogged out, hanging over his head like smoke a moment before it dissipated. He pulled his head under the blanket, too.

He slept but he did not dream. Despite the circumstances, sleep had come easily. When he awoke it was morning and he could hear a sharp tapping on his window. He pulled the blanket off his head and looked to his side, squinting in the early morning sunlight.

A sour-faced man stood outside, wearing thick brown coveralls and a red checked hunting cap. He held a black-gloved hand against the window. In the other he carried a rusted tire iron. It was difficult to say how old the man was. His face was hard, and his chin was dotted with bristly patches of white whiskers. His skin was red from the cold. It did not seem wrinkled, but it did not look young. The man scowled.

"You stuck?" he shouted through the window.

"Yes – well, no," the young man said. "I'm out of gas."

"That's what I thought. Looked at your tires, but they all look good."

"They should be."

"Then get out and help me. I'll help get you hauled away."

"That's really not necessary."

"That's all right," the sour-faced man said. "Now get out and help me before I freeze my ass off."

"You got a name?" the sour-faced man asked in the truck twenty minutes later, the other car pulling along behind. "They call me Walker."

"Frank," the young man said after a moment.

294

Walker did not react.

"My name is Frank," the young man said, louder this time.

"Heard you."

"Listen. Thank you for helping me out back there."

Walker seemed to be ignoring him.

"You can just let me off at the first gas station we come to," the young man said.

"No gas stations around here. I'm takin' you to my house. I got some gas there."

The young man paused before speaking.

"Thank you," he said finally.

Walker did not look at him.

"What you runnin' from?" he asked.

"I'm sorry?"

"You're in the middle of nowhere by yourself and got no suitcase. Looks like you're runnin'."

"I'm not running from anything."

"It's how it looks to me."

"Then you're not looking at it correctly."

"How should I look at it?" Walker said, and turned his attention toward his passenger.

"You shouldn't look at it at all," the young man said. "You should look where you're driving."

The young man gazed out the window at the passing landscape. The sunlight only accentuated the fact that the fields, the hills, everything, was painted in dead shades of brown and gray.

"How long you been out here?"

"I don't know. Since last night. It had been dark for a while by the time my car ran out of gas."

"How long?"

"I'm not sure. A few hours, maybe. I hadn't been checking my watch."

"So it coulda been early in the night?"

"I suppose so."

"You shoulda drove out here next week. We turn the clocks back in a couple days. If you'd done it next week your car mighta stopped when it was still light out."

"If I had done what next week?"

"Whatever it is you done."

"Who said I did anything?"

"I did."

"You should mind your own business," the young man said. "Besides, it wouldn't have mattered if it was still light out. I still would have been stranded."

"Yeah," Walker said. "I guess you would have."

The house was small. It was unpainted and its shutters were closed. The land on which it stood was devoid of vegetation, or any other signs of life. Two or three small sheds sat nearby, empty, doors wide open. The wind blew loose scraps of paper across the yard. If not for an uneven trickle of white smoke from the tiny chimney, the place would have looked completely abandoned.

"Here we are," Walker said. "Let's get in the house."

"If it makes no difference to you, I'd just like to buy some fuel from you and be on my way."

"It does make a difference to me. I'm cold as shit and I ain't had no breakfast. It should be ready by now, so why don't you get your stupid ass outta this truck, huh?"

The wind gnawed at the young man's face and hands as he approached the house. Walker moved like a gorilla and emitted low grunts with each step. He did not walk so much as stomp. He opened the door and shouted inside. "Get another plate, dammit! We got company!" He turned back to the young man. "Hurry up and get on in here. We're lettin' the warm air out!"

The young man stepped into the front room, the kitchen. He closed the door behind him and caught his breath. It was filthy. Dirt clung to the cupboard doors, and the walls were stained brown. Orange and yellow water spots swirled across the ceiling. The floor was gritty, like walking on chicken feed. Even though there was food cooking on the stove, the whole room smelled like dirty clothes.

Walker was still yelling. A young woman stood before him wearing a faded orange dress that hung loose on her small frame. A white apron was tied around her waist. Her dirty blond hair was pulled back and wrapped in a bun, and although a strand of it hung permanently over one of her eyes, she never moved to fix it.

"Set another place," Walker was saying.

The young woman spoke softly into her chest.

"We got no other chairs," she said.

"Then it looks like you'll have to wait to eat," Walker answered. He glanced at the young man. "Don't worry about her. That's just Laura."

She went back to the stove.

"You better not have burned them eggs," Walker said.

Laura said nothing.

"Siddown," Walker told his guest, and sat himself.

The young man sat. His chair was sticky, like it had been painted with syrup, but he did not stand up again. He looked at the table. Four places were set. Not one dish or piece of silverware matched. Most looked as though they had been fished out of the garbage.

"I'm not really hungry," the young man said.

"Bullshit," Walker said. "Them eggs done yet?"

"Yes. Yes, I think so," Laura said.

"Then serve 'em up."

Laura was silent as she scooped chunks of scrambled egg onto each of the four plates. She then went to the tiny refrigerator and retrieved a bottle of milk, which she placed at the center of the table.

"That it?" Walker asked.

Quickly, Laura grabbed part of a loaf of bread off the counter, and set that on the table as well. She stood by, waiting as Walker brought a fork-full of egg to his mouth. He began to chew. Laura held her breath. Closing his eyes, still chewing, Walker nodded once.

"Get the kids," he said.

Laura left the room.

"Start eatin'," Walker ordered.

"It's really okay," the young man said.

"I ain't askin' you."

The young man speared a bit of egg with his fork and brought it slowly to his mouth. He sniffed it. The egg did not smell rotten, but it did not smell fresh, either. His stomach turned.

"Eat it," Walker said.

The young man took a small bite and began to chew. The eggs were terrible. They felt like slime in his mouth.

"They're good," Walker said. "Eat 'em all."

As he continued to chew, the young man heard the sound of approaching footsteps. He looked at the door to see Laura returning, followed by two people. The first was a large boy dressed in overalls, who looked to be in his late teens or early twenties. He was tall and strong, and all but filled the doorframe. He had a heavy brow, and huge hands with big knuckles. He stomped to the table and sat next to the young man and began to shovel food into his mouth.

A young girl came next. She was dressed in a stained white nightgown and had thick, shoulder-length brown hair, which twirled in her fingers. She stood there, vacant, staring toward the floor.

"Siddown," Walker said and pulled her by the arm to the table.

The boy's eggs were gone within seconds. He grabbed a mittfull of bread and ate that, too. Then he grabbed another, knocking over the bottle of milk in the process.

"Goddammit, Laura!" Walker shouted.

Laura took the bread from the table and put it back on the counter. She then wiped the table with an old rag.

Walker shook his head with disgust.

"Fuck!" the boy shouted. "Shitfuck!"

"You ate already," Walker said. "Now you just set there."

"Shitfuck!" the boy shouted.

"Be quiet!" Walker yelled.

The boy looked around for a moment before grabbing some eggs off the young man's plate.

"I told you to eat 'em," Walker said with a laugh.

The young man sat back as the boy continued to steal his eggs.

"These are ours," Walker said. "Laura's and mine. That's Jonah," he said pointing at the boy, "and that's Mary," he said, indicating the girl. "They're seventeen and thirteen. Around that, anyhow."

Jonah grabbed the remaining eggs from the young man's plate and gobbled them up.

"Fuck!" he shouted once he had finished. "Shitfuck!"

"That's about all he can say, is swears," Walker said. "Mary don't talk at all."

"Son of a bitch!" Jonah shouted.

"Shut up, goddammit!" Walker shouted. "I'm talkin' right now! I ain't tellin' you again!"

Jonah reached over to Mary's untouched plate, but Walker smacked his hand away.

"No," he said as though he were speaking to a dog.

"Bastard!" the boy shouted. "Shitfuck!"

"No!" Walker shouted.

The boy began to whine and pound on the table.

"Goddammit, get out!" Walker shouted. "Get out!"

He stood and pulled his son up by the collar, dragging him to the door. He swung it open and pushed the boy out.

"Go run around," he said. "And stay away from them vehicles!"

The boy began to circle the tiny house, flailing his arms and swearing, seemingly unaware of the cold.

"Speaking of which–" the young man began.

"Forgot to say earlier," Walker announced to the room. "We got a guest. Calls himself Frank. Don't know his real name, but that's what he's callin' himself."

"About the vehicles," the young man said.

"I know you're outta gas, but I ain't gonna fill it yet. I wanna set a while."

"That's not what I was going to say. I have a proposition for you."

"Yeah?"

"What would you say to our switching vehicles?"

"I'd say it was a stupid-ass idea."

"I just want you to think about it. I would take yours, you would keep mine, and then you could sell it. You could buy three more trucks with what you could get for it. Three more at least."

"Don't need three trucks. I already got one."

"I'm not telling you to buy three trucks. I'm saying that you would get a lot of money for my car."

Walker smiled. "Is it yours to sell?"

"I'm selling it, aren't I?"

"We both know that don't mean a whole hell of a lot. Don't we, now?"

"Just take a look at it," the young man said. "That's all I'm asking."

"All right," Walker said. "But you stay inside when I check it out. I don't want you pushin' me to trade when I'm lookin' it over."

"That's fine with me."

"Has to be," Walker said as he left the house.

Laura stood against the sink, arms wrapped around herself.

"I'm sorry about all this," the young man told her. "I can see it's a big inconvenience for you."

Laura turned so she could not see him.

"I'm sorry about your breakfast," the young man said. "I wouldn't have taken it, but your husband..."

The young man thought he heard her say something.

"What?" he asked.

Again she spoke, too quiet to hear. The young man stood and took a step toward her.

"I'm sorry? Could you speak up, please?"

"He's not my husband," Laura said. She continued to look away from him.

The young man relaxed. "That's all right," he said with a smile. "I don't care about that kind of thing. What you do is your own business."

Mary had begun to eat her eggs. Her fork clinked against her plate. It was the only sound in the room.

"I am sorry about your breakfast, though," the young man said. He dug inside his jacket pocket and fished out the half-eaten Hershey bar. "Here," he said, and placed it on the counter. "I know it isn't much, but it's all I have."

"No, thank you," Laura said.

"It's okay. If you want I can take the wrapper back when you've eaten it. He doesn't have to know."

Laura looked down at the candy.

"I've never had one before."

The young man watched as she picked it up, slowly removed the wrapper and broke off a piece. She turned it over in her fingers.

"It's smooth," she said.

"Try it."

Laura put the piece of chocolate in her mouth. She looked down at her hands as she chewed. Her back seemed to tense up. After she had swallowed, she wrapped the foil back around the candy and slid it across the counter.

"What's the matter?" the young man asked.

"It's too sweet."

"Save it for later, then. Maybe you'll like it better the second time."

"Thank you. No."

The young man took the Hershey bar off the counter and slipped it back into his pocket. He glanced at Mary, who was still eating.

"Is she deaf and dumb?"

"I don't know," Laura said. "I don't think so."

"She's pretty."

"No she ain't. She's horrible. She's the worst thing I ever seen."

The young man waited to speak.

"When I was gonna have her I thought maybe she'd be what I needed, but she just made things worse." Laura had not yet looked at the young man. "She ain't a girl. She – well, she's sort of a girl and she's sort of a boy. When I saw it the first time I said to go throw her out. Throw her in the trash, throw her in the field. Just get rid of her. I don't wanna see her again. It was the last thing I ever asked for."

The young man remained still.

"We didn't know she was more girl 'til about a year ago. Before that we didn't know what to call her."

She turned and looked at the young man for the first time, her eyes widening in panic.

"Don't say nothin'. I'm sorry I told you."

"You don't have to worry. I won't say anything." He looked back at the door.

"He'll be out there a while," Laura said, relaxing again. "Since I was a little girl he was like that. Any time he's gonna buy or trade somethin' he takes an hour or so to make up his mind."

"You've known him a long time, then."

She nodded. "My mama died when she was havin' me. It's always been just us two."

The young man felt dizzy. He removed a handkerchief from his pocket as he sat down, and used it to dab his forehead. Laura turned back to the sink.

"What'd you do?" she asked after a moment.

"I'd rather not say," the young man answered, still wiping his brow.

"You've done it before."

"Yes."

"How many times?"

"I don't know," the young man said.

"A lot?"

"I suppose so."

"Why did you do it?"

The young man laid his handkerchief on the table.

"You know how it is," he said.

"Yes."